URBAN MONARCHS

By

Timothy Dempsey

Copyright © 2020 Timothy Dempsey
All rights reserved.

ISBN: 978-1-7356357-1-2

Dedication

This book is dedicated to my younger brother. Connor, at this turbulent point in your life, I want you to remember that this is your life, and you need to live it in the way that brings ***you*** the most fulfillment. Do not let somebody else define you; only you have that power.

Acknowledgments

I would like to thank my beta readers (especially Trevor, who I annoyed ceaselessly), my editor, Jennifer, and my cover designer, Olivia, for all their contributions to this book.

Contents

CHAPTER 1

BASSES AND BODIES DROPPING

The man leaned back on the cracked, grime-covered wall of the night club. He was olive-skinned with mid-length braided hair, and he was dressed in a finely tailored inky-black suit. His ruby-red eyes were locked on the woman standing in front of him. She was a Varse, a species native to this half of the planet. The woman, like all the other patrons of the nightclub, had gray-white skin, black eyes with white pupils, slits for nostrils, holes for ears, no hair anywhere on her body, and sharp, pointed teeth lining the inside of her mouth. She was wearing a deep purple cocktail dress.

The club's music pumped along with uneven beats as beams of obnoxious purple light filled the air. The atmosphere was palpable; one could almost physically feel the sense of mania that was characteristic of Outer Varisia in the air. A legion of Varse swung wildly on the dance floor. Between them were two large buffet tables, each lined with platters of gel-like orbs, alcohol, and the occasional stray pill or two.

The woman, Vara, leaned on the wall across from the man while the two of them waited for their boss to make his inevitable, overly bombastic appearance. A large smile ripped its way across Vara's face.

"So where is she, Patho?" Vara asked, her eyes darting into the crowd before fixing themselves back on the olive-skinned man across from her. "Does this treacherous bitch have any idea what's coming? What was her name again?"

"Her name is Elledia," Patho replied with a smirk. "And no, she has no idea."

"What kind of name is that!? That sounds like a Human name," Vara laughed, abruptly pausing for a second as her eyes portrayed a glint of confusion. "Wait, is she a Human? When did a Human join the Marauders? How did I not know this?"

Vara put a hand to her head as Patho shook his.

"Do you see a Human here, Vara?" Patho sighed, his patience already growing thin.

"Well, other than that skin you're wearing, no," Vara remarked, snidely referring to the Human-like appearance of Patho.

Patho shivered in disgust. "Do you really have to call it *skin*? You and I both know it's a touch-realistic hologram, not some Human's skin that I wear like a suit. I'm not *that* depraved, Vara."

"Hey, but you're pretty close. It's not my fault that your actual appearance disturbs people," Vara teased, as the music grew obnoxiously loud.

"I hate this type of music," Patho whined, his holographic face mimicking an expression of annoyance. "There's just no soul in it, you know? No emotion involved. Only the primal need to expel excess energy from one's body."

"Not a fan of techno, Patho?" Vara inquired, her gruff voice barely rising over the sound of the bass dropping. "You always did like older things, like rocks and stuff."

"That's true. The future always seemed disgusting in comparison to the past," Patho sneered. "Still, I much prefer this *archaic* future to the past, even with you creatures of flesh walking about. I just happen to think the music suffered for everything else."

"Jeez," Vara chuckled, a grin breaking out on her face. "And you said *I* worded things uncomfortably." Patho only shot a smug smile back as a response.

The two stood silently in the doorway as they waited; the other Varse in the club continued their jubilation, ignorant of the floor show that was about to happen. The mass of people writhed and jiggled in tune with the song, earning another disgusted look from Patho.

"What are we celebrating again?" Vara suddenly inquired. She looked over at Patho, her mouth hanging slightly open.

"We just chased a large Yelo cell out of Lentald. Don't you remember? You killed their lieutenant yourself," Patho responded, scanning the crowd with his illusory eyes. "Serves them right for trying to edge into our territory."

"Jeez, Patho, I kill a lot of people. I can't remember them *all*."

"I share that sentiment, Vara, but this happened two days ago. All of these unnecessary parties are blending together."

Vara shrugged. "I don't mind them. Besides, they make Bishop happy, and it's not like Yelo has that long left anyway. It's only a matter of time until they are nothing but a bad memory. So why not enjoy the fruits of our labor?"

"Yes, but we don't need to invite every Marauder from every district to all of these different parties. I think *one* party would be more than enough."

"Like I said, Bish likes to throw 'em."

Vara groaned loudly. "You see my little brother anywhere? I'm, like, ninety percent sure Bishop wants him here."

"Knowing Artex, he's probably cleaning up a mess somewhere, or spending time with some street girl," Patho responded with an eye roll.

"You mean a prostitute?" Vara gasped, losing her composure and breaking into laughter.

"How am I supposed to know what they're called?" Patho shrugged. "This city's lust for them confuses me."

Vara smirked. "You're just mad that they sell as well as what you cook up in the labs." Her smirk strengthened. "No need to be jealous of nature for providing people with what you can't."

Patho closed his eyes and shook his head.

"Vara, you test me."

She grinned. "Still waiting on that rematch."

Patho flashed a smile on his false face. "I'm sure the opportunity will present itself one day, 'Provider' willing," he laughed. "By the way, is Bishop even here yet? I've yet to see him."

"Yeah, me and Bishy rode together on our motorcycle. He's probably planning his entrance in the back. You know him, always wanting to impress the hoards."

"Most of the gang isn't even here. Why go to all that trouble to impress just a handful of us?" Patho muttered with disappointment audible in his voice. "I still struggle to believe he's actually going to hold six more parties this week. He's turned into quite the showman these past few years."

"What's that supposed to mean?" Vara asked with a frown, one of her eyes squinting and the other widening. "What are you trying to say, Patho?"

"Oh, nothing, just that he's not the same man who ran his arm through my abdomen all those years ago."

"Patho," Vara breathed, slamming her fist into the wall and causing several cracks to spider out from the point of impact. "You don't know Bishop like I do. If you did, you'd be singing a different tune."

"I don't need to, Vara," he replied, unfazed. "I only need to know what I se—"

BANG! A crashing sound interrupted Patho. The two Marauders whipped their heads around toward the origin of the noise. The music had stopped abruptly as the main speaker dropped to the ground, smashing when it hit the floor. An energy bullet had carved its way through the piece of technology. All eyes turned toward the gunman.

The gun was silver with a glowing blue line running down the side of the barrel and into the receiver. A male Varse held the weapon, his arm still pointing to where the speaker once hung. His clothes were pitch-black, save his undershirt, which was dark blue, and he wore an unzipped leather jacket with the sleeves rolled up to his forearms. The man had two incredibly striking features: his right eye, which was a pale, luminous blue, with a white sclera instead of the normal black of a Varse's eye; and his gun arm, a silver, gleaming appendage that gleamed under the purple lights.

Bishop's thin, Varsian lips curled into a smile that revealed his sharp teeth and blue gums, as he tried to project an air of confidence. He waved the gun over the silent waiting crowd.

"Did he really just shoot the speaker out?" Patho inquired, raising his mirage eyebrows further up onto his forehead.

"Yeah, but we have a few more in the back," Vara answered, her voice rising to a yell.

Having heard Vara's comments over the silence of the crowd, Bishop turned his head and quickly winked his black eye at her. He turned back to the crowd and began to speak with an authoritative voice.

"Ladies, gentlemen, and Marauders of all ages," the gang leader exclaimed, his large grin still resting on his face. "I would like to congratulate you all on a job well done. Our efforts to kick our old rivals out of Lentald have resulted in us securing our territory and keeping a firm grip on the nutriorb factories. This has resulted in another complete victory for us over Yelo. So tonight, my fellow Marauders, indulge yourselves! Feast to your little blue hearts' content! You've earned it. Everything is on my tab, so enjoy it to the fullest! That's an order!"

Bishop turned to walk away as the crowd around him erupted with cheers. He stopped in his tracks as he was halfway out the door. The boss held up his non-metal hand, index finger extended toward the ceiling.

"Actually, there is one more little thing!" he yelled. An older man in the back of the crowd began to move forward.

Bishop spun on his heel and faced the crowd. His eye's white sclera was expanding and contracting wildly around his pupil as he scanned the crowd for his target. He lifted his metal hand and pointed to a woman in the middle of the group. Her face immediately dropped when she realized where he was pointing.

"Elledia," Bishop spoke her name slowly, with a barely hidden hint of malice, savoring her expression. The old man was now standing right behind Elledia. The man's gray-white skin had begun to drop and sag from age. His outfit was composed of a pitch-black material that seemed to muffle all sound his movement would have made. His ancient eyes still glinted with fearsome intelligence, having not been dulled by age. He held an energy pistol at the back of the distracted Elledia's head. "You are the lowest trash on the face of Mekebe," he growled.

A small pellet of blue energy flew from the gun at an imperceptible speed and shattered the head of the hapless Elledia. The front of her head exploded outward, spraying blue blood and brain goo all over the dance floor. The man in black stepped over the gooey mess and handed the gun to Bishop.

"Thank you, Silt," Bishop said with a nod, holstering his other pistol. "Don't know what we'd do without you."

"Have cleaner floors, presumably," The old man chuckled.

Vara looked smugly over to Patho. "You still think he's a showman?"

"This *is* a show, Vara," Patho replied, slightly smiling. "Although it is my type of show, I will admit to that. But he still should have done it himself if he had really wanted to make a point."

"Elledia got what she deserved!" Bishop hollered to the shocked crowd of gang members; his voice was stained with his vitriolic hatred. His smile returned to his face while his eyes held a hint of true satisfaction and forced confidence.

"She was a spy for Yelo, but she neglected to properly cover her own tracks. The poor idiot got what she deserved. If any of the rest of you betray us, you will be delivered straight to Patho. Then you'll *wish* you were shot in the head." Bishop's voice held the same suave, celebratory tone that it had when he first walked in.

"Is it bad that I'm almost hoping for a few more traitors, now?" Patho laughed and looked over to Vara, who was completely ignoring him. She had already started walking forward toward the silent crowd.

"Can somebody clean this mess up?" Vara growled, annoyed. She cupped her hand around her mouth and screamed. "Not only are we generously paying you to host us, but you know damn well we don't have to be paying you at all!"

Vara sauntered toward Bishop as the club staff began to clean up Elledia's corpse. The crowd of Marauders was now intermingling amongst themselves, either sitting at tables, standing in groups, or pursuing the buffet.

"You remember our promise, right?" Vara said as she pressed herself up on Bishop, flirtatiously placing her hand on his chest and squeezing as he pulled her close. "We are both gonna regret this night in the morning."

Patho watched the couple. Bishop and Vara began passionately kissing one another while the club staff raised a new speaker to the ceiling a few feet in front of them. His patience was quickly thinning.

He nodded his head in acknowledgment to the passing Silt, who was on his way out. "Say 'hi' to the grandkids for me," Patho requested.

"Will do," Silt replied.

Chapter 2

A Normal Drive

A lone black car sped through the cluttered, gloomy streets. There were only two sources of light in the area: the luminescent gleam of the car's headlights and the dim neon glow radiating from the haze above. The driver wore a blue leather suit with a matching hat. The most striking feature of his attire was a bright blue tattoo that adorned his left cheek. The tattoo was of a stylized "M"; the driver rubbed it absentmindedly as he navigated through the darkness.

The driver saw no one as he scanned the streets, aside from the occasional "lady of the night" looking for some quick cash. He didn't have time to fool around though. "C'mon Artex," he muttered to himself. "Don't look up from the road." Above the paved streets lay a veritable spider web of temptation: tons upon tons of advertisements for shitty wonder drugs, weapons, alcohol, you name it. And most of these vices were funded by his own gang. Artex, knowing his lack of self-control, was determined to not become another fly in the web. Not tonight, at least.

Any other night, Artex would have considered the city's wicked canopy to be beautiful, in an ugly sort of way; but tonight, he was too angry to take in any of Board City's sacrilegious scenery. He was in the slums of the city known as the Southern District or "The Brooks Maze," and like many others before him, he had become lost in its labyrinth of alleyways and backstreets.

The Southern District seemed like one incredibly dark and twisted road to him. He had heard that there weren't any streetlights in this section of the city because of the incredibly desperate scavengers. He had never thought that the stories were actually true; at the very least, he doubted they would ever become his problem.

Artex glanced around at the tightly packed apartment blocks that formed the walls of the maze. The people in those apartments lived lives of sore joints and little privacy. A terrible life, to be sure, but a life was a life out here. That's just how it was. Some of them would stay here; others with enough ambition and backbone would leave and try to carve out a better existence for themselves.

Artex didn't feel bad for any of them, though. He would have killed for an apartment like that when he was younger. Instead, he just got a lot of black and blue marks from his mom, a dad who left, and a sister who ran with a bunch of blood-crazed monks. An unusual upbringing, to be sure.

One freaking night club, the thought repeated itself endlessly in his head, his gloved hands gripping the leather of his steering wheel tight enough to leave imprints. "How much of an idiot am I? I can't find one dingy little night club?!"

Artex let out a deep sigh, reaching his hand into the passenger seat as he grasped blindly for his phone. He felt something long and hard, and he let his eyes drift momentarily from the road to see what he was holding.

It was a gun with a long barrel and an even longer frame. It was made for a two-handed grip, and it had three different Raiga crystals loaded in its chamber. It was a Rapid-fire Energy Gun, standard model, and also an object that was decidedly *not* his phone. He had left it in the chair for easy access if he needed it for any "impromptu self-defense," as Vara liked to call it.

"Meh," he groaned, carelessly throwing the gun back into the seat and reaching for his phone once again.

This time, he found it. He lifted the phone close to his mouth and pressed the top button, and a robotic voice emanated out of the speaker.

"How can I help you? Ace."

"Text Elle—" Artex began. Suddenly, a laughing man from above his car threw a stack of paper at his windshield. "Pa-pa-paper!?" Artex exclaimed, swerving to get the sheets off his front window.

"Okay. Texting Patho," his phone replied.

"What? No!" Artex shouted in a panic.

"Sending 'What? No!' to Patho."

Artex cursed under his breath. He angrily threw his phone next to the gun.

"Patho never checks his texts anyway," he grumbled to himself.

He continued to drive aimlessly around throughout The Brooks Maze, pondering how he managed to end up in these situations so frequently. He had hooked up with Elledia a few times in the past few weeks, so he figured he could trust her to give him proper directions. For some reason, she hadn't texted him back. It was starting to look like either Elledia was terrible with directions or he had pissed her off somehow.

Artex squeezed the black leather of the steering wheel tighter, his frustration beginning to creep up on him.

"Zillagarz?" Artex whispered to himself as he tried to remember the name of the club. "No wait, was it? No, it was a . . ."

Artex pulled over to the nearest sidewalk and began to slam his arms onto the horn, swearing violently. The honking rippled through the city block. Lights flickered on and off as people looked out at the noisy vehicle. The tantrum continued uninterrupted for several minutes, until a rapid tapping on the window interrupted the raging Varse.

Artex felt safe in the car. Every material that made it up was reinforced in some way or another during the construction of the vehicle, so he didn't really hesitate to look out the window. But instead of a cop or an angry Maze denizen, he was greeted by a familiar smiling Varse.

"Zoog?" Artex asked, a puzzled look on his face. "What the hell are you doing out here?"

Zoog stood half-cloaked by the darkness of the streets, his face illuminated by flickers of pink from the hanging neon sign above him. The sign read "SVALS SLICKERS: Prettiest Girls in The Maze."

He was a tall Varse man with thin, sunken cheeks. He possessed arrays of small blue marks that made a zig-zag pattern on his forearms. He wore a white T-shirt with yellowish sweat stains around the neck, baggy blue pants with large pockets, and no shoes. Shimmering brown droplets were forming on the sides of his eyes.

"I live around here," Zoog responded, almost laughing at the question. "I walk to Monochro from here, man."

"You walk. From here, which is The Brooks, to Monochro," Artex rolled down the window. "Man, it really smells worse than it looks down here."

"Yes," Zoog nodded his head. "Monochro has the best stuff around, you know that."

"Know it," Artex responded, rapping his finger against the reinforced metal of the car. "I'm part of the gang that makes it, Zoog. You know that."

"Yeah, yeah, I know, I know."

"Just making sure." Artex looked Zoog in the eye as he prepared himself to ask him his next question. "Zoog, do you know any night clubs around here?"

"Yeah, I've been kicked out of a few."

"You think you could show me how to get to one?" Artex asked with a wince. "I've gotta meet up with some friends, and I'm having a bit of trouble finding my way around."

He knew this was a bad idea, but he wanted to say that he had *truly* exhausted all of his resources before giving up and going home.

"Yeah, of course, Artex." Zoog walked in front of the car, momentarily casting a long silhouette in the headlights as he approached the passenger door.

"Zoog," Artex yelled out the still opened window. "Back seat, man."

Zoog pulled open the door and slid into the back seat. Artex put his window up and once again began driving through the silent streets of Board City.

"Zoog, how did you know it was me?" Artex asked, raising the area of skin where an eyebrow would be, and glancing at his passenger.

Zoog was sitting, twiddling his thumbs with a mild expression on his face, which was about all Artex expected from his favorite drug addict.

"Oh!" Zoog sprung to life after some kind of cognitive delay. "I recognized the car. Honestly, I'm surprised you're driving around here and not with the others at Mellows Hollow."

"Huh?" Artex's eyes widened, the color draining from his already pale face. He turned his head to the back seat, looking Zoog dead in the eyes. "Did you say Mellows Hollow? Isn't that a club in Monochro?" His eye began to twitch rapidly, the tattoo on his cheek changing from a light blue to a bright red. "Why the hell did Elledia send me here?!"

Artex turned back to his original position. He curled his gloved fingers into a fist, tightening them until the leather created an awkward squeaking that only stopped when he slammed his hand on the steering wheel.

"Stuff like this always happens to me, Zoog! You know that?" Artex screamed, pulling into an alley and turning the car around, before speeding off toward where he thought the exit from The Maze was. "Every time I think I'm getting somewhere with a girl, I go and do something to mess it up and they pull some petty revenge trick on me. I never freaking end up knowing what I did wrong! Do you know how hard it is to be near my sister and Bishop all the time? They have been together for years, and I'm always alone! Patho can ignore it because he's an unfeeling nucleus of crazy that only wants to hurt people and invent shit in his little lab, but it really gets to me, you know?"

Zoog sat awkwardly as he listened to Artex rant about his relationship problems. Artex was a close acquaintance at best, and at worst a guy who would hit him with a pipe in a back alley for money. Their relationship was complicated, but most relationships in Outer Varcia were. At the end of the day, Zoog knew two things about his relationship with Artex. He knew he could count on him to get things done when push came to shove, and he knew that they were nowhere near close enough to be having this conversation. So, Zoog did what he did best. He became a background prop, a fly against the wall, and cursed himself internally for getting into the car.

"Like, don't get me wrong, I love them all," Artex continued, gripping his leather wheel as he sped down the street. "I'd die for them in a heartbeat, but geez, can you just stop rubbing your happiness in my face for *one minute*? Again, I'm happy they're happy, blah, blah, blah, but I'm pissed that I'm so *unhappy*. No amount of empty hook-ups will bring me any closure. Just a fleeting sense of physical satisfaction. Not to mention I'm the only one of us without a thing! Patho has his magic, Vara has her Bruteil, as costly as it is, and Bishop is somehow bio-enhanced. Me? I just have a lot of guns to compensate. Hell, I even asked Patho for a new one like a year ago, and he never got back to me! I had a cool name picked out and everything! On top of all that, whatever I did to make Elledia mad must have been really horrible for her to screw me over like this."

Artex gritted his teeth, attempting to stifle the tears that were beginning to run down his face.

"I really appreciate you listening, Zoog. The next time you owe us money, I'll cover it for you." Artex whimpered, wiping his face with his sleeve.

"Oh, you know me, man," Zoog stuttered, mentally noting the lack of a monetary cap on that offer. "Always here to help."

"Thanks, man, I'll remember that."

Zoog winced hard at that. "Provider help me," he muttered to himself.

CHAPTER 3

ROYALTY

The melodic sound of a violin echoed across the dark waters of the Board City reservoir. The twin moons of Mekebe hung silently in the sky, with only the brightest of stars breaking through the city's massive light pollution. One of the moons, Scarlent, had its glow completely suppressed by the light and thus appeared dull and faded in the luminous sky. The other moon, Malig, radiated a bright, silver light that mixed elegantly with the pollution of the Board City skyline.

The violinist stood on a small, motorized raft, playing his distinguished melody. There were five others on the raft with him. Three of them wore large, teal shawls and yellow masks that completely obscured their faces. The masks had large glass goggles where the eyes should be and buttoned flaps over the mouths. Each of the three figures carried a silver energy rifle, which they cradled in a militaristic stance.

Another of the six men sat atop a large wooden throne. It was ornately decorated with images of snakes coiling around one another, and it was topped with the wooden serpents slithering into the neck of a single hissing cobra. The man that sat on the throne wore a large, ornate yellow robe with patterns of writhing cobras sewn into the sleeves. His eyes gazed lazily forward at the bridge running over the canal. The man's head had a grotesque blue scar that ran across his right cheek. The stylish royal was Hastul, the leader of Yelo.

Hastul leisurely held out an empty glass toward the last figure, who carefully refilled the glass with red wine. This man wore a yellow dress shirt and black pants with black suspenders. He wore no mask, only a pair of mustard yellow goggles and a pair of bladeless hilts on his waist.

Hastul lifted the wine to his mouth and took a swig as he listened to the violinist play. He relaxed his arm on the rest of the throne, placing his head into his palm. He held the wine glass up toward the bridge so that the streetlights would shine through the wine. The regal Varse spun the wine in the glass as he spoke to the pourer.

"Any minute now, the trap will spring, and we will have the head of the Marauders' chieftain on a stick." Hastul chuckled before taking another sip of the wine. "Isn't it wonderful, Lawndel?"

"Elledia was an excellent spy, sir. We did not tell her that her cover was blown, as you instructed. We did not want to risk her returning to Sinistus and causing a panic among the enemy," Lawndel replied. "Once the chieftain is dead, the weakness of the Marauders will be on display for all to see."

"Oh yes, then we will move forward with the rest of Cassilda," Hastul stated, once again swirling his wine. "Thanks to the efforts of our loyal infiltrator we know exactly how to strike against our foe and will soon have them looking into the mirror of defeat."

"May those men who died rest well, knowing that they have served Yelo." Lawndel saluted by holding his right arm up straight, his middle and index finger extended.

"May they rest knowing that they have helped to bring order to this ungrateful city," Hastul finished his wine. "And eventually to all of Varcia, from the Inner, to the Mid, and of course to the Outer."

The sound of a violin echoed across the water, while the light of Malig shined down upon Hastul and his men. It resembled a grim, silver shroud.

"Removing Artex from the equation is just the *start* of my vengeance," Hastul smiled, looking down at his palm. The ruler's hand was glowing with a yellow light. "There is nothing they can do to compete with my power. Even if my plan somehow fails, it won't be long before the whole city sees the shake."

CHAPTER 4

BLUNDERBUSS

The inconsistent roads of The Brooks tightened around Artex as he carefully attempted to retrace his steps. The unforgiving maze of unlit streets was not cooperating with him.

"Geez, Zoog. How do you find your way outta here?" Artex asked, as he carefully turned his tenth corner.

"Well, once you live here for a while, it becomes pretty easy to worm your way out," Zoog replied, a prideful smile breaking out on his face.

"Why did you phrase it like that?"

"Phrase it like what?"

"You said 'worm,'" Artex glanced back at his passenger. "It's just a strange way of saying it, man."

"Dude, I mean that *literally*," Zoog replied, nodding his head.

Artex paused for a few seconds, allowing the quiet to fill the car, before finally breaking the silence with another question.

"Can I do it with a car?"

"No."

"Then Zoog, I beg you with all my heart, *please* don't tell me what the hell 'worm' means."

The pair continued their aimless drive throughout The Brooks. Artex let out a long sigh as he reflected on his budding relationship with Elledia and what he could have done to cause it to fail. Zoog sat in the back, playing with the window. He watched it slide up and down, again and again, never growing bored of the sliding glass. Each time Artex heard the glass rise and fall, the idea of slapping Zoog became more and more attractive.

The road in front of them resembled a large tree with branches and roots spreading out in an overcomplicated mess. The car made a sharp right turn on one of the roads and hit a curb. Artex swore under his breath as the car's left side partially lifted from the ground before landing with a soft thud.

"Ah," Artex looked back as his passenger with an embarrassed glance. "I, uh, didn't see it."

"See what?"

"The curb."

"Did you hit a curb?"

"Zoog, one day I'm going to figure out what's going on in your mind, and when I do I can almost certainly guarantee that I will spend the rest of my life screaming."

"Hey, whatever floats your boat, man," Zoog shrugged, uncaring. "Live and let live."

Artex first met Zoog when Zoog was wandering around Lentald dressed in a leotard that read "The magnificent" on the front in an ugly purple color. He didn't realize it was him until he met him again (without the leotard) in Monochro, where he was looking to buy drugs.

"You watch *Vivvedell's Blossoms*?" Artex asked his passenger. "It's a great soap from Inner Varcia. It's about the only good thing to come out of there, in my opinion."

"No, I don't own a TV."

"Oh, I see," Artex fanned his fingers on the wheel. "It's a really great show. I actually have a bet going on with an acquaintance of mine about who Vivvedell is gonna end up with. My friend thinks it's gonna be Garn, an outer Varcian roughneck, but she's forgetting the different sensibilities of Inner Varcia. She's gonna end up with her childhood friend, Stelvo. They are absolutely perfect for each other, and they have a special bond like no other. Hell, Stelvo even left his other love interest to confess to Vivvedell. That fifty Zel note is as good as mine."

"Okay."

A bright yellow light flooded in from behind them, causing Zoog to jump like he was being shocked by a defibrillator. They were not alone anymore; another car had started trailing behind them.

"Hey, barely anyone in this district owns a car, right?" Artex asked, a smile growing across his Varsian lips.

"Yeah, most of us can't afford them, and quite frankly, they're too much trouble."

"Ha, could you imagine being this guy, the *one guy* in the whole Maze to end up in traffic? That sucks so much. It's almost like he fell into our trap." Artex laughed as another car pulled out of an alleyway in front of them and boxed him in.

"Oh, now I see what's going on," he said, his smile dropping off his face like an anchor.

Zoog looked out the back window, trying to get a good look at the occupants of the tailing car, but the bright headlights prevented him from seeing into the vehicle.

"Oh Provider, Artex, are we going to die?" Zoog whimpered, his eyes having grown into large, black, wobbly saucers.

"There's a good chance," Artex whispered through gritted teeth as he tried to remain as calm as he could while driving. "If they have anything bigger than a pistol, we are absolutely fucked. The car's exterior is reinforced but it can only take so much, and they have us in too tight a position. Hard to get away from. The only option we have right now is to follow them and hope that we think of something that could get us out of here still breathing."

Zoog's face lit up.

"What if we take another turn real fast!"

"If we do that, the guy behind us will rear-end us immediately," Artex replied, the tattoo on his cheek glowing a deep red. "Then we will be literally sandwiched between them and probably will be killed immediately."

Artex followed the car in front of him as it led him through The Brooks. Unlike Zoog and the car behind them, he could make out the details of some of the passengers thanks to his headlights illuminating the back of their car. There were four men in the car, each one wearing an identical yellow mask and goggles. He knew who they were, and he knew that this situation would only end with bodies on the ground. Who would end up on the ground though, was what he hoped was up for debate.

The mind of the Marauder raced as he tried to think aloud of a way out of this. "If I drop the windows and throw my rapid fire to Zoog, then maybe we could take out some of the guys behind us, but then the guys in front will just open fire on us. Dammit!" Artex slammed his hands on the wheel in his rage.

Zoog unbuckled himself from the seat, hyperventilating. He climbed down into the space between the seats, wrapping his needle-marked arms around his legs until he was in the fetal position.

"I don't want to die, Artex," the addict wept. "Not like this!"

Artex adjusted his mirror to see the crying man, a face of disgust crawling over him at the now even more pathetic sight of Zoog. "Why, would you prefer to be as high as a Conortionist sky ship, on a couch, in a back alley somewhere?" he growled.

"Yes," Zoog whimpered through his tears.

Artex turned to vent more of his anger at Zoog. That's when something in the back caught his eye. Behind Zoog's head, underneath the passenger seat, there was something white that stuck out amidst the gray of the car's interior.

"Zoog, what the hell did you drop in my car?!"

"I didn't drop anything!" Zoog screamed pathetically.

"Then what is behind your freaking head?!"

Zoog weakly turned his head toward the object, and then he reached for it. He pulled out an obsidian black box with a note taped to it. The weeping man sat back in his seat, his face returning to one of innocent wonder at the sight of the box in his hands.

It was at this point that Artex could see where he was being led. The car in front of him was leading him out of the district and to the bridge that connected The Brooks to the rest of Board City. If the situation was different, then he would have kissed the driver in front of him.

The bridge itself was a large gray expanse with stone guardrails on its side. The absolute minimum of effort was put into creating this bridge, which put it in direct contrast to the shining abyss of rainbow light that was Board City proper. Though, if there was one thing that the bridge had over The Brooks, it was that the bridge actually had streetlights lighting it up . . . as spotty as they were.

Artex heard a click from behind him and turned around to see a wide-eyed Zoog holding an open box on his lap, a note in his left hand, and a metallic black flintlock-looking pistol with a blue circle on its side that was divided into five pieces in his right.

"Uhh man," Artex asked with concern and confusion in his voice as they neared the beginning of the bridge. "Whatcha got there?"

Zoog looked at the letter. "Hold on, I'll check."

"Dear 'Ace.' I know that it's been months since you asked for this, but here you go," the dazed addict read. "'Enjoy your 'Blunderbuss' -Patho."

A large, joyous grin spread onto Artex's face. This gun was more than a gift found late, but it was also their best chance at getting out of this—at least, it would be if Patho made it like he had asked.

The trio of cars had reached the bridge and began to drive under the uncertain lights that bathed it.

"You call yourself Ace?" Zoog asked, with an innocent look.

Artex responded to the question by throwing his rapid fire into the seat next to Zoog.

"Give me the Blunderbuss!"

"What?"

"Just give me the gun!" Artex screeched, rage filling his eyes and his tattoo.

"Here, here!" Zoog yelled, throwing the gun forward.

Artex caught the gun in midair, and he grabbed the blue circle on the side of it. His smile showed a little bit more mania as he spun the circle with his fingers; it produced a clicking sound as it snapped back into its original position.

"Zoog, Imma need ya to grab the gun next to you and start shooting like a madman at the car behind us once this window drops," Artex commanded, turning the volume knob under his clock all the way up.

Zoog grabbed the gun, his arms shaking.

"What do you mean, 'windows drop,' Ace?"

"The windows will fly off of the car, and don't call me Ace."

"I'll try my best!" Zoog yelled with a nod.

Artex breathed deeply and then sharply exhaled, his eyes focused on the car in front of him. It was them or him who would die on this bridge tonight, and he wanted them dead. He pulled on the volume dial on his dashboard, causing it to pop out, and twisted it all the way to the right.

"Ready!"

"Set!"

"Go!" Artex screamed with all his might as he slammed down on the dial. At that exact moment, the windows shot off of the car, leaving the dynamic duo inside unprotected from both wind and bullets.

Zoog screamed incoherently and began to wildly fire the gun as the windshield flew through the air above him. Blue energy bullets sprayed out in a shower of destruction, making a sharp hissing sound as they exited the barrel. Some of them smashed into the gray rock of the road and others ricocheted off of the side of the car before dissipating into the air, while the rest easily penetrated through the windshield of the trailing car. The spray had an even easier time ripping through the flesh of the Yelo members in the driver and passenger seats of the car.

The corpse-driven car spun out of control, crashing violently into the guardrail with enough force to flip the car into the abyssal canal below. It landed with a mighty splash before slightly bobbing on the surface, and finally being sucked below.

At that exact moment, when Artex was facing down against an endless blast of howling wind, trying to aim the Blunderbuss at the car in front of him, he could swear that somewhere underneath all the rushing he could hear a violin playing an off-key note. Artex steadied his arm, his face twisting into a manic slasher smile as he pulled the trigger.

The Blunderbuss fired a single dark blue pellet from its barrel, which provoked the circle on the side to pop out, one fifth of it no longer glowing. The orb flew through the air, smashing through the window of the unprepared Yelo members' back seat. The car that was leading them to the bridge was immediately engulfed in a massive midnight blue explosion.

"AHAHAHA!" Artex cackled as he narrowly and violently steered his car out of the way of the burning wreckage. "THAT EVENED THE ODDS A BIT, DON'T'CHA THINK ZOOG?!"

The sudden jolt of the turn caused the still shooting Zoog to fall backward and smash into the back of the passenger seat, knocking him unconscious.

***

Hastul dropped his wine glass as he watched both his plan and his men go up in flames from his barge in the canal. His eyes widened with a fury he had not felt since the Marauders' first incursion into Board City.

"Such insolence!" the robed man screeched, standing up and raising his right arm toward the night sky. "You will not get away unscathed! Nobody escapes the fate that I write for them!"

A yellow energy began to flicker around Hastul as he gathered his magic. Since he used a yellow color Mage, he specialized in blunt force projectiles, and he was about to help those projectiles acquaint themselves with the car of that brat on the bridge. A pill-shaped object began to form a few feet above the Mage's hand. Hastul swung his hand down and fired the object toward the speeding car. It made a whistling sound as it rocketed through the air.

"Take me home," Hastul spoke, collecting himself. "I require sleep, and maybe something to eat. I must recover from this unpleasantness. Oh, why did we only send Bans for this job?!"

***

Artex had never felt his eyes burn as much as they did at that moment, but neither that nor his freezing face could ruin his mood. Zoog was unconscious in the back seat, and even better than that, the Blunderbuss was amazing. Just a bit more and they would be back in Monochro, and this whole thing would be behind them.

A whistling sound barely foretold the sudden impact on the side of the car. Artex spun the wheel fruitlessly as the car spun out of control. His eyes were pouring like waterfalls. The car slammed into the guardrails and produced sparks as he smashed his foot down on the brake and rubber was ripping and burning from the wheels. Finally, it all came to a stop, and Artex sat panting in the driver's seat, trying to collect himself. This moment of peace was interrupted when his phone dinged, with a message popping up on the screen.

"Patho: ???"

CHAPTER 5

THE STATE OF THINGS

Bishop watched the Marauders dance and drink in the club, a dull, glazed look in his eyes. When he first started hosting these, he'd often come here to the back and focus hard on the dancing. He'd be able to hear each individual step hit the dance floor, like heavy rain on a rooftop, and it used to reassure him that what he was doing was right. Now, all it did was exacerbate his growing sense of redundancy and annoy him.

He had five more identical parties to plan after this, more if he got the initial projections wrong, but less and less people were attending lately. This was all he could do nowadays to feel like he was contributing anything anymore. It had become an endless cycle for him. The Marauders chased Yelo, or some weaker gang, out of their territory and then he would reward them with a shindig. When it first started, he'd meticulously plan each one as a separate, unique event—that was until he realized that nobody would care if he just hosted the same one over and over. At least, as long as he had food, alcohol, and other things that made them feel good. Although, he really hoped that nobody was noticing—he would occasionally overhear a comment from one of the party goers.

He glanced down at the glass cup of golden-brown liquid in his hands; the drink was swirling mesmerizingly inside it, and the purple light of the club glinted off of his reflective metal hand. Bishop lazily scanned the crowd again. Somebody here had a bit too much to drink and had gone outside just to puke it out. He could still smell it quite well over the noxious cloud of perfume and cologne that filled the club. The sense of smell was definitely a low point of his enhanced senses, especially since he couldn't figure out how to turn this one on and off. With the others, he just had to apply focus or clear his mind, but this one was always active. It was a fact he had to painfully get used to in the past few years. He could even smell Vara's rose perfume from wherever she was in the club; it was a very strong perfume, but he did really like the smell of roses. So, he guessed it had its upsides.

He could remember the first time he smelled that perfume. It was when he met Vara and Artex for the first time. It was still hard for him to believe that the three of them met in a very ugly bar fight that Vara had started when she broke a chair over his head, because in her own words, "it was too calm in there. Somebody had to liven the place up, and a good old chair smash has always done the trick for me." The three of them had been inseparable ever since. The Marauders had been born in that fight, even though the three of them had no idea at the time. It was the start of the best times of his life, times of excitement, danger, and a whole lot of gunfights. Sadly, the good times always seemed to be more short-lived than the bad for Bishop.

The level of overwhelming predictability in his life almost made him physically sick to his stomach. When he was younger, it was just the same. A repeating sequence of events over and over and a feeling of powerlessness about the whole thing, although the company around him at present was undeniably much better than back then.

His life before the Marauders was not an especially pleasant one, but it wasn't an absolutely terrible one either. It was probably the average life of anyone growing up in a small Outer Varcia town. He knew plenty of people that grew up in much worse circumstances than he did. What did bother him about it was mainly two things: the way his father controlled him and everyone around him even if what he had them do would hurt everyone in the long run, and the nightmares he still had about what happened right after he left.

Bishop shook his head when he felt his heart starting to beat slightly out of rhythm. If he let himself think about the past for too long, then he knew it would swallow him whole, and he really didn't know if he could climb back out. Besides, the present was presenting its own set of pressing issues for him.

Life wasn't what he had expected it to be after he clawed his way to the top of Board City. The very gang he created had grown to a point where he barely had any direct say in how things went. He knew that if he really wanted to, he could still send out orders and move the group around as he saw fit. But things were working so well for everyone as they were, and he didn't want to fix what wasn't broken, just so he could feel a teeny bit more fulfilled in his life. No, it was better for everyone if he let things go on as they were; this prosperity wasn't just for him after all.

He lifted his left hand, pointing to a man sitting in a glass booth, and then snapped his fingers. The man nodded and flipped a switch. The music became quicker and more intense, and the lights changed from solely purple to a rainbow of quick-changing colors.

"Enjoying your party," a smooth, deep voice asked. "Blue-eyed Bishop?"

It was Patho, his overly formal dress and Human appearance cutting a strong contrast between himself and the rest of the raving Marauders.

"More importantly—" Bishop answered with another question, "—are you, Red Demon Patho?"

Patho smiled lightly with his dark lips. He had always found the epithets that the notorious of this city ended up developing a bit silly.

"As much as one who cannot consume can enjoy an event organized around the act of consumption, I suppose," he responded in a jokingly sarcastic tone.

"Sorry about that," Bishop chuckled, taking a sip of his drink. "I'm afraid I have to plan these with most of the participants having mouths in mind."

"Such is the plight of an Ethereal in a non-Ethereal world," Patho responded, shrugging sarcastically. "All your people think about are eating and mating, while the technology looks like it's been made by children. Although I can't lie—the attitude you Varse have toward life is much more interesting than that of my own people."

***

Patho joining the gang was a day Bishop could never forget. That was mostly because he had never seen anything like Patho before in his life. Underneath that face he wore is the true face of Bishop's friend—a face unlike any other in the world. They had stumbled upon Patho by chance one day; he was terrorizing a small village, while the three of them were out looking for supplies and members to add to their struggling smaller group. Luckily, after trying to kill them, Patho agreed to join up as long as he could use some of the metal from Bishop's arm.

Bishop took another drink of his liquor before speaking, his mood having returned to a more sour state. "I've been wondering something for a while now, Patho."

"And what would that be?"

"Do you miss them?" Bishop looked out into the crowd. "Your kind, I mean."

"Certain individuals I miss greatly," Patho answered in a matter-of-fact tone, his false face falling completely void of emotions. "But as for the whole of them, I've honestly never been that much of a fan of them. As I've told you, I've always had very different priorities in life compared to the majority of my kind. Their extinction does not bother me."

Patho slid his piercing gaze to Bishop. "Why do you ask?"

Bishop locked eyes with him for a second before his eyes retreated back into the crowd. "Things like that—" he gruffly answered, "—losing a lot of people at once . . . I know how they can take a toll on a person."

"You're putting too much thought into it," Patho responded, with a small laugh. "All I'm sure of is that most if not all of them are dead, and that it happened a long time ago. If nature destroyed them, then it was meant to be."

Bishop opened his mouth for another question, but he was cut off by the sudden appearance of an arm that wrapped around his neck. Vara swayed from side to side, steadying herself on his shoulder as she poured more whiskey into his cup, causing it to overflow.

"Yuh looked a little low," she blurbeled.

"Wow," Bishop blurted out in shock. "It looks like I have a lot of catching up to do."

Patho reached into his pocket and removed the thin black rectangle with a blue luminous diamond pattern on the back. He held it away from him like it would jump and bite him at any moment.

"Hmm," he remarked, poking the rectangle a few times and sliding it back into his pocket.

"I think Artex butt-dialed me, or butt-texted, rather."

Bishop raised his brow at Patho. "You know—" Bishop pointed out, as he wrapped his arm around Vara's waist to further steady her "—I've never actually seen you use that until now."

"I like to keep its use to an absolute minimum; any type of recorded communication is a liability in our field of work."

Bishop rolled his eyes. "I know that, that's why we don't talk about work on them."

"Any information can be a vulnerability, Bishop."

"Well, we have to keep in contact with one another somehow."

"I agree on that, but there is a better way."

"And what would that be?"

Patho smirked. "You'll see some, I promise you that."

Vara began drunkenly poking Bishop in the cheek with the head of the bottle. "Bish?" Vara blurted out, annoyed. "Why are you still talking and not drinking?"

"Vara I often wonder what the monks would think if they saw you now," Patho inquired through pursed lips.

Vara threw her head backward before whipping it back to Patho. Her eyes were half shut, and her mouth hung slightly open.

"Look, Red, the Bruteil monks believe that getting drunk on violence is a preferable thing to alcohol," she replied, pointing toward the ceiling. "I, however, recognize the greatness of both ways of thinking."

Vara tightened her hold on Bishop. "Bish," she slurred, poking her finger into his chest. "You told me that we'd get shit-faced together, but here you are talking to the guy who's too afraid of losing to have a proper rematch with me!"

"Vara, that was seven years ago," Patho reminded her, moving his head closer to hers with no emotion on his face. Besides, we both know that I would beat you to a bloody blue pulp without breaking a sweat. It would be as easy for me as it would be for a trident to press through weak flesh."

Bishop stood silently, listening to the two of them threaten one another. He knew he could interject, but he didn't have enough faith in his own words to do it.

"You and I both know that you don't have sweat glands," she spat. "You bitch."

"Well, on that rude note," he said, returning to his usual perfect posture. "I think I'll be leaving this party. I've had enough of this ear-grating music."

Vara looked up at the silent Bishop as Patho walked off, a huge grin on her face. "I hope you're ready to *really* regret tonight, tomorrow."

CHAPTER 6

GOLDEN ROSE

Black jackets slid down the conveyor belt, each one exactly nine inches from the others. Robotic arms reached down from the ceiling, grabbing the jackets and sewing in additional heat-resistant mesh layers into the cloth. Once they finished, they placed the jackets back on the belt, where they were soon after dumped into large gray carts. Varse dressed in all white and wearing filtered masks wheeled the carts out of the room and to the trucks, which would send them to shops all across the city.

Lode watched the machines do their rhythmic dance over and over, a small smile on his thin lips.

The clothes made here were a Marauder's best friend, and their heat resistance allowed them to wear black in Outer Varcia without sweating themselves into mummified husks. That didn't mean he was a big fan of seeing the same basic design created over and over again. Still, the sights and sounds of the assembly line were quite pleasant, like a mechanical lullaby.

The room Lode sat in was dark; the only sources of light were small nodes of gold on the floor that barely lit anything up, and the sterile light pouring in from the assembly line just barely beamed in through the large observation window. Lode sat at a finely cut wooden desk that was bare of anything but the briefcase that he was crossing his gold trimmed gloved hands on top of. Standing by the window was a man dressed to the nines. His suit was a navy blue and was bedazzled with gems—very garish. He had his hands crossed behind his back as he watched the line do its work.

"I see you've made some changes to your outfit," the man suddenly stated, breaking the silence and referring to the golden rose vine patterns sewed into Lode's uniform. "Are our designs not to your liking, Mr. Agel?"

The man's face was slightly sunken in. Copious amounts of skin colored makeup was slathered on his light gray face, mostly around the eyes, but failed to completely hide the specks of dried brown ooze that had leaked from them.

"Oh, not at all," Lode responded, giving a friendly smile, "I simply love to customize. We aren't Yelo, Bando. We all have real personalities and are encouraged to show them."

Bando slightly tightened his face at Lode before relaxing it again. "No matter," Bando sighed. "Clothing isn't why you are here today anyway."

"Oh yes, but I'd still like to thank you and your company for being valued partners of the Marauders," Lode cheerily interjected. "'Bando's Best' makes the most breathable clothing in all of Board City, and we really do appreciate it."

Bando cracked a smile of his own as he approached the desk and pulled out his luxuriously cushioned chair. "Well, our little deal with you benefits us as well, don't forget," Bando replied. "Only paying a tenth of the protection money to you that we paid to Yelo has really helped me reinvent our brand into what it is today."

Bandolier locked eyes with the cheery man in front of him. "So, Lode," he said, excitedly rubbing his hands together, "what exactly do you have for me today?"

Lode clicked open his briefcase. "Something brand new, actually."

Bando's black eyes widened, his white pupils twinkling like a child who had just been given their first toy.

"New?" he asked, his voice breaking slightly.

"Oh yes," Lode nodded his head. "A brand new Patho original. We call it Crimslo."

Lode removed one of three syringes filled with a clear liquid from within the briefcase. The syringes were internally segmented with five small dividers.

"Crimslo?" Bando eyed the concoction intently. "What does it do?"

"It'll make you feel like you're riding high on a sandstorm," Lode answered in an upbeat tone. "Downside is you'll be completely catatonic for the duration of the dose."

Lode motioned to the dividers. "You *can* take the whole thing at once, but you'll be unresponsive for days."

Bando nervously played with the gems on his forearm. "How much for it?"

"Oh no," Lode responded, motioning with his free hand. "No zel for this today, Bando, this one is a free sample. Gotta see if people like it before we put a price on it." Lode handed the syringe to Bando, who greedily grabbed it.

"So, how addictive is it?" Bando inquired, looking up at Lode with wide eyes. "I just kicked the Andblin. I just wanna have a good time and not get hooked like a fish, ya know?"

"I couldn't tell from how giddy you were," Lode responded, smiling. "But congratulations on overcoming your beast. Crimslo is our first, and the only Non-Addictive being sold in all of Board City."

"You're kidding!" Bando yelled excitedly.

"Oh, not at all. Still, do be careful, Bando; I'm sure overdoing won't be that pretty of a sight."

Lode closed the briefcase, and stood up from his seat, slightly hesitating at the thought of leaving.

"If you'll excuse me, Mr. Bando, I really must be getting home," Lode chirped as he made his way to the exit. "Please do let me know what you think of the new product at your earliest convenience."

***

Lode walked out of the factory. Two Marauders stood guard, holding rapid fires. They nodded their heads at their gold-embroidered comrade, and he waved back with a large smile.

Grandmin was the heart of manufacturing for Board City, as a result of that, it had the least active nightlife and the darkest skies in the city. One could almost see the moons through the ever-present cloud of light.

The buildings all had hard edges, and some even had visible crystal batteries filled with the unmistakable blue of Raiga energy. The very center of town was the source of it all, and held a massive Raiga power plant which powered the whole city like a beating heart.

Lode's eyes darted around nervously, but he relaxed when he didn't find whatever he was looking for. Going home had started to become harder work than going to actual work for him. His lover, Butler, had become unbearably clingy, and he was beginning to fear that Butler would start trying to restrict his movements. Lode's grip tightened around the handle of the briefcase; he knew he had to end this for his own sanity, but he didn't know how to let Butler down easily. He still cared for him and didn't want to destroy the man.

Lode's car was bright red with a gold pattern of gold vines painted onto it that looked like they were coiling around the car. He went to reach for the handle, but a loud ringing sound interrupted him. Lode pulled out his phone reluctantly. His face twisted in an involuntary expression of disgust, but relaxed as soon he saw what name was on the screen. He let out a sigh of relief.

"Artex!" Lode exclaimed, answering the phone in his usual chipper tone. "Are you calling about the Vivvedell finale tomorrow?"

His relief was noticeable in his voice.

Lode leaned up against his car.

"What kind of situation?" Lode asked, raising a brow.

Lode's eyes widened into charcoal dinner plates as he listened to Artex explain.

"Well, thank the Provider you're still breathing," Lode responded, his voice hoarse. "Who did you say was with you, again?"

Lode began to pace around his car as he talked.

"No clue who that is," he turned on his heel, joy and relief filling his eyes. "I'm assuming you need me to pick you up."

"Oh it's not a problem at all—in fact, you're helping me out more than you know," Lode began laughing. "Monochro sounds lovely this time of year," Lode laughed. "I'll drive anyone anywhere at this point if it means I can stay out longer."

CHAPTER 7

THE MORNING AFTER

Vara awoke to a dry, warm blast of morning air. Her world was spinning, and her head was throbbing madly. The bed that she was laying in was covered in soft blue sheets, although they were now drenched in sweat. The room itself was very plain, with a dresser on the left side right next to a wide-open door. The blinds were open and the large window that they should have been hiding was smashed open, allowing the light and air of the morning to enter in. The Varse woman sat up in the bed, holding her pounding head tightly in her hand. She'd been through worse.

"I couldn't have been that drunk last night," she moaned painfully, moving her head toward the source of the light that was vexing her eyes, and seeing the shattered window. "Oh, I guess I was that drunk."

Vara stumbled out of the bed, her hangover making her weighted dress feel exceptionally heavier than it was. She carefully avoided the shards of glass scattered on the ground.

To her it was a great mystery, and she never actually remembered any of the incidents in question, but according to others she was not a big fan of things that shattered easily when she was sloshed.

"Where are my shoes? Where's Bishop? Whose apartment is this?" she asked herself as she swayed toward the door, catching her balance on the dresser. "Oh shit. What did we do with the owners?"

Outside of the bedroom door was a set of stairs, which she proceeded to go down by pressing her hands on each side of the walls and carefully trying to keep her balance.

Making her way out of the bedroom, she could not help but notice the unmistakable smell of something burning— a smell that was growing ever stronger as she descended deeper into the apartment.

What the hell did I do? Vara thought, wincing her face in preparation for what other property damage she had surely caused during her drunken escapades.

Reaching the end of the stairs was a lot harder than it should have been, and she found herself in a small hallway leading to the kitchen. The smell of burning was growing stronger with every step. Vara looked around the kitchen, a pained acceptance filling her before she even entered the room.

The room was an absolute wreck; the sink was ripped out of the wall, water was spraying everywhere, there were food capsules mashed onto the walls creating stains in varieties of greens, browns, purples, blues, and lastly, a variety of utensils were scattered around the counters—some of them clean and some of them dirty with what was either blue jam or blood.

In the very corner of the room, Vara identified the source of the burning. An orb warmer was pluming smoke from its top, helping to solidify her already strong opinion that neither she nor Bishop could cook in any state of mind.

"Wow, I was a lot drunker than I thought," Vara sighed, looking across the wreckage. "I hope I didn't kill anyone. That would be a lot of trouble to clean up."

"Not that I'm gonna clean any of this up," she said, stepping over the clutter and toward the living room.

Vara had always been what some would call a "violent drunk." Her specialty in the Varcian Martial Arts school of Bruteil did not help make the situation any better for anyone. She drank anyway of course, but usually only enough to get tipsy. That was a decision she made after a night she didn't remember when she allegedly threw at least three people through the same wall. She was sure that they deserved it for some good reasons, but replacing the wall was a real pain in the ass. Although, if the wall had three people thrown through it, it probably deserved it too.

She stumbled into the next room, and she was immediately met with two bodies lying on the ground. One body was lying on the ground near a TV in a puddle of a clear, foul-smelling fluid, and the other was mostly under a green couch, his metallic arm sticking out limply.

Vara walked over to the couch and put her right hand underneath it. She could feel how gritty the fabric was, which reassured her further that she didn't own the house.

"Bishop," she groaned as she lifted the couch. "It's time to get up."

Bishop's eyes flipped open; an expression of absolute terror on his face, he silently mouthed something before he noticed Vara, and shifted to a calmer, more hungover expression.

"Couldn't you leave me a bit longer?" he groaned, grogginess filling his voice. "We could both climb under there and go back to sleep until the world stops spinning so much."

"I'd love to, but we have a bit of an issue," Vara said, pointing over toward the man in the puddle. "There is a dude."

"Well, I'll be damned," Bishop exclaimed, rubbing the sleep out of his eyes. "There is indeed a dude."

"Yeah," Vara replied, stumbling over toward the man in the puddle. "Any idea who he is?"

"None."

"Great," Vara sighed.

She knelt down near the mystery man and sniffed. Her nose stung at the pungent scent of the concoction. It was a blend of both alcohol and urine. She didn't see a bottle near him, so she didn't know how the alcohol got there, but there was a lot she didn't know right now. This was just another unnecessary mystery to add to the list.

She watched his nostrils flare slightly; she stood up, trying not to wobble too much as she did.

"Bish he's alive."

Bishop's expression changed to one of bemusement.

"I-is that good?" he asked, still fighting off the urge to climb back under the couch.

"I guess," Vara shrugged. "We should probably just leave him here. If he's not a corpse, he's not our problem."

"I couldn't have said it better myself," Bishop responded, satisfied with his girlfriend's answer. "Now let's get home before this guy wakes up and asks questions."

"Agreed." Vara nodded.

"You think we should pay for the damages?" Bishop asked coyly.

Both Bishop and Vara began to laugh hysterically at the idea, only stopping when their headaches forced them to.

"Yeah, and we should put him in charge of the gang too!" Vara cackled, trying to ignore her brain as it tried to escape her skull.

The Varse couple continued to painfully laugh on and off before being interrupted by the clicking of the front door. Someone was unlocking it.

"Oh crap," Bishop whispered under his breath, as a young Varse woman opened the door.

She wore the black leather greaser-like outfit that was the typical attire for a member of the Marauders. Her one arm held a brown paper bag that was filled with various nutriorbs and other foodstuffs, while she struggled to pull her keys out of the lock with her other hand.

"Just a minute guys," the struggling woman announced, as she finally pulled her keys out of the lock. "This stuff will get you guys good as new. We just gotta brew it first!"

Vara watched the horror creep over Bishop's face as he realized who this was.

Bishop reached for his face and began to pull the skin down so hard that his metal hand was actually cutting into him. She had always thought this habit was cute, though it looked extremely painful.

"Pawna! Do you live here!?" Bishop screeched, his voice projecting his shock and horror across the room, and daggers into Vara's head.

"Y-yes sir!" A wide-eyed Pawna nervously answered as Vara sidestepped to cover up the urine covered mystery man.

"Pawna!" Bishop continued to yell as he walked toward the nervous Marauder, blood trickling down his face and steam pouring from the already healing wound. "We are so sorry, Pawna! We are so incredibly sorry!"

"Oh, don't be sorry," Pawna cheerily responded, all fear vanishing from her face. "I couldn't let you guys drive all the way back to Monochro Tower like that. So, I brought you guys back here—I figured it was the least I could do."

"Yes, of course! I remember now!" Bishop exclaimed, a nervous expression on his face. His wounds were healed entirely.

His eyes shifted from guilty and nervous to calm. To Vara it looked as if he flipped a switch in his head. Bishop addressed his fellow Marauder, taking the bag out of her hands.

"Pawna, I'm afraid Vara and I have made a bit of a mess in your home," Bishop admitted, while Vara continued to block the urine-soaked man from view. "We really don't want you to see what horrible guests we were to you, even if we were drunk out of our minds during our stay. Would you please leave and come back later when we have the place in order?"

"Oh!" Pawna chirped. "Yes, of course sir, will do!"

Pawna handed him the bags before turning and walking into the bustling Board City day.

Bishop spun on his heel till he faced Vara. He held both his hands up, giving a thumbs up to her.

"Sometimes truth is the best medicine," he proudly stated. "Especially when you don't go into detail." Then the orb warmer in the other room exploded. Bishop jumped several feet back and dropped the bags onto the ground.

He held his chest as he apologized. "Sorry, Var, you know how I get with explosions."

"It's fine, I'm just happy she didn't see the inside."

She let out a breath of relief and fell backward onto the unconscious Varse. This spurred him to wake up with a gasp.

Vara placed her hand on his head and rolled her eyes. "Go back to sleep," she sighed, lifting his head a little before smashing it back into the ground.

CHAPTER 8

KING IN HIS KINGDOM

Hastul awoke in a massive bed rife with yellow silk blankets and pillows embroidered with exotic shapes and patterns.

His eyes drifted lazily across the room while he enjoyed the comfort of his silken sheets. His bedroom was large and cathedral-like in design. Every inch of it was bathed in a different shade of yellow, his favorite color, and large windows tinted the morning light as it poured into the room. The floors were made of expensive metal tiles that had gold melted over them, creating a pathway from the bed's foot to his serpentine throne, which sat on the other end of the room while it awaited its master.

Hastul reached under one of his many pillows, and he produced a mirror from underneath it. It was his favorite; it was golden-hilted, with a serpentine cradle. It felt almost like a part of himself. Although it sounded ridiculous, sometimes he could swear that he could feel which pillow it was hiding under. It was the first mirror he'd ever bought for himself after founding Yelo and taking up magic. He had never parted with it since.

He looked upon his own face, his eyes full of admiration. He ran his black-nailed fingers over his light gray skin. He had created the Yelo and given those too weak to run their own lives a purpose that made them thrive. The weak exist to serve the strong. That was a fact of life. Through his guidance, the weak had forged his citadel of Sinistus—for their own good as well as his own. His hand stopped when it reached the ugly blue scar that blemished his perfect face.

The day he got that blasphemous scar was the day that everything in his life began to turn sour. The day that the Marauders came to Board

City and challenged his rightful claim to power. No, 'challenged' wasn't right. They stole it from him, leaving him with only a few small neighborhoods that were tightly under his control.

His drug trade was badly hurt, Varse trafficking was still going decently well, Mercenary work was out of the question; the more territory they lost, the more extortion money dried up. The Marauders had slurped up everything that they lost but the trafficking, and they were growing rich from it. They were depriving Hastul of his eternal golden age. He'd never forgive them for dirtying his face like this.

Hastul returned the mirror to where he found it, mixing the pillows over it, and pulled himself from the comfort of his bed. The self-styled king pulled his yellow robe off of the foot of the bed and began to walk down the golden pathway toward his throne.

The robe was styled after that of a Magician, the highest level of magic-user that a color magic-user like Hastul could ever attain. Once somebody reached this level of power, they become the truest version of themselves and gained a robe made from the light of their soul, a robe the same color as their magic. Hastul planned to achieve this greatness, but the Marauders had made it impossible for him to focus on the internal journey that was an integral part of the process. So he guessed he'd have to rely on physical practice by using them as screaming targets.

Magic was not something unique to him among the Varse. In fact, it was quite the opposite, every race on Mekebe was capable of magic in some form or fashion, with every individual a possible user. The deterrent for Varse was twofold, though. The normal deterrent was the difficulty of magic, and the often treacherous journey into the recesses of oneself often leads to stagnation or suicide. Varse, however, had a secondary deterrent: magic was a large part of Human, Lean, and Undling cultures, and the Varse hid behind their "divinely gifted" technology to distinguish themselves and give their species a greater sense of identity.

Although Hastul did not believe in the fabled "Divine Provider," the result of this aversion was most fortuitous for him, as it led to most Varse not knowing about Magic's availability. And even if they did, they'd be too caught up in their own cultural aversion to get anywhere with it. Magic made him stand out, and others rightfully feared and respected him for it. Provider be damned.

Hastul sat upon his wooden throne, the same one as the night before, and stepped on a brick beneath him, causing it to sink into the ground. The throne flipped through the wall with Hastul included.

The throne room was large, with stone columns connecting floor to ceiling. A massive door separated Hastul's sanctum from the outside world. All was yellow, of course.

Lawndel was waiting for him on the other side. He held a bowl of small, gelatinous turquoise orbs in his hands.

"Refreshments, sir?" Lawndel asked, holding the bowl out to Hastul.

"Yes. Thank you," Hastul replied, picking one of the marble-shaped balls out of the bowl and throwing it into his mouth.

The orb tasted like a mix of mint and steak. It was his favorite, and the concoction immediately removed the sleep from his mouth.

"How long have you been waiting here, Lawndel?" Hastul asked as he chewed.

"Three hours, sir," Lawndel answered. "I waited for you to wake up before reporting, just as you had instructed me."

"Good, good," Hastul nodded, swallowing his refreshment orb. "Your ability to follow my instructions is by far one of your best qualities."

"Thank you, sir."

Hastul began to walk forward toward the large, gold-plated doors at the other end of the room. "Lawndel, how are our funds holding up?" he asked, not taking his eyes off the door.

"The way things are right now, sir," Lawndel answered, trying to keep the pace with his master, "we should be able to support things as they are for about another two months. Then we will have to start cutting corners to keep things the way you like them."

"Excellent." Hastul pressed his hands against the doors and began to push them open. "Two months is more than enough time."

The doors opened up, allowing the sunlight to leak into the throne room. Hastul stepped out onto the walkway where two of his elite Lem guards stood, and he looked down upon the village beneath him. The village was made out of several dozen sugar cube shaped white apartment blocks, a large greenhouse, and a massive yellow painted wall mounted with large turrets that surrounded the whole brutalist style compound.

Inside the walls was a concrete forest compared to the unforgiving jungle of Board City. Faceless low-ranking Yelo members, also known amongst themselves as Bans, scurried around, doing their assigned tasks like ants in a colony. All this to keep things running smoothly. All this to keep things as they were. All things at the behest of Hastul.

Hastul smiled. The weak need the strong. They cannot live correctly on their own, not without the will of one greater than themselves pushing them to action. These people were disenfranchised from Board City and other places like it, and they gave themselves to him so that he could alleviate them from the burden of thought. Sure, one defected every now and again, but most would rather return to the utopia he created for them than try and strike out on their own. Those ungrateful ones did bother him, though. The thought that people could worm their way out of his grasp infuriated him to no end. At least he had his loyal hunter to drag their corpses back to him.

He moved his eyes over the wall. Beyond it was the city. Miles away and in the middle of the Varcian desert sat Board City, which shined like a magnificent rainbow-colored jewel at night. Nobody had ever fully conquered the former Varcian city-state, but he had come the closest. It was a jewel that Hastul was determined to dye entirely yellow.

Board cities and the other Husk cities of Outer Varcia were once-thriving city states that pledged fealty to the monarch of Inner Varcia. After revolting and then warring amongst one another, they became isolated, and the nobility that ruled them fell to the people. Anarchy was birthed from this, and it was swiftly filled by the gangs that formed soon after to fill the power vacuum. It had been this way as long as anybody alive could remember, or at least, anyone he knew that was alive.

"Lawndel," Hastul called, not moving his eyes from the city. "I believe today is the day to continue testing the waters to see if we can put Operation Cassilda fully into motion."

"Yes sir," Lawndel answered dutifully. "The locations listed in the cell phone have been given to our agents in Monochro; they will strike as soon as they are commanded."

"Good," Hastul yawned, the night before having taken its toll on his restfulness. "See to it that it goes smoothly. I am going to return to my quarters for the afternoon. I want you to make sure that those sub-

Varse mongrels see their faces in the mirror of defeat. If this goes well, we will move on to phase two. If not, back to the drawing board, and do send an update to Overseer Thirty-Two in Yellow Light. They must be ready to jump into action as soon as we call."

"Of course, sir."

Chapter 9

The Redder the Better

Patho stirred the fluid in his beaker, humming to himself. He stuck a syringe in the concoction and sucked up the clear odorless fluid. It was nothing more than a common anesthetic, but it was an essential element in his next project. He would be needing a lot more than this batch if his calculations were correct. Sadly, it would have to wait; he had a guest coming, and she was not somebody who would tolerate being treated like an afterthought.

The lab was a fairly large room filled with blinking and whirring machines, each one designed for some scientific purpose or whatever Patho needed them for. A table holding a demonic-looking set of armor made of a beautiful silver metal sat in the middle of the room. On the other end was his assistant's little area of illegible notes and odd mechanical parts. The very back of the room glowed a soft red from his energy forge, which itself greatly resembled a lava lamp. Boxes of shimmering charge Raiga crystals surrounded it; they were his most valuable available equipment. Lastly was the newest addition to his little sanctuary, an unconscious man tied to a hospital bed. Patho had borrowed them both from the infirmary.

He was placed next to the door, and he was also the reason the Patho needed the anesthetics. Patho set the beaker down, turning his attention to one of his humming machines.

He walked over to the coffee maker, picking up the cup from underneath it. Patho returned to his table which held the armor, and he placed the cup on it. He didn't drink coffee, but a lot of his guests did enjoy the drink. Plus, a little bit of homey comfort helped to not deter others from talking to him. Another nifty plus was that his assistant, Rook, talked less when he had something to drink.

The mechanical door to his lab slid open. A Varse woman walked into the cold, metallic room. She was wearing a large black overcoat with gray rags randomly sewn into it, and hooked chains hung from her head like hair would on a Human woman. She had a small blue scar underneath her lip and a large blue lumi tattoo of flames crawling up her neck, but most striking was the rusted prosthetic claw where her right hand should've been.

She refused to give others her real name for reasons unknown to Patho, so instead, he and others addressed her as Claw. It was a name she seemed ambivalent to.

"Here for more Raiga shells?" he inquired, expecting the usual requests from his guest. "You do know that you're the only one that uses such dangerous ammunition, right? It takes me a while to get around to making more of them. People usually want their guns to fire solid Raiga, not liquid."

She responded to him promptly by throwing a metallic vest with leather hooked chains attached to the back onto the floor of the room. The vest made a loud clang as it slid on the metal floor of the lab.

Claw looked Patho dead in his holographic eyes. "How do I use it?"

"Well," Patho sighed with a shrug. "I need to know what it is before I give you any advice, Claw, and if it's what I think it is, there's a club for that kind of stuff down the street."

"And what do you think it is?" Claw snarled.

"An object for your personal use," he responded nonchalantly, his eyes moving from the vest on the ground back to his guest. "Claw, I have no interest in your personal life, and I don't know why you thought I would.

Claws face became a mix of rage and embarrassment. "Wait, I know what you're inferring. You know I'm not interested in—"

"I made coffee; do you want it?" Patho interrupted not allowing the chain-haired woman to finish her sentence.

Claw shut her eyes and clicked her metal fingers together before exhaling. "What kind is it?" Claw responded. Having calmed herself down, her eyes drifting from the coffee to the silver armor next to it.

"Is that made of eatherium?" she asked immediately, forgetting the coffee.

"Yes," Patho answered with a devilish smile crawling across his face. "It's my most precious pet project at the moment."

"Precious is an understatement. So what does it do?" Claw pressed, as she studied the ultra-rare metal on Patho's table.

"It's simple body armor, no technology internally," Patho answered. "You should know by now that despite my position here I don't actually enjoy using technology for my personal defense."

"That's actually a good transition back to my original reason for being here." Claw sipped her coffee. "The vest isn't technology, it's an artifact."

"Like an *artifact*-artifact, or like a mundane historical kind?" Patho replied, his interest peaking.

"The magic type," Claw responded, carefully placing the cup back on the table with her left hand. "I want you to tell me how to use it."

Patho pursed his lips. An attempt at any kind of magic was a rarity for a Varse. Artifacts were especially rare on the continent of Unos for that very reason. This conversation was going to be an interesting experience.

"You do know the seriousness of what you are asking me, right?" Patho sighed loudly as he asked this question. "If you choose the wrong type, you will end up offing yourself."

"I thought that was a myth," Claw said, her stoic demeanor beginning to slightly crack. "Don't you just pick one and go to work?"

"Magic is an intensely personal process, my friend. To violate your innate leanings is to create an unhealing wound in your soul—a wound that will end inevitably in your death."

Claw shifted uncomfortably. He knew that she had been in her fair share of life-threatening situations. That was life in Outer Varcia, but the thought of suicide made her viscerally uncomfortable. She didn't live through all those fights to die over something as small as giving herself a slight advantage in life. His train of thought was suddenly interrupted by the sound of muffled screaming from behind her. The man in the hospital bed had woken up and was struggling against his restraints.

"Oh, sorry about that," Patho calmly said, standing up with the syringe in hand. "Artex came back this morning pretty roughed up. That man was with him, and he happened to fit the exact needs of an experiment that I've been working on, so I helped myself."

Patho stuck the syringe into Zoog's arm, adding another needle mark to his left arm. He injected the terrified Varse with the anesthetic, and watched his body swiftly fall limp as a drug-induced sleep came over him.

"Don't worry, it's non-addictive," Patho reassured Claw who showed not even the remotest sign of caring. He walked from the hospital bed to the table, picked up one of the clawed gauntlets, and began to run his fingers around it.

"Claw, this is made of the strongest and sharpest metal that has ever been created. A truly perfect metal." Patho put the glove onto his hand, flexing his fingers with an incredibly satisfied look on his face. "The walls of my lab are a reinforced steel alloy. Now watch."

Patho placed his clawed index finger upon the wall and pulled down with force. It looked as if the wall itself was pulling away from the touch of the glove.

"I get my supply of this wonderful metal through the efforts and sacrifices of a dear friend of mine. My reasons for using it are not as kind as its source, however." He held his hand out toward Claw, palm splayed. "I am a user of color magic, specifically red magic. A magic that increases the potency of physical impacts." Claw watched as a deep red aura began to surround the claw like a blob of violently churning water.

"Claw, there is nothing in this world that brings me greater pleasure than the feeling of ripping something alive apart with my bare hands. That is why I chose red, or you could say red chose me," Patho mused. "As a friend, I'll warn you now. If you really wish to pursue magic, put a lot of thought into your decision. Then come back to me. Otherwise, it will feel as if a trident pierced your very soul, and you will certainly destroy your life."

"I prefer guns anyway," she muttered under her breath as she stormed out, having barely touched her coffee.

"Do come again soon," Patho shouted. "Next time, I'll be sure to have an errand for you to run." The Marauders' chief scientist turned his attention to the unconscious Zoog as he removed the glove from his hand.

"Now, how long does it take for the worst withdrawal to set in again?" he wondered aloud.

CHAPTER 10

THE TOWER

Monochro Tower stood tall in the very heart of Board City. The building looked like a large monochromatic needle, and was tipped with a penthouse. Altogether, it looked like a sewing needle with a black and white cork covering its tip.

Although it was an impressive sight to behold, the tower actually only consisted of two real areas on the surface: the social area on the ground floor and the penthouse on the top. Beneath the surface, however, was a series of floors that served as gyms, Patho's lab, an infirmary, and a myriad of other things.

Bishop and Vara strolled together toward the looming tower, arms locked. The couple entered the building. The lobby of the tower was used as a large auction house by Yelo, and way before that they heard that it was a vacant unfinished building that was going to be used as an administrative area for the crumbling city state. The Marauders converted it into a massive sea of cushions and couches; it was much more fun that way. Thanks to Patho's beautiful mind, the reinforced windows of the lobby doubled as massive TV screens, although they could only play in blue and white. Several Marauders were scattered about on the couches; some were watching Human things broadcasted all the way from Dagroum. A large group was gathered around another screen watching the marathon countdown to the season finale of *Vivvedell's Blossoms.* Others nursed their hangovers with ice packs and annoyed faces.

"Good to see everyone enjoyed their night," Bishop whispered to Vara with a smile. "I think they all needed this. Next time, we will hold another one for the guys in Grandmin—we know they need it. Especially Mivrail."

"That guy always looks like he's about to explode," Vara chimed in. "I don't get how he can be with someone like Lode for so long and still be that stressed all the time."

"Love works in mysterious ways, I guess."

Bishop perked up and began to look around the lobby. "Speaking of mysterious ways," he pointed out, almost lamenting the state of the room. "I'm surprised the twins aren't here."

"I'm glad they aren't," Vara grumbled.

"What?"

"I said I don't think Pawna's house deserved that," Vara returned the smile from earlier.

"Don't remind me. I feel terrible about that," he groaned. "We are the last people that should have put her through that."

"By the way, which one of us is going to call Pawna when the cleaners finish up?" Bishop asked, as he and Vara began to part ways, each heading toward separate elevators. "'Cause it looks to me like you're going to go run around in the basement, and if you're doing that, then I think it should be me who makes the call. On account of the noise and all."

"Yeah, I'm going down to work on my form for a bit," Vara laughed. "I hope that these cleaners were worth the bill."

"Well if they aren't, it's our job as dissatisfied customers to give them some 'constructive criticism,'" Bishop replied, pressing the up button on the elevator as Vara pressed the down button on the other.

Bishop stepped into the elevator. He pressed the button for the top floor, and the machine began to lift him there with a soft whirring sound. He could see sparse images of Monochro in between the bars of steel that intermittently interrupted his view and cloaked him in shadow.

Monochro was the cleanest and safest part of Board City, with a number of shops, cafes, restaurants, and pretty secure drug dens that all claimed to function just as they would in a classier Inner Varcian town. The streets were a pitch-black that matched the shade painted on some of the various buildings that surrounded it, with the other buildings being a stark white. The sizes ranged from large towers that reached greedily for the diamond shaped sun to small, box-like structures where cafes and other small businesses took up shop. Right next to Monochro Tower there was a large building consisting of several large garages. They were Marauder-owned and Marauder-used.

There was still a lot of crime here. Hell, the gang was the largest part of it, but the Marauders didn't really abuse their positions as much as the other governing forces of the city had when they had their time in the limelight. People usually got a warning about not paying on time instead of just being immediately shot. That business model never really seemed sustainable to Bishop.

The elevator door slid open smoothly. The top floor was a living quarters shared between him and the other original members, although he had no clue what Patho used his room for since he didn't sleep. He probably stored more of his half-finished pet projects in there.

The floor of the penthouse that Bishop was on contained a large living room with cream-colored furniture. A massive television hung from the ceiling, suspended by strong, thin wires, and stairs leading up to the next floor sat right next to a small kitchen and bar setup. The walls here were made of a Patho-designed, reinforced glass that was made with Vara in mind. A dart covered Yelo poster hung loosely on the wall; it depicted three masked figures looking proudly at a large golden sun that was setting over a city. And the floor shifted from a beige carpet to similarly colored tiles depending on where you were in the room.

Bishop walked forward toward the window, not paying any attention to the elevator behind him descending. He pressed his metallic hand on the glass. While he stared down at Monochro, his mind was racing like an energy bullet through the open air.

He recruited members, armed them, and led them all for moments like these—moments where they weren't just members of some giant gang, or when he wasn't just some crowd-pleasing warlord, but a group of people who had a place to actually call home and live their own lives the way they wanted to, thanks to the strength they built together. Every one of them deserved it; every one of them earned it. What he didn't expect was that the same growing power and stability that allowed the others to thrive would be the very thing that made him feel like he was completely useless.

His thoughts drifted to his close friends. Those individuals had been with him since the beginning of his new life, and those had stood with him shouldering the burden of the Marauders' dream when it seemed like a fun impossibility.

He envied their growth. Vara became more skilled in Bruteil, Patho picked up science scarily fast, and Artex learned how to channel his anger constructively, mostly. Bishop had just become a face to a gang that pretty much ran without him, and planned parties to try and keep everyone in a good mood to not notice how redundant he was—a task that he knew he was failing at.

When things got quiet like this, his mind would always rush back to dark places, specifically back to his birthplace of Nod. That and explosions always made his heart flutter. When the Marauders were still wrestling for dominance of the city, he was able to fight them off, but now he felt them creeping into his head a little bit more every day.

Vara was the only one who knew anything about Nod, and even then, nowhere near the whole story. She was the only one that Bishop knew he could confide in without them trying to force him to deal with what took place. For some reason unbeknownst to him, she had faith in his ability to work it out on his own.

Everyone had their demons. Bishop knew this, but it didn't comfort him. Nothing could undo what happened. He could only try to safeguard the future for those he cared for before his guilt eventually dragged him down to the hole where he belonged.

The elevator behind him dinged, thankfully interrupting his train of thought.

Artex stepped out of the elevator, and somberly walked toward Bishop. "Bish," Artex called out. "I think Elledia might be a spy."

"No shit."

"Huh?" Artex blurted in utter shock, his jaw almost hitting the ground. "Di-did you already know that?"

"Yeah, didn't you?" Bishop chuckled, feeling a little hurt. "I swore I texted you the details, like, four nights ago. Did you not see it?"

Artex went pale. "Did you say *four* nights ago?"

"Yeah."

Artex opened his mouth and wagged his finger at Bishop as he prepared to speak. "I uh … I was, you know, uh . . ." Artex snapped his fingers. "I was in the same room as Elledia for an extended period of time four days ago, and I could not find my phone after said period of time." He took a breath. "But she did seek me out later the next day to return it!"

"Wow, Artex, that is the weirdest way you could have said that you sle—"

"What I did or did not do is not important," Artex screamed. "Bishop, what are we going to do? I think she read through my phone." Artex whimpered, his legs having grown weak from the realization. "I can only imagine what she knows now. Oh shit, Bishop! She probably read through my other contacts too. Bishop, she knows what we've all been talking about, and who knows where she's sending it! That's probably why I didn't see the message."

"Well, for one thing, Artex, she's not sending any of it anywhere at present. Silt put a bullet in her head last night," Bishop soothingly announced to his pale friend, trying his best to calm him down. "And for another thing, the last thing I sent you before that was a picture of Vara with twelve nutriorbs in her mouth, and besides, all the important conversations between the Leadership take place in person. You know that."

Artex caught himself on the cream-colored couch just as his knees were about to give. "Oh thank goodness," he loudly exhaled. "I can't imagine what she could have gained from this, then. Hopefully nothing."

Bishop hated seeing Artex like this. He was always much harder on himself than he needed to be when something went wrong, even if the situation had nothing to do with him. He was the exact opposite of his sister.

"Art, how did you find out she was a traitor if you didn't get the message I sent you?" Bishop asked out of a combination of pure curiosity and hoping to move the topic to something that would end Artex's guilt trip.

"She had me in The Brooks," Artex began. "And if it weren't for a new gun Patho had made for me a while back, I would've died on a bridge at the hands of some Yelo scumbags."

He should have double-checked with everyone about Elledia, but no, he just had to plan for last night instead. What happened to Artex was his fault, and it wouldn't have even happened if Bishop had done his job right and checked in with his gang's organizer.

"Artex didn't die," he told himself. "All that they have to do is to strike back at Yelo hard enough for them to get the message and screw off. Then everything will be fine."

Bishop inhaled deeply before exhaling sharply. "Well, the important thing is that you survived, and that we now—"

Bishop's phone buzzed in his pocket. "Excuse me for a minute, Artex," he said, checking the phone. "Ahh, the cleaning's done. I gotta make a call real quick—then we will finish talking about this. Your sister and I made a bit of a mess."

Artex nodded hurriedly. Bishop called Pawna, and she luckily picked up swiftly. "Hey Pawna, you can go home now the cleaning is done."

"Oh that's great news. I'm with Lode right now and I'll head home when—" she suddenly gasped, and Bishop heard the sound of glass shattering.

Bishop heard Pawna shriek before the sound of a blast rendered her silent and sent his heart on a roller coaster. He began to shake violently while holding the phone.

Multiple blue explosions began to erupt in the streets of Monochro. Several of the smaller buildings and one high-rise parking garage completely collapsed in on themselves. People running in the streets were being mowed down by rapid volleys of energy bullets. Blue blood and bodies were quickly filling up the streets. The aggressors were indistinguishable from those they were attacking. Several Marauders came running out into the streets, their own weapons drawn as they began firing at those who they thought were responsible for the attacks. Energy bullets filled the air as one by one the aggressors fell to the Marauders' guns, but not without taking a good number of the responding Marauders out with them.

The two Marauder leaders in the penthouse stared at the carnage below them in complete silence, not knowing how or why this was happening. The whole debacle could be heard over the phone. Thoughts of Nod began to flicker into Bishop's head. It was so similar, yet so different, that he could feel his perception of reality falling apart. He saw the single sand-dusted street of Nod as if he were still there. Then he saw the lent house and the fear in Artex's eyes.

"Bishop?"

CHAPTER 11

WHAT'S YOUR NAME?

A group of Bans walked through the streets of Monochro, one after the other in a perfectly straight line. They lacked their signature yellow Yelo masks, and they were dressed so that it would be impossible to tell them apart from an ordinary citizen of Board City. One of them, a young woman, reached up and caressed the gray-white skin of her face. It had been years since she was last allowed to remove her mask; the fresh air felt weird on her skin.

The mission they were on was essentially suicide, but it was hammered into her that no price was too high to ensure the future of Yelo. Despite this, it felt like a pit was forming in her gut. The feeling was very familiar. She was sure she had felt it at some point before, but she could not place her finger on exactly when that was, or what it was.

She walked silently at the back of the line. The other Yelo members in front of her were similarly silent, with the exception of their operation leader. He was a Lem, or a higher ranking member of the gang, and he was reminding his underlings of the importance of their mission.

She had heard around the compound that a mission like this was being planned, but never in her life did she think she would be selected for it. The whole thing started with a cellphone that was stolen from one of the Marauder higher-ups. That's how they were able to get the locations in Monochro that they were going to strike—from the conversation logs with other Marauders. None of the locations were actually officially affiliated with their rivals, but they were expected to have a high Marauder concentration inside during this time of day. The mission was called for by the glorious leader of Yelo himself.

The Yelo members had spent two days in Monochro preparing for the operation. They did not get to enjoy much of the city life while they were there, though; a strict code was written for missions that required the shedding of the normally mandatory mask. The code that had to be followed to the letter, or the superior officers would discipline their subordinates by removing an eye from the offending party. All mirrors in the rooms they were staying in must either be destroyed or removed from the premises. No Yelo members may interact with nonmembers, and they may only interact with one another in the presence of a superior officer, and even then, they must only speak when spoken to.

A lump began to form deep in her throat as the group got closer to their target. It felt like someone was squeezing the base of her neck. The pit in her stomach had grown deeper, yet she still could not identify the alien emotion that vexed her.

Back in Sinustus, her assigned role was as one of the greenhouse workers. This was a far cry from that, but she would do anything that was asked of her by the organization that had given her so much. She had lived a comfortable life.

She had been a member of Yelo since she was a teenager and had not looked back. Time felt like a blur of comfortable monotony leading up to this point, when she was asked to fully repay all she owed.

Her right eye began to leak water. It dripped down her face while the other two feelings continued to worsen.

The streets of Monochro were almost vacant, save a few non-aligned Varse and Marauders that lingered outside of some of the businesses. Once in awhile, someone would walk out of a building and stumble into another. Monochro was notoriously more active at night, on account of it mainly just being a seat for whatever gang held power at the moment, and its business only existing to entertain them and the Board City Elite that befriended them. She had never been here when Yelo held power, but she doubted that the bars did anywhere near as well then.

The female Ban looked around Monochro. The tower in its center played host to the enemies of her people, but it was once a great auction house. She fondly remembered those auctions, since sometimes they would be broadcasted on a great screen in Sinustus for the Yelo to watch while they worked. This all changed when the Marauders challenged Hastul's great vision for the city and took that small pleasure away from them.

Each Yelo member that was here held a large satchel on their sides. Each one held some grenades, and either a rapid fire or a pistol—whatever vice-commander Lawndel thought they were most fit to use. She herself had a pistol. She had never shot a gun in her life, but she thought throwing a grenade should be easy enough.

The group walked by an alley, and they found themselves in front of a restaurant with large windows. She peeked inside the restaurant. She saw an assortment of Varse inside. Some were eating actual foodstuffs like meat or vegetables, while others were dining on sweet pastel-colored nutrition orbs. The water was running out of her other eye now, and the feeling in her stomach and throat we're getting to be unbearable. She blinked the water away, and she noticed something else in the window. One of the Varse had stood up and walked to the window. The stranger was looking directly into her eyes; the woman's eyes watered, her mouth a frown, and oddly she was semi-translucent. She recognized this girl. It was her reflection.

It had been years since she had seen herself. She was an average looking Varse woman with ovular eyes, and a slightly smaller mouth than normal. Her body began shaking uncontrollably, she barely noticed the group leader yell out his order of attack.

Instinct took over when she realized what was actually about to happen. There was no glory in this, and Yelo saw no qualms about throwing her life away to feed whatever goal they were aiming for. It dawned on her just how replaceable she really was. She didn't want to die here.

Queenie acted on pure instinct. As the others began to open fire on the diner, she sprinted into the alley and tried to duck behind the restaurant's dumpster. She slid on some muck and fell to the ground while the world exploded around her. Tears were pouring out of her eyes as she curled into the fetal position. Queenie recognized the emotion now. It was one of many that she was deprived of during her time in Yelo. Sadness.

Chapter 12

Marauders

Zoog struggled uselessly against his restraints as he watched the suited Human man sort through crates of what looked like raw Raiga and boxes of disjointed machinery. He had no idea where he was or how long he had been here, he did know who that man was though. It was Patho, the Marauders resident psychopath.

Zoog twisted and turned his head until he was able to dislocate his jaw. Getting out of binds like this had always been a talent of his, and he finally slipped out of the rag that was covering his mouth.

"Help!" Zoog began to feebly scream as soon as he freed his mouth.

Patho slowly turned around. He held a syringe in his hand, and an impossibly wide smile on his face.

Zoog strained harder against the bed, watching the grinning Patho slowly approach, like a lion stalking its prey. "Stay away from me!" he screechedh his voice barely coherent, while trying to shake the bed away from the scientist. "Get that needle away from meh you freaking mammal!"

***

The smile on Patho's face grew to the very limits that the hologram would allow, his false pink gums completely exposed as he reached the restrained Varse.

"Are you sure you want me to keep this away?" he gleefully hissed, leaning over Zoog, needle pointed at his arm. "You seem like quite the needle enthusiast to me."

Patho pierced the arm of the screaming man and pressed down the plunger. Once again, he watched the panicking Zoog relax into an induced sleep.

"Delightful," Patho hummed to himself, as he went to continue playing with his machines. "I should probably make a stronger anesthetic than this."

A ringing soon filled the room. It was a basic tone more similar to an alarm than a standard ringtone, but Patho knew the sound was that of his wretched phone. He picked it up warily and answered.

"Hello."

"Patho, you gotta come up here," the panicked voice of Artex buzzed through the phone. "There was some kind of attack outside, and Bishop's freaking out like I've never seen! I have no idea what's gotten—"

Patho hung up the phone, his face showing almost no emotion. The grim news did fill him with concern, of course, but he knew that listening to Artex yell about it wouldn't help the situation actually resolve. He placed the phone back on the desk. He wouldn't be needing it any time soon; he had something much better in mind.

Patho stepped out of his lab, making his way toward the elevator. The hall was narrow, with fluorescent lights hanging from the ceiling that lit up the metal-tiled floor and walls. Patho calmly pressed the up button on the elevator.

The door opened with a slick sliding sound. A light gray hand with black nails darted out of the still opening door. The hand wrapped around Patho's face and easily yanked him into the elevator.

"Hurry up!" Vara yelped, releasing Patho's face from her iron grasp. "The others need us!"

Patho collected himself. Although he was of course concerned about Bishop's well-being, the gang as a whole had just been hit with some kind of large-scale attack. He could not watch this iteration of the Marauders fall apart like the last one. That was his top priority: making sure that order was restored, and that this smear on their name was avenged with the utmost brutality.

"Bishop will be fine, Vara, we've gotten through worse situations than this one," he said, starting to reach for the back of his neck. "This is just another obstacle that we must overcome."

Vara anxiously tapped her foot while the elevator lifted them out of the basement. "You don't understand," she responded as she stared at the elevator door with laser focus. "We got attacked on our home turf. I'm more worried about what impact this will have on Bishop."

"Such things happen, Vara," Patho sighed, grasping the touch realistic hologram generator attached to the nape of his neck. "It happened a few times to the first iteration of Marauders. It's just a part of life."

"I know this happens, Patho," she retorted, her white pupils darting to the scientist at her side. "The issue is that this has happened before to Bishop too, and it didn't leave a good taste in his mouth."

"Such things rarely do, but you have to move past them to prevent more." The elevator dinged as the duo reached the penthouse floor.

Artex paced around the room, mumbling to himself. Artex stopped as soon as he noticed their presence, a weary smile coming to his face as he jogged to the other two members of the quartet.

"Oh, thank goodness you two are here," he panted as they walked out of the elevator. "Right after all the explosions, he started panicking and shit. I know he's always hated them, but I've never seen him do anything like that before. Then he locked himself in his room."

Patho ripped the generator from the back of his neck, causing the image he had been wrapped in to shatter from his frame. The generator's crab-like legs unfurled as it deactivated. Patho appeared as a six-foot tall featureless and smooth outline of a male Humanoid; he was a semi-translucent red color, and he wore no clothing.

"What exactly happened here, Artex?" he asked, his voice seeming to just radiate off of him without the solid frame of his hologram to channel it out of his mouth.

Vara couldn't focus on what her brother was saying, it didn't matter to her right now. She needed to help Bishop, any way she could. Her priority was only the four of them. It always had been. Everything else was a fun hobby as far as she was concerned. She enjoyed the other Marauders, but they weren't her family like Artex was, and the other two became. They did not come first.

She tightened the muscles in her legs, and then she sprung. Bruteil was the single largest part of her life, not that she had much of a choice about that anymore. The practice involved using the springlike physiology found in some of the muscles of the Varse body to increase the strength and speed of the practitioner exponentially. It was an art form considered by many to be too risky as it was much deadlier to learn than to use, and it was mighty deadly when used. If one were to ever stop training their body for a long period of time, their muscles would begin to rapidly disintegrate. To Vara, though, the boons had always seemed worth the downsides. She'd practiced it for most of her life.

The second floor of the penthouse was covered in a deep blue paint, and a carpet of a similar hue. The room had a table with four seats in the center and three doors each to a different bedroom. On the wall next to the stairs was a red glowing keyboard with a small red screen, and a trident symbol floating from edge to edge was projected on it.

Vara ran to the door of their room and she knocked on it rapidly. Bishop opened the door a crack, wide enough to allow Vara to catch a glance of the large iron wardrobe on the right wall. He had told her to never go in there, that it was something he couldn't part with, but was too painful for him to ever see again. She wondered if it was connected to what was happening now.

"Vara, I can't talk right now. I just need some time alone," he whispered, his words sounding rehearsed and his face contorting from one pained expression to another.

Vara felt a pit form in her stomach. Every word out of Bishop's mouth was tearing into her like a knife would meat. Even if he had to be alone, there was no reason he had to *be alone.* He needed them all, and she knew that. All of them needed to be close by while he pulled himself together; she knew they'd do it for her, and vice versa. This emergency thing outside could wait. All those people . . . those strangers could handle themselves for a little while. They were all mostly adults anyway. The other two would understand, or she'd have to make them.

"Vara, I'm sorry I can't talk anymore," he stammered to her in a whisper. "I'm going back in."

Vara moved with purpose as she left Bishop in the room, shutting the door behind her. Her eyes were set on the keypad in front of her. It activated a protective veil around the penthouse, cutting it off from the rest of the tower—keeping all in or out. The downside was that once it was activated, it would stay for forty-eight hours. She entered the code without a second thought.

Patho and Artex watched as a red blob of energy slid down from the roof, temporarily dyeing the interior of the room a bloody crimson. The blob of energy turned from a deep red to clear as it finished its descent.

"What the frig?" Artex asked, a look of utter bewilderment on his face as he stared out at the protective field. Patho began walking toward the stairs.

"Don't worry," Patho assured him. "I made this so that the same code that starts it would reduce the time to three hours if put in backwards. Think of it as some planning time instead of a horrible delay. That's what I'm going to do."

Vara met Patho at the halfway point of the stairs. She whispered a cacophony of swears to herself. She didn't know that entering "PITCHFORK" backward would reduce the time.

"You are not entering that code, Patho," Vara yelled to Patho, who had begun to climb his way up the stairs.

"I think I am, Vara," he responded, trying to force his way past her.

Vara moved to block his path. "Patho, Bishop needs us here with him," she pleaded with the red outline. "If we aren't there for him then who will be."

"The gang is in disarray," Patho stated coldly, trying to shove past the Varse woman once again. "Bishop can wait, we need to focus on what's most important before we deal with his psychological issues."

Vara's face contorted with rage, and she placed her hand on the smooth red shoulder of Patho, grasping it firmly. Then she violently flung him across the room. He smashed into the reinforced glass.

Artex heard the loud smack, and he watched a very angry Patho slowly slide down the glass, landing perfectly upright.

Patho moved his featureless head to Vara. "You are forgetting the place we hold in this gang, Vara," he hissed, his forearms and legs becoming cloaked in a fiery red light. "Must I remind you that duty always comes first."

"Our place!?" Vara yelled, reaching into the back of her dress and producing twin silver hilts; each one had a blue and black gem implanted into them." The real Marauders are the four of us, everyone else is just an accessory!" Vara flicked on her energy daggers by pressing the black gems inward on the hilt. Blue light poured out forming into blades concentrated in Raiga energy.

CHAPTER 13

QUEEN OF THE ALLEY

Queenie sat in the alleyway for what felt like an eternity. The sounds of gunfire and explosions had finally stopped. Despite this, she felt no new comfort. Her eyes were still watering.

From what she could tell, the Marauders had switched into full panic mode after the attack. Her mind was still struggling with the reality of her situation, former and current. If she could stay curled up in this alley for one thousand years she would, but Queenie did not have a thousand years.

Despite the amazing accomplishment of not dying, Queenie still had a massive problem on her hands. She had just dug herself out of years of horrible brainwashing, and done so seconds before she was supposed to go and die for the ones who brainwashed her—she still had to get out of this alleyway without being confronted by the currently blood-lusting Marauders, who she was assuming that by now had noticed that all the attackers wore the same exact design of satchel.

She still had the weapons inside hers, of course, but Queenie was sure pulling them out of her bag was a great way to ensure that she would swiftly get a bullet in her head.

Queenie had no idea what move to make; she knew that the first step in any possible escape was getting up off the ground, but she didn't feel ready to forsake her sanctuary—smelly as it was. She leaned herself on the side of the dumpster. Queenie pinched her left arm to stifle the tears.

She remembered what initially led her to join up with Yelo. A string of bad occurrences had left her with nowhere to go but the streets of The Brooks. It all started when her parents had died of a freak fire, and as a result of her late father's gambling habits, she inherited his debts to the Board City Zingers. Although eventually she did end up choosing the comforting presence of a desolate alleyway in her life over the cold ease of having her life lived for her in Yelo. At the time, it felt like it was the right choice for her to make, and they did end up removing the Zingers from her old neighborhood, which was a cathartic plus.

Queenie let out a deep sigh. She had no idea where she would go from here. The world was full of new and familiar possibilities for her to discover, or find again. The choices she made, as scary as it was, filled her with an excitement that felt like a fire burning within her chest. She briefly began to wonder if she had inherited her father's habits. The sudden sound of approaching footsteps snapped her back to reality.

She peeked her head out from behind the vomit green wall of the dumpster, trying as hard as she could not to be seen by whoever was approaching. There was a man walking down the alleyway. From the silver energy pistol in his right hand, she guessed that he wasn't looking to make friends.

The man wore the normal Marauder attire that she was used to seeing, but with a white lab coat that draped over his shoulders. He moved skittishly down the alleyway, muttering to himself with each step as he willed himself forward. The gun was shaking badly in his grasp. She watched him grab his right arm with his left to stabilize it, but he failed immediately at this when his left arm started shaking soon after he grasped his right.

Queenie reached into the satchel at her side, grabbing her own pistol. The Marauder was going to find her back here if he kept walking, but she wouldn't let herself be found unarmed. There was no way in Hell. She slunk behind the dumpster as the echoing footsteps grew closer and closer.

Queenie shot her arms out, gun in hand, and pointed at his head. "Drop it," she whispered, putting all of her confidence into those two words.

The Marauder man dropped his gun with a sharp clang. He put his hands straight up in the air. His eyes bugged out, and his face shattered into an expression of pure and absolute panic.

"Be quiet," Queenie intimidatingly whispered. "Anything more than a whisper from you and I shoot. Got it?"

Queenie did not want to have to kill this man, but she was trying to mentally prepare herself to pull the trigger if he didn't comply. Even if the sound of the gun alerted others to her presence, she should at least have enough time to climb into the dumpster and hide.

"Don't shoot. Don't shoot. Don't shoot. Don't shoot." The Varse man whisper-yelled, looking as if he was about to soil himself.

"Get down." Queenie motioned for the man to sit beside her, where the dumpster would block him from the view of those on the street. She kept the gun on him the whole time.

He quickly moved to where she had motioned. "I'm sorry," he whispered to her, a genuine but confused look of regret in his eyes. "Please don't kill me."

She couldn't believe this guy was a Marauder. He was shaking like a leaf even now.

"Wh-who are you?" Queenie asked, exhausting her confidence.

"M-my name is Rook," he squeaked.

CHAPTER 14

THE REMATCH

Artex watched his sister and Patho lunge at one another, magic and daggers in hand. He, however, knowing how things could go when these two got worked up, was cautiously ducking behind the couch.

The two Marauders met in midair, and Vara swiftly dodged a magic-covered swipe from Patho. She maneuvered herself in the air as the two were about to rocket away from one another. She used her unnatural speed to slice off Patho's right arm. The blue energy of the blade easily cut through the smooth red matter.

Patho crashed into the staircase, his disembodied arm evaporating into a red gas as it hit the carpeted ground with muffled thud. An identical cloud immediately started spewing from his wound, which condensed perfectly into a new arm.

Vara landed smoothly on the other side of the room. "Really, Patho?" Vara laughed, turning to face him with a sarcastic grin and holding her arms out tauntingly. "You're actually holding back against little old me."

"I don't want to kill you, Vara," Patho calmly stated before his tone shifted to a more agitated one. "But I think I could get away with breaking your body to the point where you'd stop being a problem, don't you think?"

Her smile dropped as Patho held his hand toward her, his palm splayed; red energy began churning wildly around it.

"Shit."

Vara sprung upward, dodging the first blast of magic. It burst violently against the window, creating a small explosion of red energy and a large crack in the reinforced glass. She turned her body upside down and kicked off the ceiling to avoid the second blast which landed with similar results to the first. This time she landed on the large television that hung suspended in the air, finding her footing on the top of it.

Patho wrapped the bottoms of his legs with magic before firing off a third blast. Vara once again leaped into the air as the third blast destroyed the television. She twirled in midair, looking back to where she remembered last seeing her opponent. He wasn't there.

Patho slammed into the distracted Vara midair, wrapping his magic-cloaked arm around her waist before launching her into the couch.

Artex, barely seeing this in time, scurried away from his hiding spot just before his sister slammed into it. He stood up and looked at Vara, who was already pulling herself out from the stuffing-strewn wreckage of the couch. He knew she'd be fine, but what wasn't fine was the TV.

"Come on guys, not the twenty-footer!" he yelled to his distracted comrades, internally lamenting the loss of his recorded episodes of *Vivvedell's Blossoms*, and his chances of seeing which Bachelor Vivvedell picked on the big screen.

"It was just the four of us in the beginning, Patho!" Vara grunted as she wound her shoulders. "We're all a big happy family, and those bonds shouldn't be placed on the back burner for people who aren't even close to being a part of that family!"

"You have always been blind to the bigger picture, Vara," Patho confidently responded, striding toward the readying bladesman. "Besides, would a happy family really beat the life out of one another like this?"

Vara smiled as she got into a sprinters position. "It builds character." She laughed before launching herself toward him, becoming only a blur of purple and white. She reached him just as he was attempting to raise his magic-covered hands up to block her.

Vara moved the blue blade of the dagger toward his neck, cutting through it in one swift motion as his dissolving head fell from his shoulders. Vara grabbed onto his shoulder, using it to change direction midsprint so that she was facing behind him. She thrust her other dagger through his back; its tip punctured through the front of his body. She spun the first dagger in her hand before repeating the process while she watched his head reform.

"Let's see how you like being thrown?" she yelled with a giddy smile on her face. However, to her utter dismay, when she tried to throw him, the energy knives cut straight through his torso and took off his left arm instead.

Patho whipped around to Vara, reducing the magic around his hand to a dull glow before delivering a powerful punch to Vara's face. He felt most of her teeth break from the impact.

Vara slid back a few feet and grasped her face for a moment, before taking her hands away and spitting out the pieces of broken teeth. Blue blood was dripping from her mouth and nose slits.

"You're still holding back," she panted with a broken smile.

"Forgive me," Patho sighed, using magic to leap away from the bleeding Varse. "Allow me to correct that mistake."

Artex's mind raced as he helplessly watched them beat the shit out of one another. He knew that they had to compromise, but he also knew that they weren't actually fighting over the Bishop problem. Both of them loved to fight, and they couldn't live a life devoid of violence even if they wanted to. Artex knew and accepted this, but these two had been looking for a rematch since they first met. Now they found one, and Yelo would be hysterically laughing at them if they knew the state that they had devolved to.

He was by no means in the same league as them, or even Bishop. This fact ate away at him every day, but there was one thing that he had on all three of them—one little quality that he could provide to the Marauders that none of the other founders could ever dream of doing as well as he could. Artex could mediate. Artex knew what he had to do. He reached into his jacket.

"I think it's time we stepped this up a notch!" Vara shrieked gleefully, as she pressed down the blue gems in her hilts. The energy daggers became energy swords, and grew a foot and a half longer with a flash of light.

"Curing the paralysis I inflict on you is going to be an interesting side project Vara. That is *if* I can cure it!" Patho raised his voice in retort as his red aura flared across his entire body like an inferno.

The two ran at each other, a psychotic grin of anticipation slowly spreading across Vara's broken face. Patho's fists opened into claws. A dark blue marble flew in between the two. The orb brought a brief pause to them, right before it exploded into a large, dark blue blast.

Patho and Vara jumped back just in time to avoid being caught in it, although the carpet was gone and the metal floor underneath it was now scorched black. Confused, Vara looked around the room for the source of the explosion. Eventually, she settled on a pissed-off looking Artex, who was holding a type of gun that she had never seen before. He had fired the Blunderbuss.

"You two need to stop this bullshit!" Artex scolded, spittle flying out of his mouth as he barked at them. "Do you think that beating the crap out of each other is going to somehow prove one of you right?! What kind of childish-ass logic is that?!"

His eyes began bugging out of his head while he scolded. "You ever consider that maybe you're both right! Huh?! Maybe you both have a point, and that you need to CALM! YOUR! SHIT!"

He looked at Vara, gesturing the gun at her. "You need to understand that just because you value the inner circle more than the rest of the gang, it doesn't mean that everyone else in it doesn't matter, and that we don't owe them for getting us here just as much as each other!"

Artex turned his attention to Patho next. "And you, learn to empathize already! Her lover, and our friend, just turned into a sniveling, helpless mess at the absolute worst time, and I'm guessing that's why she put the field up in the first place. You can't really expect her to think straight after walking into that!"

He lowered his gun. "You are both gigantic children that need to learn that you don't always need the fucking violence. I'll concede to you that it fixes most situations around here, but inner group conflict? NO! It just makes a shitty situation worse!" Silence fell over the room as Vara sheathed her swords, and Patho dispelled his energy.

"Now, if you two are done with your tantrum, let's get to work and try to fix. This. Mess."

"Well, I'm very happy to see you finally found the gun, Artex." Patho added. His demeanor had returned to a state of total calmness.

CHAPTER 15

WALK A MILE

Queenie had Rook helpless, and in the palm of her hand! But she didn't know what to do with him. When she came to Board City, she had the agenda that Yelo had given her, but now that she was on her own, there was nothing to guide her actions besides her own rusty sense of reasoning.

The Marauder beside her sat with his teeth chattering, and his whole body shaking with them as he stared at Queenie. She didn't know for sure if the shaking was coming from fear, anger, or both. She had a strong feeling, though, that it was mostly fear.

Queenie wracked her brain for what to do with this man. She could question him, but what would she gain from it? Another option would be to try and kill him quietly, but that seemed like a waste to her. Something had to be done though—she knew that she couldn't just take a hostage and do nothing with them. That would be odd.

"Who are you?" Rook whispered, taking his captor off-guard.

"What?" Queenie asked.

"Who are you?" Rook repeated, the shock of Queenie making him feel braver. "I think I have a right to know who's pointing a gun at me."

The longer she sat here with him, the more she felt like she took a knee-jerk reaction to this whole thing.

"Uhhhh," Queenie began, as she tried to carefully select her next words. "I'm Queenie."

"Hey!" she quietly yelped at Rook, pressing the gun toward him." I'm the one supposed to be asking the questions."

Rook visibly lost what little confidence he had gained.

"Okay, okay." He frantically motioned for her to calm down as he spoke. "What questions do you want to ask?"

Queenie felt a tinge of panic when she realized what she had said. There were no questions for him. It was too late now. She had already told him she had questions. The words began to fall out of her mouth in the order that she thought them, and as soon as she opened it.

"Are you a Marauder?"

"Yes."

"Why?"

"Why?" Rook repeated.

"Yes," Queenie nodded, trying to pass off an air of certainty.

Rook paused for a moment. "Well, why would anyone join a gang like this? For the perks that come with it."

The answer was not what she was expecting. Although she could understand why some like Rook would be attracted to power, she couldn't believe that he'd sell his soul to this gang just for that. However, she really didn't have room to talk. She needed to end this situation quickly.

"Here's the plan, Rook," Queenie announced to her hostage as she began to remove her satchel. "I'm going to let you go, but in return for my kindness you won't tell anyone about me having been in Yelo and you will let me—"

"You're in Yelo?" Rook said cutting Queenie off, his voice full of a quiet surprise. "Yeah, that makes sense, now that I think about it."

Queenie felt her momentum die as soon as it had started up. She had assumed he knew from the satchel, but it seemed like she was just overthinking things.

"Formerly in Yelo," she loudly corrected. "I quit the gang."

"Well, good for you," Rook's eyes began to drift behind her head. "Quitting your job and sticking it to the man. Like a real champ!"

"There's no reason to be sarcastic about it," Queenie grumbled. "I quit and now I'm free. Do you accept my terms or not?"

A large smile spread across his face. "No."

"What do you mean, no?!"

"I mean you should have responded a bit quieter," Rook started to laugh, his eyes fixed on something behind her. "Monochro is absolutely crawling with us right now."

Something heavy hit Queenie across the back of her head. She fell to the ground, hearing Rook's voice along with the voice of a woman and the rattling of chains before losing consciousness.

Her head was spinning when she returned to the world of the waking. Queenie couldn't move her arms. She began to look around and saw that she was tied up and sat in the middle of the street surrounded by a horde of angry Marauders. They were hurling rocks and swears at a bound man that was dressed similarly to her; his jaw was limp and broken.

The streets were filled with rubble. Bloodstains had turned random splotches of the concrete blue, and corpses of both factions were strewn about randomly, with some civilians mixed in there too. The mob that surrounded her and her limp-jawed former colleague were chanting threats and curses at the incapacitated duo. She knew why they were doing this, and she didn't blame them. At the end of the day, Queenie was just happy to die as herself and not as an expendable pawn living in someone else's game. She wondered if the man with her had a similar change of heart to her own, and if he felt similarly about his own death.

One of the Marauders knelt down, grabbing a piece of rubble from the street. "My brothers are dead because of you!" he screamed in between sobs, while hurling the rubble at Queenie. "You yellow-suited—"

She couldn't hear the rest, as the rest of the mob began jeering loudly when the rock hit her in the side. Her decisions had led her to this point. She accepted that.

More rocks were being thrown at them. A large one hit the man in the chest and she heard the air leave his lungs. Many of the larger ones missed her, but most of the smaller ones hit their mark.

A loud sound erupted from the crowd, quieting down the unruly mob of Marauders. A woman in a large black trench coat, a mechanical claw for a right hand, chains implanted into her scalp, and a large blue imitation of flames on her neck, had moved into the center of the crowd. She pointed a high-powered, shell-firing energy rifle into the air, a blue energy trail still rising from the barrel. Queenie could see the words "Cherry Picker" beautifully engraved into the side.

"Are you all a bunch of morons?" she angrily asked the hushed crowd. "Don't forget that we need at least one of them to be able to speak."

The crowd began to mumble to itself, debating the merits of Queenie's life. The chain-haired woman rolled her black eyes, having obviously had enough of this emotion-fueled nonsense. She turned herself toward Monochro Tower and heaved her gun into a firing position. She pulled the trigger, causing a loud boom to emanate from the gun as it shot a Raiga shell from its barrel.

The blue streak blasted through the air toward the penthouse windows, only to be met by a suddenly visible red wall when it got within several feet of the glass. The shell exploded violently off of the wall and sent down streaks of pure Raiga to burn through the concrete below. The wall returned to its translucent state just seconds later.

"That thing is keeping the leadership locked up," the chain-haired woman yelled to the crowd. "So in case it's too hard for you pea-brained morons to comprehend, I will say it again. Do not waste your time killing the captives before we interrogate the one that can still speak."

Queenie knew that she was going to die or get beaten brutally for information. One of the two was certain, so she decided to try and save her own skin while she still could. This would either speed the process up or possibly get her out of this bind in one piece, if she were lucky.

She struggled to stand up in the middle of the distracted crowd, and the other Yelo members looked up at her with their now-blackened eyes.

Queenie took a deep breath and yelled with all of her might. "I am defecting to the Marauders."

The mob was silent for a minute; then they all started laughing. Queenie felt her face turn blue. Living your life behind a mask for seven years and then having a group of people laugh in your face once you take it off was not a very fun feeling. The man limply yelling at her feet did nothing to help her sense of comfort.

The chain-haired woman fired a rapid fire into the air this time. "Okay, problem solved." The chain-haired woman looked her dead in the eye. "There's no harm in big words as long as you prove them."

Chapter 16

A Melodic Memoir

"When I reach the zenith of my very being, I will become bathed in a cloak of my very own soul. All the world will know the name of 'Hastul!'"

Hastul twirled and danced in a windowless, subterranean, yellow room. There were twenty concrete pillars laid out before him, each about six feet tall and one foot wide, five of which had been completely decimated and reduced to rubble. In the back of the room, three other members of Yelo stood and watched their leader twirl. Two were members of his elite guard, the Lems, and the last was a Ban who was manically scribbling Hastul's every word into a notepad that they were holding.

"I will take flight upon my ascension to Magician-hood, as other exceptional individuals have before me!" Hastul lifted up his left arm, a yellow aura flaring out of it and forming into two egg-shaped constructs that floated a head above him. He flung them both with a graceful flick of his arm, obliterating two of the concrete pillars.

"And I will take my rightful place, through righteous war and well-spilled blood, atop the throne of Inner Varcia."

Hastul fired a beam of yellow light from his hand, blowing apart another column with ease. "I will unite the continent, and all of the Varse who live upon it, into the single great nation it was always meant to be—all of it under me. The ways of Yelo will be exported far and wide. All will lose the burden of their own terrible self, all but I who will carry that impossible burden for all Varse everywhere." He danced further across the room. Then he returned to his original position with a flurry of waving arms and scrambling legs.

He fired another ovular blast into a pillar. "Yelo, as grand as it is, is only the first step in my grand and righteous mission of true unity and absolute prosperity." Hastul stopped his dance suddenly.

He shot a look toward the scribbling Ban. "Are you getting all of this?"

The Ban nodded silently but enthusiastically. Hastul smiled and waved for them to continue writing. He then inhaled deeply as he serenely moved his silk covered arms above his head, forming the shape of a "Y" with his body. Yellow magic began to swirl around him.

"From a young age, it became apparent to me that people as a whole were unable to make the correct decisions for themselves, and that only a select few could really know how to live a proper life. The vast majority would always prioritize paltry things like pleasure over what is really important."

A swarm of magical projectiles began to form around Hastul, popping into existence from his aura in the air around him. "Then one day, I had a grand realization. If nobody was going to take the reins and be the shepherd that the world needed, then it would have to be me who led both the flock and the lesser shepherds around me. I am fully aware of what a great task this is, but do not weep for me. I do this because I hold deep in my blue heart a deep and unfathomable love for all of you. Together we will spread the dream of Yelo to each and every corner of Unos."

Hastul threw down his arms, releasing the building storm of projectiles. The remaining concrete columns were turned into a gray haze by the rain of yellow ovals, and the wall behind them now had several large craters in it.

The aspiring magician's arms fell limp to his sides. He stood panting and sweating, with a smile stretched long across his weary face.

"That was quite the display of power, my master," a voice rasped from behind him. "I return to you bearing gifts and good news."

The Lems had instinctively pointed their rifles, Raiga blade bayonets and all, right at the head of the new arrival. Despite this, he didn't show the slightest bit of discomfort. People like him were an uncommon sight in Outer Varcia. He wore a much darker variant of the normal Yelo uniform, with dagger-covered straps wrapped around his chest. His mask was cut to reveal his mouth, a slim but focused rifle was slung across his back, and his teeth, yellow and crooked, hung from a mouth surrounded by green and black scales. A powerful tail with an identical complexion slammed into the ground behind him. He reeked with the scent of smoke and burning, and in his clawed hand he held three Yelo masks as if they were sacks. Each mask was full of something and had large blue stains forming on the bottoms.

"The heads of the three traitors, as you've requested, my lord," the Huntsman proudly proclaimed to the room of Varse, a small puff of black smoke escaping from his mouth.

Hastul's smile grew a little bit wider, and he turned to face his minion. "Excellent, they got what they deserved," he cheered. "I'm going to take a wild guess and say the good news is that the attack on Monochro went well."

The Huntsman gave Hastul a crooked toothy grin. "From what I was told by the Vice-Commander, the Marauders are in total chaos and their leaders have yet to take even the slightest action regarding the attack."

"Yes!" Hastul screamed.

"Oh Cassilda, my sweet, sweet Cassilda. Oh, how I've crafted you from my wildest fantasies. Now, that the Marauders are reeling, I can execute you and bring you into fruition." Hastul was almost drooling as he whispered this to himself.

"You two," he yelled at the Lems guarding the entrance way. "Gather the rest of your numbers by midnight, then come straight to me. I have important orders that must be handed out."

The Lems saluted almost robotically before heading up the stairs past the reptilian Huntsman.

Hastul then turned to the Ban. "You go and find Lawndel. Tell him the same." The Ban did the Yelo salute and ran, almost tripping on themselves up the stairs.

Wisps of smoke coiled around the Huntsman's figure as he smiled with his yellow teeth. "And me, sire?"

"Go find someone to give me a massage."

CHAPTER 17

JAMMED UP

The setting sun was a red diamond-shaped blot on the horizon. Orange light was flooding into the wrecked penthouse, and the lights of the city were beginning to flicker on, a weakly glowing rainbow compared to the overwhelming orange of the sun.

"Elledia!" Vara hollered through her busted mouth, violently shaking her brother back and forth, his lumi tattoo creating a small streak of blue.

"Dad didn't kill Mom for you to throw your life away on some ingrate like her," she ranted, her eyes wild. "He didn't die so that we'd make the same mistakes he did!"

"Geez, Vara, why do you gotta bring Dad into this!"

"Why!?" She pushed him out of her grasp and into the bar. "You know damn well why!"

"No, Vara," Artex said, steadying himself. "I don't. Besides, it doesn't matter right now." Artex grasped onto the side of the bar to steady himself. "We can't focus on the past right now! We are literally stuck in a cage, Vara!"

"Well," Patho chimed in, "you did set the dominos in motion."

"Oh, so the 'great magical one' has finally decided to bless us with his opinion," Artex snapped at the red outline. Besides, if we want to talk about dominos, then this would all be Vara's fault anyway."

"What?!" Vara howled. "How in the name of all the brothels in Yellow Light do you think you can blame me for this?!"

"Well, Sis, we wouldn't be in this mess if you didn't miss your shot," he hissed. "If you killed Hamstrum back at the music hall, then we wouldn't still be dealing with this Yelo crap."

"Hastul," Patho swiftly corrected. "And that was years ago, hardly relevant to the situation today."

"You gave me that gun anyway, and you know that I'm a terrible shot," Vara added in, arms crossed.

"Vara, you ripped the rapid fire out of my hand, and then you just started firing the gun and screaming," Artex looked directly into his sister's eyes and trying his best not to look away. "You ruined the whole plan with that."

Vara shrugged. "What can I say? I was excited."

"Yeah, and I was lonely!" Artex angrily retorted. "We all have our downfalls, Vara!"

"Your loneliness almost got YOU killed in an obvious trap," Patho interjected. "I don't even know how you fell for that; all you had to do was ask literally anyone else in the gang where we were meeting and you would have never been in that situation."

"Oh, yeah! Well, aren't you lonely, too, Patho?!" Artex mocked. "You are the last Eatherial alive, right?"

"Artex, what the hell?!" Vara screamed, after hearing her brother's comment.

"What? Are we going to keep ignoring it?!" he continued, whipping his head to Vara. "He is literally the only one that we can prove is still alive! How can he call me lonely if he's the only one left?!" Artex wore a crazed smile, trying his hardest to rationalize what he was saying as more than just a dig.

Patho slowly walked toward the angry, whining Varse, causing Artex to shrink back. "As much as I'm enjoying this, don't we have larger issues to deal with?" Patho firmly stated, his voice conveying a coldness that his featureless face could not.

Artex was pressing himself so hard against the bar counter that he could feel the cold metal of the bar through his jacket.

"Patho, you're right," Artex croaked, forcing the fear from his voice. "What options do we have?"

"We could try and contact someone on the outside," Vara exclaimed with a snap of her fingers.

"That won't work," Patho replied, backing away from his nervous comrade. "My Trident Field blocks all signals going in or out."

Vara's head slowly turned to her red friend. "Patho."

"Hmm?"

"Why?"

"The energy making up the field had to be sufficiently thick in order for it to sufficiently repel fire from heavy weaponry." He shook his head, and then said, "it was either the signals go down in an emergency or we do."

"So we can't watch TV now?" Vara sighed disappointedly.

"Well, that's . . . one of two reasons," Patho answered, looking toward the wreckage of the television.

"Okay, okay," Artex began pacing back and forth. "It will take three hours to take the field down altogether, we can't communicate with the outside world while we are in here, and Bishop is still out of commission."

Artex inhaled deeply and opened his mouth to speak. A blast of blue rocketed toward the window and was immediately and silently neutralized by the suddenly visible Trident Field. The room was painted ruby red for a few seconds as the Raiga shell's debris fell to the ground below.

"Frig!" Vara jumped spastically. "What the hell was that?!"

"I think I might have an idea," Patho said, walking toward the window. "I'm pretty sure only one Marauder opts for that much firepower at her hip—or jacket, in this case."

The other two ran to the window. A doughnut-shaped mob had formed in the street, with Marauders on the outside and two civilian-looking Varse on the inside.

"What are they doing?" Artex asked.

"Having all the fun without us, obviously," Vara quickly responded.

"A damn shame, that is." Patho tapped his fingers on the glass. "We do so much for this gang and they can't even wait up for us to form a lynch mob. Life is cruel and unfair."

"You're both awful people, you know that?" Artex looked at his comrades wearily.

"Yes," they answered in unison, their eyes refusing to be peeled away from the mob.

"You're no saint yourself, Artex," Patho added.

"I've killed my fair share, but I've never got off on it like you two."

"You should really try it sometime," they both replied.

Artex began pacing once again, peeling himself away from the window.

"So, what we are gonna do is wait an hour, and then Patho will enter the backwards code," Artex stopped walking and pressed his hands together. "Patho, is there a way to take the jammer down before the Trident Field as a whole?"

"No."

Artex blinked a few times. "No?"

"I cannot take it down entirely, no. Neither can I weaken it enough to allow cell phone signals through, but another type of signal might just work."

"What kind?"

"A brand new kind!" Patho exclaimed proudly. "I've been working on a solution to the cell phone issue, which you Artex have so beautifully proven to be real, and that signal might just be able to slip through after a few adjustments."

"That's real swell, Patho!" Artex replied with his arms at his sides. "But is there anybody to even receive this new signal?"

"Yes, of course! What kind of scientist would I be if I didn't test things? Several select Marauders have been using the prototypes. I luckily keep mine in my room."

"Great. Are there any other projects like this that you aren't telling us about?"

"Artex, if you can be sure about one thing on all of Mekebe, let it be that the answer to that question is yes."

"Fine with me, as long as they don't kill everyone."

"They most certainly probably won't."

Artex turned to Vara. "What about you? Are you good with this plan?"

"Yeah, I guess, but if Bish is not better after this, I'm staying here with him. You can fix your mistake with Patho."

Artex bit his tongue, not wanting to reignite the tensions in the room. "That's fine. You do you."

Patho wrapped his legs in magic and headed for the broken stairs while Vara watched another streak of blue fire arc into the sky.

"Claw is really going at it out there," she commented.

"If anything interesting happens out there, please tell me," Patho pleaded, hopping to the second floor.

CHAPTER 18

BISHOP

The air conditioner roared cold across the room while Bishop huddled, clutching his head, in a nest of bedsheets he had thrown from the bed to the floor. His mind was overflowing with memories of the past, and his eyes were fixed on the iron bolt-littered wardrobe in front of him as he rocked back and forth. Locked within that wardrobe was the last reminder he had left of his past life. A single relic from the annihilated village of Nod.

Bishop was the only one to survive the massacre of Nod, but he considered it a different type of death for him. Bishop stared down at this metal-skinned arm. His alterations were the only good thing to come out of that day.

Bishop always knew that this day would come. No part of him wanted to do this. He wanted to keep running away and pretending like "Bishop" was the only person he ever was, but he had to face it. Even if it destroyed him, he had to at least try.

He stood up and began to shakily walk toward the wardrobe, the small, almost invisible blue veins of his black eye now visible from the strain.

A small amount of light from his enhanced eye was reflecting a small blue smudge of light back at him from the door of the wardrobe. He had literally no way to properly describe the man who gave him this eye; the only word that came close was "fleshy." The meeting was fast, and it included the awfully distracting event of his friends and family being slaughtered right behind him.

Every time Patho asked about his arm, Bishop would say, "I was a bit distracted when it happened." Patho never liked that answer, but that's all he ever felt like saying. Bishop cracked a weak smile at the thought of Patho getting into a huff about the eatherium. He'd always asked when he was harvesting it from Bishop, a very painful process, but the metal was promised to him in order to get him to join.

He smacked his hands into the metal wardrobe, slightly denting it. Bishop looked toward his night table; he kept a helmet in there. He had Patho make it out of some kind of weird-tinted, reinforced plastic. He could see out of it perfectly fine, but anyone on the outside would just see gray, though. Bishop wore it when he expected things to get ugly. He'd recovered from all types of wounds, but he was pretty certain that a good shot to the head would kill him. So, a helmet and some body armor seemed like the best solution to the problem. He hadn't worn either in a long time.

The helmet had come to represent the opposite of what was in the wardrobe to him. One was the degraded leader of the Marauders, Bishop. The other was Knigh, a coward of a much higher degree. Knigh was the name that Bishop was born with and had tried so hard to forget. Thinking of it again after so long filled him with a sad nostalgia.

He felt his emotions twist into a painful knot in his stomach. It felt like somebody was stabbing him and stirring the knife in his entrails, but it was much more metaphysical, and much less like when he first met Vara. His legs were starting to shake.

Bishop let himself fall backward into his nest of covers, and he shut his eyes after landing softly on top of them. His memories were a poison that he spent years trying to expunge and hold behind a dam of fake identity. Now he could feel them all flooding back as an unfocused wave that was threatening to drown him. Bishop knew that it was too late to stop them, but he had to condense them into something that wouldn't absolutely annihilate him. He had to relive it all.

He tried to focus on his memories, letting himself drift back into the river as softly as he could. He could smell the familiar scent of the homemade alcohol in his sister's bar. Bishop heard the sound of his baby nephew crying, and he could taste the brew of a sour liquor he hadn't had in years. He could also feel the heat pouring in from the window and onto his cheek. When he began to use his mind's eye to finally truly visualize it in front of him, Bishop could see the cold interior of the dirty little bar. His father was sitting directly in front of him.

Knigh looked around the rundown soggy bar. Lev's Watering Hole was his sister's passion project, and it was the meeting place for the first gang that he had ever been a part of, the Nodding Canes.

King was an older Varse man. His face had begun to droop, and large dark bags had formed under his unflinching, pride filled eyes. He wore a large black slug leather cowboy hat with a crown of blue feathers surrounding its middle. And, of course, he wore the signature piece of any Nodding Canes ensemble: a large black long coat made of a thin, breathable fabric, with the gang's initials woven into the right sleeve in white thread.

Several other members of the gang, all armed to the teeth with energy pistols, rifles, rapid fires, and even some of the more daring ones with rickety bootleg grenade launchers, stood guard over King like dogs ready to bite anything that got too close to their master.

"We shouldn't have done this," Knigh softly remarked, before taking a swig of his whiskey. "They're gonna come back with a hell of a vengeance, you know. The Church of Conort doesn't let stuff like this slide." The bar was silent except for the sound of the infant, Nave, crying in her baby carrier.

King sighed, looking at Knigh with an incredibly stern and tired look in his eyes.

"Knigh, I've protected this town for my entire life. I'm not going to let some damned missionaries sweep in and enslave us," King replied, his grim face not showing a hint of regret. "They were going to kill us all anyway, it's either in a gunfight or force us to convert away from the Provider and kill us in our hearts. It's better to die free than to die in the service of slave drivers."

Knigh shifted nervously in his chair. His father had always been a brick wall of a man. His hardheadedness made him a good leader at times, but it also landed the whole of them in hot water if he was left unchecked more times than he'd like to say. Because of this, Knigh always made it a point to question his father's hasty decisions, much to King's chagrin.

"Death is a part of our life. I know this," Knigh acknowledged, while fiddling with the embroidered right sleeve of his long coat. "But this isn't just our lives! It's all of Nod that you put at risk with this big statement of yours! Sir, you can't seriously think that this is justified?!"

"Nod was doomed the moment they walked in here with their banners out," King reached across the table and grabbed his son's unfinished drink. "Besides, we have a hostage. That should buy us some time to evacuate the town. The Church wouldn't want to kill one of their faithful, now would they?"

King finished the whiskey. Then the old Varse man motioned his hand over to the corner of the bar. A Human man with dark black hair, a swollen black eye, peach skin, and a good blue eye was tied to a chair with a rag gag in his mouth. The man was wearing a standard missionary's uniform, which consisted of a white onesie with a large green and gold shawl bearing three straight yellow lines being intersected by a line running through the middle of them. The missionary was straining against his restraints, a look of absolute hatred filling his uninjured right eye.

"With him, we can bargain for time," King placed the empty glass down loudly in front of Knigh. "I think it's time you took a break from all the thinking, son. Leave the worrying to me."

Knigh took a deep breath before standing up from his seat. He looked into his father's eyes, then walked out of the bar. It was a bright day outside. The wind was lightly blowing the desert sand into small puffs that moved through the town's single black street; gray concrete buildings were spattered in worn metal and bathed in the sunlight. The Varse inside huddled together in fear of the inevitable retribution his father had assured that the Conortionists would rain upon them.

Knigh placed his hands on his face and began to pull his skin down. King always had to be right, about everything. Even with stakes like this, his father was still going to dismiss every counter-argument in favor of acting like he had the foresight to see every possible outcome. When he was wrong, King would always twist the situation so that he was right in his own way. Knigh felt like he was screaming at a statue almost every time he spoke to his father.

His footsteps echoed throughout the town as he strolled from one end of the massive street to the other. It was a walk he took often, and pretty much the only walk to take in Nod. He used to like it, but now it was just another reminder that he was born into a dead end.

Frustration had been building in Knigh for years. He couldn't stand the blind obedience that the other Canes had for King, including his sister. Just because the man had survived longer than most didn't mean that every word he said was worth a hundred Zel.

Knigh knew this better than anyone, but he still struggled too long on his decision to leave or not. Now, he'd have to die along with the rest of the Nodding Canes when the Conortionists returned, so that at least some people could escape the slaughter and run into the Varcian desert just to die anyway.

"Hey!" Knigh heard a voice yell from behind him.

He turned to see his sister, Nave in hand, standing at the entrance to the bar and waving him down. Bishop's eyes snapped open; his pounding heart felt like the bass of the speaker he shot the night before.

It felt like an eternity since he had thought about King. The man was an absolute unrepentant jackass, but he was still his father. The man wasn't the sole cause of what happened in that town, but his stubbornness was a major contributor. The feelings that Bishop had for King were complicated. He wasn't sure how to actually describe them, but what he did know was that he never wanted to be him.

Tears began to stream down his face. Now he was able to stand up, some of his strength having returned to him. He walked toward the iron container once more, and slammed his head into it as hard as he could, adding another dent.

Bishop felt the blood trickling down his face, and the wound beginning to steam. He knew that he had to keep going. Bishop fell back into the pile of sheets, wrapping himself up in the cocoon and closing his eyes.

CHAPTER 19

TEAMWORK

Queenie stumbled; her hands were bound in rope. She could feel the gun pressed against her back. Needless to say, she'd had more comfortable walks.

Today had provided her with many great lessons, such as the surprising level of safety a good sturdy dumpster could provide, not seeing your own face for seven years doesn't leave a small amount of psychological scars, and most importantly, a hostage situation is much easier to reverse than one might first assume.

The one holding the energy pistol to her back was none other than the zenith of confidence, Rook, and the two of them were about to head into the guts of Monochro Tower alone. Still, it was a better fate than what was happening to the other Ban.

Queenie couldn't help but wonder why she couldn't seem to shake Rook. It was like the two had become linked by some cosmic force that only wished to see how miserable it could make her in a single agonizing day. And that it decided that the best way to achieve this was by making her into one of the few lucky individuals that get the glorious opportunity of being held hostage by her own former hostage. It was a level of equalization that Yelo could only fantasize about in their wildest propagandic dreams.

Rook, on the other hand, was loving this. He was beaming with a gargantuan sneer, the embarrassment of just a few hours ago having been replaced with an overwhelming sense of smug superiority.

"Don't you think the rope is a bit much?" Queenie asked in a cautiously hopeful tone as the pair entered the lobby of Monochro Tower. "It's not like I can just conjure up weapons out of thin air. All this caution seems kind of unnecessary."

"Don't you think trapping me in an alleyway for half an hour was a bit unnecessary?" Rook responded in a sarcastic tone, daggers in his words.

The first floor of the tower was vaguely familiar to Queenie. She had never been here in person before, but she had seen it several times during the auctions. But the platform where the slaves were sold off had been removed and replaced with an unusually large amount of lounge chairs and sofas, some of which were filled by Marauders.

It was funny. She had watched with mild enjoyment while tied-up people were sold to the highest bidder, yet now she was the one who was bound and being forced to go with people she didn't want to. She wondered if that cosmic force found this funny. "The Provider works in mysterious ways," is what her mother would always say.

The other members of the gang scattered throughout the room were looking at her with either a look of absolute disgust, or one of complete bewilderment. Rook responded to their looks with triumphant waves and a face filled with undeserved pride. Queenie had agreed to join the Marauders to save her own life, but the chain-haired lady told her that she would have to prove loyalty first. She assumed this meant giving up intel on Yelo, but apparently it just meant getting tied up and helping make the Marauder she previously captured look as good as possible while she helped him find something in his boss's workshop that might help with the red globe situation.

She wondered if she would actually end up a part of this gang at the end of this, or if they would just kill her anyway, once things were all said and done. Right now, she knew she was safe from anything aside from the current barrage of emotional damage being heaped onto her, but even then, she was reaching her bullshit threshold with Rook's waves.

After several more gloat-filled minutes, the duo stopped parading around the lobby and made their way to the elevator. Rook daintily pressed the blue button, and the metal door opened with a cheerful ding. He stepped inside and gave the rope a tug, tilting his head and widening his unflinching smile. Queenie sighed defeatedly before stepping inside.

"So, what are we even looking for down here?"

Rook's smile dropped. "I, uh, actually don't know," Rook quickly blurted out, before trying to recover from his slip-up. "But I'm sure I'll know what I'm looking for when I see it!"

"Didn't you say you are this guy's assistant?"

"Yeah, I did, why do you ask?"

"Because it seems to me like you don't really know what you're doing?"

She watched Rook tighten his grip on the rope as his posture stiffened. "I uh—"

The elevator sounded a second time, and the door opened to a silver, windowless hallway lit by small cylindrical lights on the walls. The lights gave a sterile shine to the corridor.

"I am absolutely confident in my training." Rook gave Queenie an obviously forced smile. He then began to lead her down the hallway toward a sliding door with the image of a large red trident emblazoned in its front.

The odds of them finding anything useful were dropping like rocks in the water for Queenie at this point. She had not known Rook for too long, but he had already somehow established himself as one of the least competent people she had met in her entire life. It probably had something to do with seeing him almost pee himself in an alleyway.

Rook quickly tapped a code into the keypad that was to the left of the metal door. It made a beep, then the door slid up immediately, which to Queenie seemed like a good sign.

The room was very dark, with the only substantial light source she could see being from something that looked like a giant pulsating lava lamp in the very back of the room. It was casting a deep red tint all over the lab. Small dim lights flickered on and off, humming machines filled the room, and a leather vest laden with chains caught her eye immediately. The vest rested awkwardly in the middle of the floor, and next to it on a metal table lay a very demonic-looking set of armor which was missing its right gauntlet. But this all paled in comparison to what the duo saw next after walking further in. Right next to the door was a smelly, sweat-drenched hospital bed, and next to it was a worse-smelling puddle of vomit. The bed was covered in many different restraints. To her it looked like someone had been in the bed recently, but had gotten out, somehow without having broken any of the restraints.

"What was your boss doing here?" Queenie asked, gesturing her head over toward the bed and its accompanying vomit pile.

"Hell if I know," Rook replied, with an exasperated sigh. "I've learned not to question him at this point."

Rook began to fumble around the walls of the lab, trying to find a light switch somewhere in the crimson room. Every movement he made was one of uncertainty, like he was terrified of touching the wrong thing.

She took another look around the room while he searched. Her eyes once again were drawn to the vest on the floor. Something about it seemed so out of place in this room. Even in this lighting it looked like there were divides and ridges carved into the material.

Queenie shook herself out of her trance. Patho was listed as an "unknown assist" in the briefing Yelo gave her group. She knew he was a scientist, but that was all she knew. She looked to the semi-complete set of armor that was placed on the table before her. It looked monstrous; every detail that had been forged into it was done so with incredible attention to detail. She wondered what it was, and why this low-tech looking armor was displayed so prominently in a lab like this. Something quickly passed in front of the lava lamp thing, causing the room to be temporarily cloaked in absolute blackness.

Rook swung around frantically, with panic plastered plainly across his face as he wildly pointed the silver gun toward the energy forge. "What was that?" Rook yelped, the gun once again shaking pathetically in his hand. "What did you do!?"

"I literally haven't moved!" Queenie motioned for Rook to calm down with what little arm movement that she had, but instead he pointed the gun at her face.

***

Zoog watched the two Varse from behind one of the many boxes of Raiga gems. His years in a traveling circus troupe had left him with many things, most of them being emotional scars, but one of the more useful tricks he had learned was how to dislocate and relocate most of the bones in his body. This little talent of his made Zoog one very hard-to-restrain Varse. He'd wormed his way out of much worse things than a hospital bed during his time in Board City.

He squeezed the wrist of the silver gauntlet he was wearing, trying to find the hidden switch that would turn it on. He had been finicking with this thing for like twenty minutes. There was no doubt in his mind that this thing had some crazy-ass gun in it, like the one Artex had—he just had to find it.

Patho hadn't returned for him yet, which was good. But from the looks of his new guests, it seemed like he wouldn't be the only test subject for the Human's nefarious experiments. He knew he had to do something to help that tied up woman, but since he woke up he'd had the worst nausea. It was making it hard for him to do much of anything.

This was not where he was expecting to end up when he got into that car with Artex. Though, there was a silver lining to the whole thing. Once he got out of this, Artex would hook him up for free with whatever wonderful narcotics he asked for, and Zoog intended to take complete advantage of his friend's heartfelt promise.

Zoog watched the twitchy man who was holding the gun let out a shaky groan before he lowered the weapon to his side.

"Don't let it happen again," Rook sighed. "We really need to get that sphere down."

The man's eyes turned sharp. "Especially since this whole thing is your fault."

Zoog had no idea what the guy in the lab coat was talking about, but he always knew a good opportunity to move when he saw one. He held his churning gut tight and stumbled to his feet, struggling to keep the awful cramping at bay.

Once again, a shadow enveloped the room, leaving only two thin beams of red light, which shined from behind Zoog like a pair of thin cherubic wings. He clenched his armored fist. He didn't need a gun or an intact stomach to be a hero. If he made this count, then he'd be able to escape, free the girl, and most importantly, get his sweet, sweet drugs.

Rook and Queenie stood shocked, covered in Zoog's lanky silhouette. Rook began to raise the gun toward the hunched figure at the other end of the laboratory, but Zoog had already begun a sloppy sprint toward the terrified scientist.

He fired out an energy bullet, only missing the shot when Zoog coincidently crouched over in pain mid-run. The bullet bounced harmlessly off the reinforced glass of the energy forge, and then it ricocheted harmlessly into the iron wall before dissipating. Queenie watched the sweat-stained mystery man collect himself and continue his sprint to Rook, who himself was trying to aim the pistol for another shot.

Zoog felt the vomit rush up his esophagus as soon as he raised his armored fist. The punch connected with a sickening crunching sound, right into Rook's waiting jaw. Some of his teeth were knocked out from the impact. Rook fell limp to the ground, unconscious and covered in his own blood. The energy pistol slid across the ground and under the table. Zoog immediately let out a stream of vomit on the unconscious Rook, while Queenie watched with a strange mix of disgust and satisfaction.

The sweaty man stopped vomiting and smiled at her. "You need to get out of those ropes?"

Queenie just nodded her head, smiling faintly.

CHAPTER 20

NOD

The dusty town of Nod again folded out before Bishop. Knigh opened his eyes to the sight of his sister, baby in hand and a red feathered hat on her head, waving him down from the door of her bar.

Lev was a few years older than him, but unlike Knigh, she unfortunately inherited their father's taste in headwear. The kid's father was a deadbeat who skipped town when he found out she was expecting, and he was also the catalyst for Knigh and King to go on a special hunting excursion together.

"Don't worry about Dad," she called out. "We have an evacuation plan for before they get here."

Lev was putting on her usual cheery facade, but Knigh had gotten very good at seeing through it; there was an underlying terror in her smile. She had put her whole life into this town the same as him, but with the added difference of a lot of that life being wrapped up in the concrete bar that stood beside her, and the rest of it in her arms.

For their whole lives, Nod had been subject to their father's whims while the two of them sat by waiting to inherit the mess. Lev found her way out of this scripted future by convincing King that running the local watering hole was a great way for her to listen in on conversations and uncover plots against him, of which there have been none. This left Knigh alone with the burden.

"We shouldn't even be in this situation, Lev," he grumbled, trudging toward his sister. "Him and his damned ego went too far this time. We are going to lose everything because of this, and we don't even know when!"

"We have to have faith, Knigh." Her false smile dissipated. "Dad's gotten us out of worse situations."

Knigh felt a fire light in his guts; he knew she was lying to him, and she knew it too. He looked into the glass window of the bar and saw their father watching the conversation. The sharp gaze of the old Varse locked with Knigh's desperate and angry stare.

"Lev, there are no worse situations!" he yelled, causing Lev to take a short step back. He was making sure that King would be able to hear him, and caused his nephew to begin crying. "He killed us all! Do you not understand that? I know you've heard the same stories about those fanatics that I have!"

For the first time in years, Knigh saw Lev's face entirely drop, and with it, her facade of calmness. "Knigh," she muttered in a cold cutting tone that she would only use when she really wanted him to listen to what she was saying. "We can't take back what happened yesterday. All we can do now is trust in King's judgment as the head of this town and try our best to make it through whatever comes next." She turned and walked back into her bar, and King's eyes still had not moved from his son.

This town was completely under the spell of a selfish old man. Knigh hated the dependency of the townspeople that his father cultivated, and he knew his father hated that Knigh made it a point to frequently resist his supposedly all-knowing will.

He could feel his anger churning in his chest—if he didn't go cool down right now he knew that he'd do something in that bar that he couldn't take back. Although, at this point, he wondered if that even mattered anymore.

An overwhelming sense of helplessness was quickly enveloping Knigh and replacing his anger. He looked down at the initials sewn into his jacket's wrist. He could clearly remember how excited he was when he was little to be given one of these jackets and be sworn in by his father as one of the town's protectors, but that was then. Now he knew that all he had wanted his whole life was to leave this town one day and have his own life, to be free from the choking culture of the Nodding Canes—but now it was too late. Everyone here was doomed to die, including himself.

He could feel a lump forming in his throat, and Knigh knew he could still leave. Doing so would cost him everything. He would have nothing but his gun and the clothes on his back, but he could leave.

Knigh began to walk back down the singular street of Nod as he had done so many times before. His tears, unable to be held back any longer, began dripping down his face. His thoughts began to wander, and they got stuck on his dying dreams of freedom. Just because this town was doomed to die didn't mean he'd have to be, but him leaving would mean severing the connections with those that he loved right before they died—something that felt like an unforgivable sin. Every second of his life had been given to this town to ensure that it would continue to function. The people he'd killed, caravans plundered, animals hunted, all of it was for Nod, and none of it had amounted to anything. He reached the end of the road.

Knigh stared out into the sandy wastes of Outer Varcia, the wind causing the back of his long coat to billow in the air. He debated between the painful loyalty he was bound to, and the cowardly liberation he desired. It just wasn't fair.

Knigh's breathing began to falter, his emotions overwhelming him. Every part of his being was screaming at him to take off running into the sand and to not ever look back—every part but his sentimentality, which was like an anchor wrapped around his neck, keeping him trapped in this suffocating town. He had so many dreams that he wanted to at least try and make a reality. All possibility of those dreams becoming reality was about to be destroyed by the uncaring egoism of his father, and the maddening faith of a bunch of soulless lunatics. That was, unless he ran right now.

The desert in front of him curled out into an endless array of golden dunes, and the nearest town was a few miles away. Nod survived on whatever the gang brought back from those wild sands, whether it be the carcass of a dead Zlugger worm or the food supply of a raided caravan. The Canes were exceptionally good at scavenging, and Knigh had learned his fair share of survival tips during his time with them. He fancied that he could do it if he wanted to, but being able to survive didn't mean he'd be able to live with his actions.

He took a step into the desert. Another gust of wind blew, throwing sand in the air and causing his long coat to flap more wildly in the air. Once the wind subsided, a great silence replaced it. The quiet was deafening, and it left Knigh with only the raging storm in his head to listen to. He felt as if his innards were being boiled alive by the pressure. Knigh began to pull his face down, and he shut his eyes.

When he opened them, Knigh felt something deep inside of him break; it was like a river was flowing through him. Its waters were now rushing to cover his insides, cooling them. Knigh began to run. He ran and ran, his footsteps kicking up puffs of sand as he put more and more space between him and Nod. He didn't know where he was running to, but he didn't care as long as he determined his own fate there.

Knigh didn't know if he'd live to regret this, but at least he'd live. "Life was short . . . and even shorter in Outer Varcia," he'd heard many people say. He'd seen his comrades gunned down in front of him more times than he could count, and he had eventually grown completely numb to it. But each time he saw blood hit the ground, he did wonder if they were satisfied with their life up to that point. He asked this even though he knew the answer. Knigh did not want to have the same answer when his heart finally stopped beating.

His frantic running came to a stop. Knigh turned to look at Nod one last time. It sat silently within the dunes, an oasis of gray stone and sun-bleached pavement. He could still make out details like his sister's bar. He squinted his eyes. Several silver cigar-shaped objects were moving through the sky, and they were heading his way. Knigh put his hand over his eyes to try and see them better.

"What in the name of the Provider are those?" he whispered to himself.

"Three minutes."

A smooth voice that carried both the softness of a woman, and the harshness of a man suddenly filled the air.

"Three minutes till everyone in that town dies," the voice repeated, with a matter-of-fact tone. "You made it with three minutes to spare. You must be a very lucky boy to have decided to leave right when you did, and to be here with me at this precise moment in time. My predecessor twists fate for me again. It must be tired of its duties."

Knigh whipped his head around frantically, trying to find the source of the voice, and only finding empty desert around him. "Who's there!?" He yelled, unable to hide the flood of fear in his voice. "Are you with the Church?"

Laughter erupted from all around Knigh, it sounded like a mix between a sick child coughing and a hyena yelping. "Such a blind institution as that does not find me among their congregation." A large white flower bulb burst from the sand in front of Knigh–it was throbbing with green luminous veins that formed a tree made of circles and lines. It caused him to fall backward in surprise. More and more of the strange figure slowly rose out of the sand as Knigh tried desperately to crawl away and process what he was seeing. A torso raised from the sand, draped in a thin pulsating whitish layer of what looked to Knigh to be a shroud of living flesh. Two hands coated in gray chitin came from within the living shawl, and in the left hand the figure held a golden staff. Atop the staff was a crystalline structure identical to the symbol pulsating on the bulb.

"Be not afraid," the figure tranquilly cooed in its androgynous voice. "For I come bearing a great gift for you, should you be capable of receiving it."

Knigh looked up at the bulb-headed figure. His heart was racing; his fight or flight was going nuts in the presence of this thing. Whatever this thing was, it knew about the situation in Nod, and it was claiming that the Conortionists were mere moments away from attacking the town. All of this greatly unnerved and confused the young man. If this thing was right, then he could probably get back in time to fight, an option he didn't believe he had when he left. He tightened his hands in frustration.

"Whether it be fate or intuition that brought you here to me, it does not matter. You have escaped Nod before its inevitable annihilation, and have delivered yourself to me. You are a true survivor, and I will bestow my gift upon you," the creature stated to the distracted Knigh. "Should you prove yourself even more fortunate and survive the process, you will become of a higher order than the average specimen of your barbaric race."

A loud humming sound filled the air right before the bang of an explosion. Knigh whipped his head toward the source of the sound. A large column of black smoke was rising from where one of the distant buildings of Nod once stood. It felt like a wall had slammed right into his chest. There was never going to be a fight—no final last stand for their town. No, the Church was just going to wipe Nod from the map entirely, with or without the chance of surviving missionaries.

Silver shells rained down upon the unsuspecting town from cigar-shaped aircrafts that bore the sigil of Conort on their hulls. Blue Raigic explosions ripped the concrete buildings apart at their bases. Knigh was completely paralyzed by the sight of his town, the only place he ever called home, being completely erased from existence. There was no going back now or ever. He would never be able to triumphantly return and rub his success in King's face, and never see his sister or his nephew ever again.

"Ah," the figure exclaimed, slightly amused. "Right on time."

The bulb-headed creature reached into its shawl with its right hand and produced a clear, jiggling orb. He released the orb from his loose grip, and it drifted slowly downward until it was in front of Knigh's face.

"In a show of my boundless generosity, I will allow you to witness the fate that you have so narrowly escaped."

The orb started to project a vision within itself of the bombing from the perspectives of various locations in Nod. Knigh saw the Varse that were huddling in their homes ripped apart by the volley of explosions, their pieces flying through the air like blue confetti. He witnessed the street he walked so many times be reduced to a pile of unrecognizable gravel. Worst of all, he watched a bomb blast rip through the bar, tearing an off-guard King apart as if the man was made out of wet paper. The remains of the gang leader coated the faces and bodies of his still surviving sister and nephew before another bomb reduced them to a blue goo. Knigh couldn't believe what he was seeing; he whimpered between shallow breaths. The figure above him watched with complete ambivalence.

"It is time," the figure whispered, just loudly enough to be heard over the still-repeating bangs. "Now receive my gift and break free of the limits of your biology."

The creature stomped its foot heavily on Knigh's chest, knocking the wind out of him. Then the tree-like structure on the top of the staff began to liquify and flow into the golden rod. It twisted the center of its staff, and a large pointed proboscis popped out of the bottom.

"Prepare yourself, for after this you will never be the sad creature you once were."

It stabbed the needle directly into Knigh's waiting heart. He could feel the liquid flow into him, beating through his body with every pump of his heart. As it intermingled with his blood, it felt like every part of him was touching hot metal. His right eye began to boil and burst, steam rising from the hole, while the skin on his right arm started to excrete a silver fluid out of his sweat glands.

“What do you want with me?” Knigh just managed to squeak out amidst the unimaginable burning pain.

The creature laughed, the bud on its head started to beat like a heart while it began to bloom. “How presumptuous.” The creature extended its index finger toward Knigh, the flower having almost bloomed completely revealing fleshy tendrils, tipped with smaller dripping flowers, shielding all but the edges of its green head from his sight. “A creature like you does not get to question me.”

Bishop awoke in a cold sweat, panting heavily. His eyes immediately locked on the wardrobe in front of him; his heart was beating like the dozens of drums in a massive parade.

Chapter 21

Order

Lawndel sat unmoving behind a small desk in a similarly small yellow room. A machine topped with a shimmering blue Raiga crystal sat in front of him, singing with radio static. The crackling of the radio was interrupted by the sudden emergence of a panicked voice. The echoes of gunshots and explosions filled the room. Lawndel sat unfazed, listening to the sounds intently. He reached for his canteen as he waited for the magic phrase that would let him check this off of his to do list, and he took a swig of the clear vitamin concoction inside. Finally, Lawndel heard the words that he was waiting for.

"Mission complete," the voice reported, a hint of pride glinting like shining gold. "The enemy outpost in The Brook's Maze has almost been completely cleared out."

Lawndel's hands clasped tightly into fists, and he began to grind his teeth. "What do you mean 'almost?'" he inquired to the man on the other side, trying his best to hide his disgust at this breach of protocol.

"We believe that the last few of them have retreated into the back of the building with a few rapid fires," the troop commander related to Lawndel, the concern audible in his voice. "Sir, in order to finish this we could use some—"

Lawndel immediately and swiftly clicked the radio off; he had no reason to continue listening. Once a mission had been completed, those completing it either returned home or died. Lawndel didn't need to care as long as they did what was required of them, and as long as they followed the correct protocol. There was no room for early birds here. They didn't follow it though, nor had they completed the mission. So they were on their own.

Either way, with or without a few expendable members, the whole of Yelo would continue to exist without any real noticeable change. Besides, the less mouths to feed, the longer resources would last, and the longer he had to whip Yelo into an ideal shape.

The Vice-Commander stood up from his tiny, cramped chair, stretching his powerful legs as he made his way to the door. He left his cramped, closet-like office and made his way into the massive, bustling but windy courtyard of Sinustus. He carefully shut the door to his office, which was protruding from the compound's defensive walls.

Lawndel made sure to take his time shutting the door, relishing the intense feeling of satisfaction that he got from fulfilling any assigned task. Order was Lawndel's life, and he saw great value in spreading that way of life to others that were lost in the chaos of their own terrible life choices. From his time in the Inner-Varcian military, Lawndel had learned many useful things, and among them was a most beautiful truth. That truth was that even the most lost individual could be forged into a fine soldier if they were put into the correct circumstances.

The Ban level members were running around the Yelo compound like busy yellow ants. Each one carried supplies to one of the different production plants that they were assigned to. Out of all of them, Lawndel was most interested in the printing press at the moment.

Once "Operation Cassilda" was completed and the Marauders were fully removed from Board City, Yelo would need to go on a recruitment binge. The propaganda produced from the press would be an invaluable tool in spurring that on.

Everything was going right on schedule today. It gave Lawndel a feeling that he considered to be absolutely sublime. Every day he would wake up early in the morning, stretch, and then do a quick check of the compound's various systems. Next, he would wait for Hastul to wake up so that he may give him his daily update on the gang's status, as well as receive any orders that might need to be executed. After that, he went to his office in order to oversee any active operations outside of Sinustus.

Once he completed that task, he'd usually go and train his body until it was time to eat dinner, and then sleep after that, but seeing as today held a great triumph over their hated rivals, he figured that he'd make sure that the propaganda posters and pamphlets were up to snuff. Lawndel knew for a fact that routine was the comforting mother that helped the forlorn find their way back to true productivity.

He caught a paper that was being blown around the courtyard. He crumpled it in his hand before placing it in his pocket, a disgusted look on his face. The winds were blowing with such force against the walls that the guards that walked its edges were taking refuge behind the giant, mounted defensive turrets. Whipping gusts were blowing sand into the compound in bucket loads, bringing an ungodly amount of annoyance to Lawndel.

Once this windstorm was over, he was going to have to make an unwelcome detour to make sure that the Bans were doing their clean-up jobs. They usually were, but Lawndel needed to be sure for his own sanity. The sand was by far the worst part of Outer and Mid Varcia for him. Inner Varcia was much more suitable to his tastes; luckily, Hastul agreed with him on that, and Sinustus was usually a welcome retreat away from the unforgiving and dirty desert.

Three Bans ran up to Vice-Commander Lawndel, who was halfway to the printing press by this point. Their posture and movements were stiff and rhythmless. They did the Yelo salute as soon as soon as they were exactly four feet from him. The three of them were standing in a perfectly straight line.

"Sir, there is a problem," the central member of the group announced, in a restrained but urgent voice. "We have found a thief in the greenhouse."

Lawndale began to grind his teeth again—another interruption cutting into his day would surely result in a tension headache this evening. "I see," he coldly responded, his face barely hiding his frustration. "That is indeed a troublesome discovery, however, you have neglected the rules that were placed for you in case of an event like this and reported this to the wrong person in the chain of command. The greenhouse overseer is the officer that handles situations like these. Not me." Bans could be so ambitious with their interactions, always trying to rise up the chain of command; he would need to figure out a better way to quash that later.

"Although your loyalty to Yelo is appreciated, your rations will receive a docking for at least one week due to this infraction," Lawndel continued in a painfully professional tone.

"Sir, that's the issue," the middle Ban hesitantly continued. "The one stealing rations is the greenhouse overseer."

A great rage quietly overtook Lawndel, and his teeth grinding became audible. It was inconceivable, impossible, utterly unfair, and terrible. A third interruption to his schedule! And this one would take a while to properly fix. The promoting process would have to be painstakingly thorough.

The Vice-Commander stood perfectly still for exactly three minutes before speaking, greatly unnerving the three Bans who were loyally waiting for a response in front of him. "Take me to them."

Lawndel marched through the commune, a silent fury in his every step and the three agricultural workers meekly following behind him. The Bans were parting like curtains at the first sign of the Vice-Commanders staunch approach. Between this and the cleaning, he didn't know if he'd get in even an hour of his precious and vital training time today. Even worse was the fact that an event like this would mean that the propaganda would have to be diverted to the inside of Sinustus, and the Yelo as a whole, before it could be properly exported outside. This would inevitably put a damper on the already waning recruitment numbers, and right when they were gearing up to drive the Marauders out of Board City too. All of this was completely unacceptable, and it deserved the highest level of punishment possible.

The greenhouse was a large structure that resembled an oval made of glass, and it hugged the compound wall. The whole thing was filled with many exotic types of plants that ranged from spherical teal fruits and rugged rigid purple vegetables, to feathered orange herbs that were useful in medical salves.

The rows of plants spread themselves out in front of Lawndel. He stopped his march to survey the area. The Bans tending to them all stopped what they were doing and saluted the Vice-Commander.

"We have the overseer held in the back," the central member informed Lawndel.

"Former," he corrected, a tinge of venom in his normally calm voice.

A large, bolted iron door separated the overseers office from the rest of the facility. Lawndel easily flung the heavy metal door aside, causing the Bans that were still accompanying him to jump.

Three Varse were in the room; two were Bans armed with energy pistols aimed at the overseer, who was sitting in their chair. They sat in complete stillness, aside from their hands, which were still signing the documents that would clear the food produced here for the orb processing plant.

"Good afternoon, Vice-Commander Lawndel." The overseer's voice cracked as she greeted him.

Lawndel didn't hear her, as he was hyper focusing on the documents, she still had the gall to be signing. "Leave us," Lawndel commanded the Bans, as he ripped his eyes away from the papers and fixed them on the overseer. The other Yelo members scurried out of the room.

"You have been accused of stealing food from Yelo. Under normal circumstances you would have up to five minutes to prove your innocence, but due to the second infringement of 'filing while accused of treachery,' that time has been reduced to one minute. Please present your case now."

The overseer remained silent for a short time while she took his declaration in, and then she began to speak. "I was filing to show that even under such circumstances, my loyalty is unshaken. I fully accept all punishments from the second charge, as I am indeed guilty, but the charge of stealing food has been greatly exaggerated by my underlings in an attempt to have me removed from my Hastul-assigned position."

"Exaggerated means that the crime committed was of a smaller nature than was initially suspected, not that there was no crime. Your pleas of guilt have been heard and are appreciated by the whole of Yelo," Lawndel stoically recited to the silent overseer, his silent rage boiling. "You will face two well-earned punishments for such abuses of power."

Lawndel walked closer to the frozen woman. "It was just one baggie—" was all she had time to say before Lawndel removed her mask, revealing her terrified face.

"The first punishment is exile."

She broke when she heard those words. "Please, you can't do this," she squealed, tears beginning to form in her desperate eyes. "Yelo is all I have! I put my whole life into this, please! There's nowhere else for me to go!"

"The second punishment . . . is death." As he spoke, Lawndel slowly reached for one of two bladeless hilts that rested on his belt. When he ignited it, several smaller scraps of metal floated out of the hilt, causing the blue energy of the blade to bend into a crescent shape.

In one fluid motion, Lawndel slit the woman's throat with the Raiga sickle. Her eyes widened as her throat was opened. Lawndel then pushed her chest, causing the gagging woman to fall backward, as to not get any stray fluids on the documents in front of her.

Despite how troublesome this surprise task was, he couldn't help but feel that same rush of intense satisfaction upon completing it. A thin smile found its way onto his face. He collected the documents from the desk as he prepared to leave. There was still time to visit the printing press and oversee the cleanup, and if he continued with exceptional speed then maybe, if he was lucky, he could get a spot of training in. Then the whole intoxicating cycle would begin again. Hopefully, it would do sowithout the agonizing annoyances of today.

CHAPTER 22

ANGERING ARTEX

Monochro's buildings lit up in a pattern of deep purples and bright whites, with the white buildings shining white and the black buildings beaming purple. The Marauders on the street scurried about, sorting the corpses into two massive piles. Back cars, whose windshields reflected the light back into the sky, were filling up the street with newly arriving gang members who were trying to get a grasp on the situation with their missing leaders.

Vara tapped her black nails on the splotchy green granite of the bar counter. Several empty shot glasses were dotted around her, and she had a blank expression on her face. She glanced over at Artex, who was standing with his arms crossed, and muttering to himself as he leaned against the opposite end of the counter. She could feel her boredom eating her alive like an angry, starved parasite. She wished that she could at least get into her gym or watch TV; then she wouldn't mind being trapped in here.

"If Patho can get the jammer down then we will be able to contact the outside world. Then if we can communicate with some other Marauders, we can start restoring some order to the gang. After that, we can start to plan our next move against Yelo, which will be much easier to do if Bishop fixes his shit in the near future. Once that is planned out, we can execute a counter move. After that, if we don't have a shit ton of casualties, we will be able to take their resources, which will mean that we will have more than we used to," Artex rambled endlessly, rapidly tightening and relaxing his grip on his forearms. "And then—"

She couldn't take this anymore; she'd heard him ramble enough for one lifetime when they were kids. "Oh, I know!" Vara suddenly interrupted, causing Artex to jump, his tattoo quickly flaring red. "You're a butterfly!"

He looked at his sister, a confused and angry look on his face. "What!?"

"Charades," Vara stated, as if it were obvious. "You're acting all fluttery so I figured you must be a butterfly."

"Vara," he said with an exasperated sigh, placing his head in his hands and shaking it. "I'm trying to make sense of what's happening, so I can do my job. I'd really appreciate it if you didn't screw with me right now."

Vara reached for another bottle of liquor from the bar behind her, flicking the top off and taking a giant gulp. "No shit," she belched, crossing her eyes, sticking her tongue out of her mangled mouth, and shaking her head. "Waiting like this is boring me out of my freaking mind, Artex. We used to play charades with the other kids back when we were with the monks all the time. I figured it would be a fun way to pass the time now."

"Vara?" Artex pinched the bridge of his nose and shook his head in frustration. "You do remember what happened to those other kids, right?"

Vara looked around the room, collecting her thoughts before she answered. "Oh, I remember!" She took a quick swig of her drink. "They wasted away!"

"Yes, Vara," Artex responded, with a disappointed sigh. "They wasted away to just their bones and skin. I swear we might as well have grown up in different camps, because you remember a much happier place than I do."

Vara smiled widely. "Oh, you're still mad that the monks wouldn't teach you Bruteil, aren't you?" She wagged her finger at him. "You should be happy they cared as much as they did—you would have definitely wasted away."

She let out a loud cackle, and Artex stiffened up. "Why are you like this?!" Artex yelled, before taking a deep breath trying to collect himself. "You do know that the longer we are in here the more vulnerable we are, right?"

"Aaaaaaaahhhhhh!" Vara yelled, trying her best to imitate a game buzzer, before taking another swig from the bottle. "Wrong! We are . . . completely safe up here. It's everyone down there that might be in trouble." Vara waved her hand dismissively after the statement, her eyes rolling as she did.

Artex clapped his gloved hands in front of his face in an attempt to stop himself from letting out an angry scream that would surely deafen himself. "V," he said in the calmest voice he could muster, "doesn't that alcohol burn your mouth?"

"Yep," she answered before taking another mighty gulp of the brownish gold fluid.

"You don't care, do you?"

"Oh, absolutely not," Vara said, finishing the bottle as she stood up on the velvet-cushioned stool, and began to flap her defined arms up and down. "What am I Artex? What am I?"

"An idiot."

"Oh," Vara pouted. "Now that's just being mean."

"Here I am trying to play an innocent game with my beloved brother, and he responds to my love—" Vara gestured to herself spastically "—by mocking me."

Artex rolled his eyes. "Are you really trying to patronize me over this?" He laughed, still trying to hold in his anger. "Vara, I put my absolute all into making sure this whole operation is moving in the direction it's supposed to be, and all you do is train in your little gym, drink, and occasionally carry out the odd assault or two. You contributed the least out of all of us to actually creating the Marauders. What can you possibly make me feel guilty about?"

The tipsy Vara stopped playing around, her mood pulling a one-eighty. Her eyes narrowed into daggers. She leapt over the counter so that she was standing eye to eye with Artex. Even slightly drunk, Vara still could move gracefully.

"What did you just say to me?"

"I said that I can't feel guilty," Artex answered, his fear of his sister being suffocated by his sheer cold rage. "Because I don't owe you shit."

"That's not what you said," she growled. "You said that I contributed nothing to this gang. I might not be a brainy little idiot like you, but I'd love to see you kill a Yelo Regional Overseer."

"A Regional Overseer?" Artex lost his composure, his face morphed into a painting of anger. "Vara! That's just a high level bureaucrat, how hard can it be to kill one?!"

Vara smiled. "Oh little brother," she cooed at him, her words drenched in sarcasm. "You don't know what you're talking about."

"Getting into this entire situation with Yelo, and sending Bishop into this spiral," Vara's face was void of emotion, save her eyes which radiated an intense hot anger. "You should feel guilty about that, Artex. He's only suffering right now because you couldn't contain yourself around a pretty face."

"If Bishop is having this bad of a reaction, V," Artex hissed. "Then he probably should have dealt with whatever shit is causing his little meltdown a lot sooner." Vara's eyes widened to the point that the black orbs looked like they would shoot from her skull.

"I've got the signal through!" Patho loudly called down from the broken staircase.

Vara ignored Patho, instead continuing to focus all of her attention on her defiant brother. "What did you just say?"

"I said that Bishop should have dealt with all this, whatever it is, before he decided to become the leader of an entire gang."

Vara gritted her smashed teeth into an irate scowl, causing her wounds to bleed. She opened her mouth to reply, but she was cut off by an annoyed Patho.

"And I said that the signal is going through," he loudly interjected from the bottom of the stairs.

The siblings turned to the red Eatherial walking toward them, his arms crossed. "Was there ever a part of the plan for after I did this, Artex?" Patho inquired, his annoyance still plainly showing in his words. "Or was this just to buy Bishop more time?"

"Oh, now you're starting too!" Vara yelled, the alcohol showing its influence on her movements. "Why don't the two of you show our leader a little respect?"

"I do enjoy him," Patho replied. "And I understand that Bishop has some skeletons in his closet, but who doesn't? Artex is right. If whatever this is can take this much of a toll on his psyche, and it causes us this much trouble, then he should have tried to face the metaphorical dragon much sooner."

Patho looked past Vara and down to the streets of Monochro. The Marauders on the outside were forming two piles of corpses in the street.

Civilians watched in a mixture of curiosity and fear from their windows or the surrounding sidewalks. “I mean, look at what they’ve devolved to,” he exclaimed, gesturing outside. “I can abide by and even endorse a good stoning, but now they’re just acting like idiots!”

Chapter 23

Call to Misadventure

The unconscious, vomit-covered Rook lay upon the cold metal floor, his body bathed in a deep red light. Zoog used the sharp claw of the gauntlet to easily and wobbily cut through the ropes that bound Queenie's hands.

"So, you are saying that you weren't being brought down here to be experimented on?"

"Yeah," Queenie answered, feeling some of the confidence she had in her response falter. "I mean, I don't think so."

"That's good, but why were you tied up?" Zoog asked, confused.

"Let's just say the rest of the Marauders were not a big fan of my previous career choices."

"Ahh, I see," Zoog remarked with a loud belch.

Queenie couldn't help but smile at Rook's sorry state, although her new friend didn't seem any more competent. He did seem to have a much better attitude, and that was a much-needed upgrade.

"We better get going before that psychotic freak, Patho, gets back and dissects us or something." Zoog slowly began to walk toward the exit, carefully trying not to hurl all over the floor again.

Queenie felt conflicted. On one hand her treatment by the Marauders had not been that great since she "joined," but on the other hand, her declaration of loyalty was the only thing that stopped her from getting stoned to death like some medieval Human would have been. Rook's current state wouldn't help her case either, but if she turned the throw-up guy in for it, she might be able to squeak by.

She definitely needed to get something from this lab to show that she at least tried to help. She quickly scanned the room for something that looked like it could take down an energy field. Queenie was swiftly faced with the realization that she knew nothing about science, and especially energy fields. The one thing in the room that kept stealing her attention, though, was the strange vest that sat in the center of the lab.

She grabbed it from the ground. Queenie, despite her lack of scientific knowledge, was absolutely sure that this would do nothing to remedy the problem. Still, if it was in the center of the room, it must be important, right?

"Hey, wait up glove guy," Queenie shouted, speedily walking toward the nausea-plagued Zoog. "You can't just leave me down here alone."

Zoog grinned at the name, it sounded like the name of a crime-fighting vigilante, like from the Inner Varcian cartoons. Was this how this woman saw him, a gauntlet-wielding hero?

"I wasn't planning on it, citizen!" he yelled into her face.

Queenie blinked a few times; the smell of vomit on his breath was still stinging her nostrils. She walked ahead of the odd man, now absolutely sure that she was going to turn him into the Marauders.

A sharp beeping sound cut through the soft whirring of the laboratory, and both Varse stopped dead in their tracks. The sound played again. Queenie looked behind her for its source. Whatever it was, it wasn't coming from Rook. He hadn't moved an inch.

Unsettled, Queenie walked over to the unconscious lab assistant, placing the chain vest down in the hallway as she did. She reached down and repacked into his pocket. She pulled her hand out and was holding what looked like a metal eyeball with a blinking red light at its center. Against her better judgement, she touched it.

A red holographic rectangle projected out of it. She heard a deep smooth voice on the other end, and a line in the middle of the rectangle would shake every time a word was said.

"Rook," the voice said in a commanding tone that reminded her a little bit of Vice-Commander Lawndel. "I'm going to need you to listen to me very carefully. Go to the back of the room near the energy forge and get the Sonic Maximizer, then insert this into it and take it outside, so that a message may play to the masses, and hopefully get them to stop conducting whatever inane ritual that they are conducting outside."

She had no idea what the voice was talking about, especially the part about the ritual, but she knew that the benefits of doing this outweighed the risks.

"Hey," Zoog yelled from behind her, still holding his churning gut. "You're going the wrong way."

She ignored him, walking toward the back of the red room. "Hello?" the voice asked. "You know that I don't like to be ignored."

"Yes, I'm here!" Queenie answered, feeling her heart pump in her chest.

"Who is this?" the voice asked. "You don't sound like my Rook." Queenie felt her blood turn to ice.

"No matter," he quickly exclaimed. "You probably know about as much as he does anyway. The Maximizer looks like a satellite dish with a cord on the bottom. Let me know when you retrieve it."

"Will do, sir!" Queenie's right arm flinched instinctively after saying that. "My name is Queenie, by the way, I'm brand new to the gang."

"Okay," he responded. "Did you find it?"

"No."

"Do you know how to call back?"

"Yes."

"Do that when you find it."

***

Patho hung up the eyeball and turned to Artex and Vara. "Well, that's one step forward," he exclaimed optimistically. "Rook might be dead, by the way."

Chapter 24

Epiphany

Bishop stared at the cabinet, and he felt it staring back, each bolt in its doors another unblinking eye. His trip down memory lane had only left him more confused. There wasn't a coherent thought in his head on how to move forward.

The weeks that he spent traveling alone in the desert of Varcia, killing and eating rain slugs to stay alive, all seemed like one giant blur of time to him—a blur in which all he could focus on was the guilt he felt. He was content to live the rest of life wandering from town to town and being a vagrant, but when he first ran into Artex and Vara, he realized that he could still try to live the dream he originally left Nod for.

Bishop bit his lower lip, his teeth easily puncturing through the skin and causing him to bleed. He dug his nails into the leather of his jacket, hugging himself tightly. It was all finally coming back to him; every last mistake was crushing him under their weight.

Today was an historical day for the Marauders. In the past three years, the Marauders had only been attacked twice in their own territory, but neither of those hit as hard or this close to home for him. It was an unpleasant reminder of how fleeting this all was; just like the Canes, it could all be wiped out in an instant. The thought of how many times control of this city had changed hands was always buzzing in the back of his head.

His first encounter with Yelo was when the Marauders burst into an old Monochro music hall that was frequented by Yelo. He never really could find it in himself to take them seriously after that. They all dressed like freaks, and Vara even managed to shoot their boss almost immediately after they got in.

By the time he had started hosting parties, Yelo had been dealt a losing hand, and he had started viewing them more as a calendar that bled when you'd shot it as opposed to a legitimate threat.

His fingers, both metallic and not, dug further into the leather, which caused it to begin ripping. His scattered thoughts began to focus on the other founding members. He knew that he had been using them. They got so good at their jobs that he didn't know where his place was anymore. If someone needed something done, they would go ask Artex, or if they needed something physical or a little pick-me-up, and they were very desperate for it, then they would see Patho. He, on the other hand, had just become a figurehead. All he was good for was providing entertainment; he felt like a jester in his own castle.

He began ripping and tearing wildly into the tough, airy material of his jacket, catching his own flesh in the frenzy. Bishop ripped the jacket from his body—leather and blood began to fall to the ground, and steam began pouring from the wounds.

Images of King began to force their way into his head, just like the way King forced his will onto Knigh throughout his life. That man was everything he never wanted to be—everything he tried to forge the persona of Bishop into being the exact opposite of. But now he could see the vestiges of his father's influence within himself. When push came to shove, and the gang finally needed a guiding voice again, Bishop locked himself in the room.

These feelings had been eating away at the back of his mind for years, always injecting a strand of misery and guilt into every joyful event in his life since he left Nod. His mind felt like a swirling cauldron of coagulated blood, thick and unmoving, but at the same time, constantly drilling itself further and further into him.

He shut his eyes tightly. He may have run from his old home just moments before it was blown to pieces, but realized when he relived it that he didn't regret leaving. For a few years in between now and then, he actually felt alive, and that was worth the cost to him.

Bishop's eyes slowly opened with a realization, flicking to the locked iron cabinet in front of him. All of this moping and sulking wasn't actually doing anything to remedy the situation. All it was achieving was making him feel worse and worse about himself. He had to stop. What happened could never be undone, but he couldn't keep letting it impact him like this.

Bishop stood up and let the ripped jacket fall from his frame. He had a lot to make up for, but before that, he had to put this shit behind him, once and for all. He needed to open the wardrobe.

Bishop reached for the handles. He grunted as sweat began to drip down his face. Thanks to whatever the flower guy pumped him full of, Bishop was much stronger than the average Varse, although not nearly as strong as someone like Vara. Still, he wasn't going to let himself be beaten by a glorified box. He placed his right leg on the bottom of the wardrobe and began to pull harder.

The hinges began to pop off, one after another. If he couldn't open it normally, he would just rip the whole damn thing apart. Screws plopped to the floor as an eager Bishop strained.

"Almost there." Bishop growled as he pulled.

The doors broke off of the wardrobe, causing Bishop to fall backward as the cabinet began to fall. He shot his foot into the interior of the wardrobe, catching it as it fell. Bishop was holding himself in a precarious pose when the metal doors clamored to the ground behind him. He pushed the whole thing back to its original position. His old, long black coat hung solemnly on a lone hanger.

Bishop stared at the coat for a moment, taking a deep breath before exhaling. He lifted the right sleeve to his face, which was emblazoned with the insignia of the Nodding Canes.

"Don't want that," he remarked, a look of slight disgust as he slipped on the coat. Bishop clawed the coat at the elbow joint to separate the fabric. Bishop tore the sleeve off, leaving half where the bicep meets the forearm still attached to the coat. The fabric was comfortingly familiar to him, but the feeling he got when he put it on was completely different. Despite his anxiety about what came next, he was full of resolve to see it through—no matter the cost.

"No more excuses, I have to do this!" Bishop repeated the mantra to himself over and over as he walked out of the room.

The purple and white lights of Monochro illuminated the empty second floor, turning the blue of the room into a deep indigo. The part of the wall underneath the Trident Field keypad was ripped out; the wires had been dragged out and several had been cut, but oddly the stairs were in pieces, and he could hear Artex and Patho talking downstairs.

He felt his heart skip. Going down there and facing them wasn't going to be as easy as he had hoped it would be. There was only one thing he could do to make sure he didn't crawl right back into his room.

"Ah," Bishop quietly exclaimed, taking a deep breath and walking to the other end of the room. "I'm really gonna have to do it this way, aren't I?"

He ran toward the stairwell, jumping down to the lower floor, the worn back of the long coat billowing behind him as he leapt.

CHAPTER 25

GROUND LEVEL

The black screen of the phone sprang to life with a click of a button. A finger slid across the screen, navigating through the apps with a robotic familiarity. After selecting the desired app, the screen shifted briefly to the floral-patterned title card of *Vivvedell's Blossoms*. When the card faded a red line at the bottom of the screen showed that this episode, the long-awaited season finale, was only moments away from being finished. The finger clicked play.

"No!" Stelvo yelled, flailing his arms dramatically. "It's just not possible! Say it isn't so, Vivvedell! Tell me that this is all just some kind of sick joke!"

"I'm sorry, Stelvo," Vivvedell turned away from her childhood friend, throwing her hands up and shielding her eyes from him. "Garn is the one that my heart flames for, I must end our relationship here . . . I'm sorry."

Vivvedell ran out of the well-furnished living room, crying, knocking over and shattering a potted plant as she went.

"Noooooooooooooo!" The brokenhearted Stelvo fell to his knees, screeching like a wounded animal.

Claw clicked off her phone, seeing the glow of the Board City skyline in its black glass. She was ecstatic; not only did Artex owe her fifty Zel over this, but that spineless wretch Stelvo finally got what he deserved.

She slid her phone into the metal case strapped to her hip. Claw began to head out of the alleyway she was hiding in. She looked up into the sky. The lit-up night sky looked like a lavender haze.

The other Marauders were surely looking for her. She knew she shot herself in the foot earlier by helping out that hostage. The other Marauders kept looking for her to tell them what to do, which under normal circumstances would annoy the life out of her, but under these circumstances made her almost violently angry. She could not let something as inconsequential as armed, panicking idiots stop her from seeing the season finale.

"Claw, thank goodness you're here!"

"Oh, yes, Claw, Thank goodness!"

A shiver ran up her spine. She knew those voices; she knew them all too well. "Jeff and Joff." Her tattooed flames began burning as red as the real thing, "To what do I owe the pleasure?"

The two Varse that stood under a streetlight in front of her were some of the most notorious in the entire gang. Unlike other Marauders who hammered out their reputations by exceeding in their respective fields, these two stuck out because they had the amazing talent of being incredibly obnoxious.

Jeff was wearing a shimmering bright red outfit consisting of dyed rain slug leather pants, and a coat that was much the same. Joff wore an identical outfit, but in blue. Both of them had a pistol on their hips, left and right respectively, and large sighted guns with thin, cone-shaped barrels across their backs.

"We heard that Bishop is in trouble," Joff exclaimed, his voice grating on Claw's ears.

"Aaaaaaaaand, if he's in trouble . . ." Jeff continued, his voice having much the same effect on her as his brothers.

"You can bet your ass that we are going to be there!" they both yelled in unison, stomping their feet on the ground and sneering.

Claw felt the high from winning her bet drain from her very being, and it was replaced with a very vivid feeling of disgust. "Do you two really have to act like that, now of all times?" She shook her head at them, feigning concern. "You do realize that a lot of people just died, right? Not really the time for little games, now is it?"

The twins' faces contorted into vicious grins as they began to walk closer to Claw. "You know what's more inappropriate than games?" Jeff asked, looking at his brother.

"What would that be?" Joff replied, repeating his brother's movements.

The twins were standing on their toes, trying to get as close to Claw's face as they could. Claw didn't budge. "Sneaking away in the middle of a crisis to watch a shitty soap opera."

Claw's eyes blew open. She swung her head backward, the chains in her skin jingling as she did, and brought it crashing into Jeff's face. He shrieked and fell backward, blood spurting from his nose.

"Jeff?!" Joff gasped, right before Claw nailed him in the face with a punch from her non-prosthetic hand. He fell to the ground like his brother, shifting to match his stance.

"I won't be criticized by little ingrate spies like you two." Claw wiped the blood from her face with her sleeve, leaving a blue smudge on her black coat. "Besides, you should be thanking me."

"Why's that?" an angry Jeff noisily hissed.

"Because I made sure to break both of your noses, so you can keep up your weird identical twins' shtick."

The twins growled at her as she stepped over them and out of the alley. She had heavily debated killing them and blaming Yelo, but sadly they were too good at their jobs to warrant it. For now.

The Marauders in Monochro were hard at work piling the corpses into two piles: Marauders and not Marauders. Claw knew how to silence a crowd, a shot from Cherry Picker usually shut anyone up, but she had no idea what to actually do when said crowd handed her power.

She figured the best thing to do was to build a funeral pyre, since it would take a while to do and get the others out of the chains for a bit. It wasn't like they all wouldn't just be cremated anyway, so why not get it all done at once, right?

"Hey Claw, does this look about right?" a Marauder asked, pointing to the pile of their dead comrades.

"Great!" she replied deadpan, barely glancing toward the Marauder. "Best pyre I've ever seen."

"And what about the other pile?"

Claw hadn't thought about that part. She mulled it over in her head for a second.

"Use it as target practice."

"But Claw, some of them are actual civilians."

"Yeah."

"Wouldn't that make for really bad optics?"

Claw thought it over for a second.

"Yeah, I guess you're right."

"So, what should we do?"

Claw shrugged. She turned on her heel and began walking in the other direction, leaving the Marauder to ponder her words of wisdom. If she walked far enough, she was sure that she would find a restaurant or something that hadn't closed just because a few wee bombs were thrown around.

The street was swamped with cars, Marauders, and motorcycles. A lot of Marauders came to Monochro as soon as word got out, only adding to her headache in the process. Over by one of the parking garages, several black-vested Marauders were kicking an inflatable ball to each other, and off of the face of the other, more unlucky hostage who was tied to a fire hydrant.

Ebby's Eatery might still be open, Claw thought to herself. *That would be really great, they have the sweetest orbs in town.*

As she walked, a large shadow moved to loom over her, eclipsing her own shadow completely. "Where's Lode?" a deep voice boomed from behind her.

A tall man that was built like a brick house stood behind her; it was as if he appeared out of thin air. He wore the standard Marauder apparel, although even the largest size available looked tight on his muscle-bound frame. Finally, he had two large silver rapid fires holstered to his sides.

She glanced back at him. "Oh, it's you, Butler. Aren't you supposed to be in the manufacturing district?"

"Those engineers in Grandmin don't need our help to stay safe," the giant answered, his voice gruff and deep, but tinged with worry. "Where's Lode?"

Claw took a deep breath before responding, her patience for today having already worn to its edge before running into this lovesick puppy. "Have you checked the corpse pile?"

The massive man's face dropped like a boulder in a lake. "No."

"You probably should."

She watched the giant run toward the pile, trying to blink away the tears forming in his eyes. She worked with him once or twice; he was an impressive fighter, but from what she saw and heard, he was more of a desperate lover.

"These people," she said, shaking her head and walking into the purple and white night life of Monochro.

CHAPTER 26

SONIC RECONCILIATION

Queenie sifted through box upon box of strange, half-finished electronic devices. She had been searching for the Sonic Maximizer on Patho's behalf for what felt like a half hour. Patho's lab was the definition of an organized mess, although she would have never guessed how bad it actually was when she first walked in. Once she actually dug into it, though, it became apparent that he'd just throw finished or half-finished machines into random boxes once he was done or bored with them. The man with the gauntlet wouldn't leave the lab without her following behind him; she was assuming that he was too scared to actually leave on his own. He stood "guard" by the doorway, tapping his metal fingers against the wall and enjoying the sound of the tapping a bit too much to be normal.

She pulled a metal cube with a button on its side out of the box. Then she set it on the ground next to her in the assorted pile of other gadgets, very careful not to press the button just in case it was some kind of machine that stopped the heart of whoever used it. Queenie had never actually heard of a machine that could do such a thing, but from what she knew of the mysterious Patho's reputation, she couldn't be too sure of anything.

"Tip-pity tap, tap." She heard the man giggle to himself, his eyes flickering with a childish innocence that was marred by the brown crusty stains running down the sides of his face, and everything else about him. Queenie hadn't had the opportunity to be an individual, to be herself, in years. But for reasons she didn't quite understand the moment, she had opened the metaphorical door to let freedom back into her life all these freaks waltzed in right behind it.

Another strange machine that didn't fit the description of the Sonic Maximizer was pulled out of the box—accompanied by an eye roll from Queenie. The process of searching through a box and then carefully putting everything back in just to start again with another box was really starting to grate on her. But she took great solace in Rook, who was still unconscious and coated in cold vomit. As much as it might suck to do now, if she was able to get in good with the higher-ups of the Marauders, it might just save her life. If she was lucky, they might even let her leave with her life and her limbs intact. She might not have to actually join the gang. Maybe they'd even set her up with some nice Monochro apartment to live in. She would love that. In the back of her head, she knew all this working out perfectly for her was a complete long shot, but the chances would be a big fat zero if she didn't make herself suffer through this drudgery.

She again dug her hand into the crate. She was beginning to wonder if this was the wrong box, but she'd already been through two others and a thought in the back of her head had her thinking it might even be the wrong lab.

Queenie let out a pained yelp when she felt something sharp pinch her palm. Zoog looked away from his carnival of tapping fingers just in time to see Queenie rip her hand violently from the box.

Some small strange machine that looked like a nickel-sized crab had latched itself onto her palm; it had a deep purple button on its back. She began to try and pull it off her, but she stopped due to the throbs of sharp pain it was causing—it had hooked to itself deep under her skin.

"Are you okay?" Zoog asked, concerned about his new friend.

"Just a tiny little accident, I'll be fine."

Queenie stood still for a second, trying to figure out the best way to solve this new problem. Then a spur of the moment idea popped into her head. If she couldn't rip it off, she was going to smash it off. Raising her hand toward the sky, Queenie prepared to smash the crab machine into bits. She'd worry about the hooks later.

She blasted her hand into the wall, attempting to destroy the machine, but instead of the sounds of metal shattering, she only heard a small click. Queenie sat silently, her heart in her throat as she waited for her hand to explode.

A white light began to climb up her arm. Queenie stood up and began shrieking as it climbed from her arm to her torso. She fell backward onto the ground by the time the light fully had consumed her.

Zoog watched in horror as the light enveloped her and changed her. Soon her appearance became one identical to Patho's Human disguise, outfit and all.

Queenie sat up and lightly patted her chest, making sure she was still alive and breathing. Her clothes felt different, but everything felt like it was there. A relieved smile began to creep over her now dark lips.

"Oh, I understand now!" Zoog screamed, pointing his gauntlet at her, palm splayed. "I know what you were after now! Monster!"

"Wh-what?"

"I know exactly what you are now!"

"Horribly confused?"

"You're still using her voice. Have you no shame in what you've done? Or are actions like these just a sick normal for you?"

Queenie hadn't the slightest idea what he was talking about. All she knew was that smashing whatever it was didn't go so hot, and that she was thankfully still breathing after the fact.

"You thought you were so clever, kidnapping me and strapping me to that bed. I bet you never thought I'd escape your little trap, did you?"

"Dude, what the hell are you talking about?"

"Then, when you figured out that 'Zoog the Magnificent' wouldn't come so easy, you had your little lackey bring down a spare for you!"

"Seriously freaking me out, man."

"I've heard the stories about you, Patho. Awful stories, but I'd never imagine that you were actually an immortal spirit that needs to take the bodies of others to survive."

"What!" Queenie looked down at her hands. They weren't hers; they weren't even Varse hands. She began yelling loudly, grabbing her face and feeling the unfamiliar soft skin of a Human."

"What in the name of the Provider, and all his gifts, happened to me?!"

"Nice try, fiend!" Zoog motioned his hand toward her threateningly. "You could really work on your acting skills, not that you'll have the chance. I'm putting an end to your evil ways right now, and by the way, you could never even dream of handling this body. BEAM FIRE!"

"No!" Queenie yelled back, throwing her arms up to shield her from a blast that never came.

Queenie peeked out from behind her arms, seeing Zoog finicking with the glove and swearing. Even if there were no lasers in that thing, she'd seen what the glove could do to a person. She needed a way out of this, and fast.

She grabbed the chain-covered vest from beside her and threw it onto Zoog. It landed, draping over his face. He let out a sound like a cat being thrown in water before running blindly backward, trying to get away. Instead, he just smashed his head on a wall. Once again, Zoog was unconscious.

Queenie carefully approached him, grabbing the gauntlet and the vest before running back to her pile of gadgets. In retrospect, she probably should have tried to use one of them, but something in the back of her mind wanted her to use the vest instead. Also, there was no telling if it would have helped her or just made things worse.

There were currently three problems for the former Yelo member to face. She had not yet found what she was looking for, there were now two unconscious idiots, and third, she was apparently Patho now. She sat down where she was and put her head in her hands. It had been a very overwhelming five minutes. She heard the soft click again. Suddenly everything was white, then the white shattered like glass around her. Queenie was Queenie again. She blinked a few times. The oddness was becoming more extreme every minute. This was just her life now. She had to accept it. There would never be normalcy again—only an ever-worsening bizareness that ended in a hopefully fast death.

Queenie began sorting through the box again.

***

"You sure we can trust this Queenie girl?" Artex asked Patho while he watched his wobbly sister down another shot of brandy. "I never even heard of her until today."

"Are you honestly trying to tell me that you're aware of every member of the Marauders?"

"No."

"It sounded to me like you were."

"Well, I wasn't."

"Well, it sounded like you were."

"Do you have nothing better to do right now than to annoy me?"

"I have some books in my room, but the stairs are broken and I don't feel like jumping up them again, so annoying you is all that's on the menu right now."

"Oh, lucky me!"

Vara watched a blotch of blackness leap down from the upper floor and land soundlessly behind her arguing friends. When her eyes came into focus, she recognized the blotch. It was Bishop—though he was wearing a coat she'd never seen before.

"Oh, hello there," she tried to say flirtatiously through a drunken and broken smile. "That's a, that's a, that's a nice coat ya got there."

"Vara, what the hell are you mumbling about over there?" Artex snapped.

Vara pointed toward Bishop. "Bish!"

Artex and Patho turned their heads to see Bishop standing awkwardly in the center of the room, as stiff as a plank. "Hi."

"Welcome back," Patho responded coldly. "Is your little meltdown over?"

"It wasn't that big of a deal," Bishop sighed, trying to play it off. "It was just something I had to get through."

"Well, that's good, maybe we can actually agree to leave here now instead of sitting around like useless idiots. Isn't that right, Vara?"

"Yeah, yeah, yeah," she blurbed.

"Leave?" Bishop asked with a raise of his brow.

"Yes, *leave*," Patho repeated. "After checking in on you, Vara here put up the Trident Field, and we've been floundering in here ever since."

"So we are stuck in here for three days?"

"We can shrink that to three hours at any time, and we have somebody working on strengthening communication to the masses. Artex has also informed as many as he could, via text, that we will be making an official announcement regarding the situation as soon as we can."

Bishop shook his head before speaking. "Patho, get it down now!"

"Oh! You're giving an order!" Patho exclaimed in a mix of sarcasm and surprise. "So you're finally trying to reclaim your spine, then! You picked a hell of a time to do it! Might be five years too late!"

Bishop hesitated before replying. He could feel the frustration radiating from Patho's featureless face. Patho was right; he couldn't just act like he had suddenly earned the right to earnestly issue them commands again. The respect they once had for him had waned over the years; even Vara seemed to treat him like a wounded animal at times, but that was exactly why this all had to stop. Bishop furrowed his brow. He would restore his reputation and self-respect if he died trying, but right here and now wasn't the time to be worrying about that. Real issues needed real actions; they could all argue about it later.

"Do you really think arguing about this is going to change the fact that the field needs to come down? If you were waiting on me because of Vara's insistence, then you don't have to wait anymore. Take it down."

"I suppose you're right about the timing. Besides, we have the next three hours to talk, just the three and a half of us," Patho said after a brief pause. He walked toward the broken steps with magic gathering around his feet.

"By the way, Artex," Bishop said, looking around the destroyed room. "What the hell happened in here?"

"Well, Bish," he answered, with a deep and exhausted sigh. "They finally had that rematch they always talked about."

"Oh, I see. It was always just a matter of time."

Bishop walked up to the window and pressed his metal hand on the glass. He looked out at the two piles of corpses, the collapsed buildings, the giant man sorting through the piles, and the Marauders gathered below.

"I wonder if we acted differently if this could have been prevented," Bishop lamented. "If I hadn't been such a bitch about everything, Yelo would already be done for now."

"Bish, it's all of our faults. We let ourselves grow complacent these past few years. We control more than three and a half out of six districts; our heads got too big for our own good and now we paid for it."

"Yeah, but where did that complacency start?"

Patho jumped down to the rest floor, landing gracefully. "The code has been entered," he announced, waving his hands in false excitement and walking up to join the others. "Now, all we can do is wait."

The eyeball on the bar beeped. "Did you find it?" Patho asked, neglecting phone etiquette entirely.

"Yes, but I have a small problem."

"Ah, good. Please take it outside and put the phone into the jack on the back. I will be sending a message to Rook's phone; play it when you have inserted the device."

"Path—sir—sir Patho, I really need your help with this problem."

Patho was silent for a few seconds and debated on whether he should just hang up or not. Eventually, after noticing the stern look he was getting from Artex, he decided to help the newbie.

"What's the problem?"

"A thing attached to my hand, and I can't get it off."

"A thing?"

"Yeah, a crab looking thing."

"Ahh . . . I see. I will remove it when we meet." Patho hung up the phone, and handed it back to Artex, who looked slightly confused by the girl's comments.

"One of the T.R.H. generators has implanted itself in her hand," Patho answered before the question could be asked. "It shouldn't be that much of a problem to remove."

"Patho, what on Mekebe is that?" Bishop asked.

"He wants us to talk to each other with eyeballs instead of phones," Artex answered. "I don't think he grasps how uncomfortable it is."

"It's only uncomfortable if you make it uncomfortable," Patho answered back. "Now, Bishop, about that arguing . . .."

CHAPTER 27

FACING THE CROWD

Queenie stood in front of Monochro Tower, holding the Sonic Maximiser in her hands. The crowd of Marauders had not yet noticed her, a fact she was thankful for. She didn't see the cannon-wielding woman with the robotic hand anywhere in the crowd, which she wasn't thankful for. Instead, she was greeted with two piles of corpses, and the sight of a very large man walking back and forth between them as he rummaged through the bodies, visibly muttering and weeping to himself.

She put the eyeball into the jack on the back of the device, and pressed play. A robotic voice began to blare from the machine. Queenie jumped back, wincing and covering her ears, careful not to press the button on her hand again.

"Meeting here in three hours," the voice said, in a cold, emotionless screech. "Please be present to receive further information about today's events. Do not come, and do not encourage others to come, if you or they hold a vital post elsewhere. Please be patient with us there, as we are experiencing difficulties with our defense system, and we will be with you as soon as we can be—Patho." The message repeated itself five more times before stopping. Queenie, who had never stopped moving away from the sound, found herself pressed against the wall of Monochro Tower.

The groups of Marauders that littered the streets were all now looking at the machine, and they began mumbling amongst themselves. She was really hoping that none of them had noticed her yet, and it had just dawned on her that she didn't know where she could safely wait out the next three hours so that the less friendly Marauders didn't give her a repeat of the same special treatment that she first received. Her head still hurt from those rocks.

She looked down at the thing implanted into her palm. The flesh had become inflamed, and it hurt if she even lightly touched it. It was starting to hurt if she didn't touch it too. Queenie wondered if she could use this to hide and make the best out of a bad situation. Then again, if Patho suddenly appeared after claiming he wouldn't for another three hours, it probably wouldn't work out especially great for the imposter.

She found herself standing in darkness. Queenie looked up to see the massive figure of the man who was sorting through the piles standing over her. He was at least seven feet tall, was built like a statue, and had wet tear stains running down his cheeks from large eyes that seemed to pierce right through her.

"Girl," the giant growled with a mix of desperation and anger tingeing his words. "Have you seen Lode?"

"Who?" Queenie managed to squeak out.

"Lode."

"I—uh, don't know who that is."

"You don't know who Lode is?"

"No, I don't."

He knelt closer to his face, his gaze stabbing into her like knives. His mouth contorted into an annoyed frown before he opened it to speak again.

"You don't know who 'Golden Rose Lode' is? What a damn shame that is for you." His breath smelt much cleaner than she would have assumed. "If you see a man with gold vines sewn into his clothes and a smile so warm that it can melt an iceberg, you WILL come find me before you even THINK of doing anything else."

"Yes. Yes, of course! Gold vines, great smile, I'll bring him right to you."

The man stood up straight once again. Queenie could now really see the confusing swirl of emotions painted on his face. He looked like he was about to burst into ugly sobbing, vomit, break something or someone in half, and scream all at the same time.

"Not a great smile," he growled, turning his back to her and heading toward the piles once more, "the best smile."

Queenie breathed a sigh of relief once the giant man had returned to his frantic searching. It was probably best if she waited inside the lobby. Most of the Marauders that were in there before had gone into the street by the time she left the lab, and she figured she could just hide under a couch until it was safe for her.

Queenie went inside, looked around, found the tallest couch she could, and slid underneath it. She knew how suspicious this looked, but she was screwed if a Marauder that was a little too angry found her in any position, so she might as well put herself in one where it would be harder for her to be seen.

***

Bishop exited the elevator, Artex and a Human-looking Patho following behind him. The past three hours had passed quite awkwardly, with its fair share of arguments. The full magnitude of the delayed response really sank in for him in between Patho's round of beratements. The Marauders looked weak, very weak, and Yelo would be itching to seize on that weakness. That couldn't be allowed to happen.

The trio stepped through the lobby, bracing themselves for the crowd of black that they could already see gathered outside. Then without warning, a young woman dressed in shabby brown clothes slid herself out from under one of the couches. The three of them looked at her with expressions of bewilderment as she held her right hand while hopping up and down and swearing.

"Couch girl, are you Queenie?" Patho asked, putting the pieces together in his head.

The girl looked up and smiled a nervous smile. "Yes, sir!"

"Thank you for your help with the Maximiser. Give me your hand?"

"Oh, it's no problem at all," she said, shaking her head as if to say it was no big deal. "I'm here to help." She held her hand out to Patho, revealing a very swollen palm.

"Whatever happened to Rook, by the way?" Patho inquired, inspecting the machine in her hand.

"Oh, the other guy down there knocked him out, but then I knocked him out. No idea if either of them are awake yet. I didn't see them come back upstairs."

"How did he manage that?"

"He punched him with a glove from the armor set down there."

Patho spun on his heel, leaving Queenie standing in the middle of the room with her hand out. He angrily headed straight for the elevator to his lab.

"I'm sorry for throwing a trident in your plans, everyone, but I really must make sure that my guest downstairs hasn't done anything to sully my armor. I will return to you all as soon as I set things as they should be—whether or not I'm covered in something unsightly and blue."

"Wh—what about my hand?" Queenie asked, taking a few steps toward Patho as he stepped into the elevator.

"Artex will help you."

"How will I help her? This is your thing!"

"Just rip it out," the Eatherial answered as the door closed in front of him.

Bishop watched Queenie and Artex stare awkwardly at her hand for a few seconds. Then Artex walked closer and poked the machine.

"Ow."

"Sorry, I'm new at this."

"Of course you are," Queenie mumbled to herself.

"What?"

"Nothing! I just had a really long day."

"Tell me about it," Artex replied with a groan.

"I'm heading outside," Bishop interjected.

"Sorry about this, Bish. I'd be out there with ya, but Red Boy dropped this on me, and I can't let her just stand here with this thing in her hand while we wait for the Almighty Lord of altruism and kindness to get back."

"Don't worry about me," Bishop replied, trying to assure both himself and Artex that this would go well. "I am the leader of this gang, you know."

"Yeah, I know. It's just been awhile." Artex returned to trying to help Queenie remove the machine. Bishop heard her yelp. Then he heard Artex apologize and vow to try again.

Bishop pushed open the doors and walked forward to face the mob of Marauders that were waiting for him. He could feel every set of eyes on him, every set of eyes that he had let down these past few years as he descended into his spiral of self-pity, every set of eyes that had no doubt noticed the change. The overwhelming scent of blood and dust in the air wasn't helping him feel at ease either.

All was a silent, save for the ambient sounds of Monochro as the Marauders stared at their leader. Bishop opened his mouth to speak. He had no idea what he was going to say, but if there was a single skill that he remained absolutely confident in these past few years, it was his ability to bullshit. A loud bellow erupted from the crown stopping Bishop's words in his throat.

"You! Where were YOU?!" a voice yelled in what sounded like a dreadful mix between a sob and a moan. Butler's giant form rose out of the crowd, his sleeves and hands stained blue with blood. He looked at Bishop with a desperate rage, and then charged at him with his fists clenched while the other Marauders just watched.

"Where were you when Lode died?! Where were you when my sweet thorn suckle was crushed by rubble?"

Bishop watched the giant run at him, his sclera expanding and contracting. If he allowed Butler to hit him, it would send a clear signal to everyone that he was weak, but if he moved out of the way, Butler might just go for him again, which would also just be pathetic. He had to do something—not just for the Marauders, but also to prove to himself that he was serious about everything.

Bishop easily moved out of the way of Butler's fist. Butler came around again with his other hand; he was weeping at this point. Bishop again swayed his body away from the punch. He shot his leg with a powerful kick right into the giant's side. Spittle flew from Butler's mouth as he was forced to take a few steps back. Bishop was upon him again in an instant, delivering a powerful backhand across his face with his left hand. Butler fell crying and wheezing to the concrete, a blubbering mess.

When he dodged the first punch, he felt what he thought was the familiar sensation of his heart fluttering, but when that feeling spread to the rest of his body he recognized it as something entirely different. It was his heart beating with thrill, a feeling he hadn't felt in a long time. He was ecstatic to feel it again.

"Really, Butler?" Bishop sighed and shook his head as he loomed over the fallen giant. "Now is the best time in the world to try and attack your boss? Really shows the Marauder sense of unity and cohesion in times of duress!"

Bishop turned to the still silent crowd. "Sorry about the delayed response." He began to walk as he talked. "The sensors on our defense system were a bit too sensitive, so when the buildings fell, it felt the vibrations and trapped us inside."

A grin began to stretch across his face. He was beginning to feel a little like his old self again, at least for the time being. A small one-sided sparring match in front of a crowd seemed to be just the thing Bishop needed to get his gears turning again. Although he did feel bad for Butler, and he didn't know how long this boost would last. A start was a start, though.

"But we are here now! And we are already hard at work to make sure that Yelo gets what's coming to them! I have a few ideas in mind on how to make sure that they get the message from us loud and clear. In fact, I think it might just be the last message we ever have to send those bag-faced freaks!" Bishop continued to walk forward, and the crowd began to part for him as he did, reacting to his attitude and body language.

"There are, however, a few more pressing matters, though, before we repay what we owe." Bishop looked down at the pile of dead Marauders that he now stood in front of.

"One! I need to know what this whole thing is about, and two . . . we need to get this place cleaned the hell up. Now, I'll take care of the second part, I'll have the best crews this side of Board City cleaning, fixing, and searching through rubble for our fallen comrades, but I need you to tell me why every single one of our accessible dead is now piled up in a big mound in the middle of the street. Along with another pile of corpses!"

"Claw told us to build a funeral pyre," a voice in the crowd answered, spurring a disappointed head shake from Bishop.

"Tsk. Tsk. No, we can't do that. I don't think our fallen want to be a scorched grease stain in the middle of the road. I can't think of anyone who would. Sort through them, and I mean really SORT through them, then send them off to whatever crematorium is most active in their districts. They deserve a proper send off.

"Three. Things are going to start to change around here. I will not let this gang be caught off-guard again, and I am no longer going to sit by the sidelines and plan parties. Sorry to all those that enjoyed the parties." Bishop refocused himself before he trailed off about how there would still be parties, just not as many parties, and how he specifically wouldn't plan them. "In case you haven't noticed from the smell of blood and the sight of bodies around you, the good days of bloodshed on our terms is over. We need to put this city back in its place before it knocks us out of ours—like it did to so many before us. We are not them! No, we are us! Yelo and those other gangs may have lost their time in limelight, but we won't go so quietly into the dark. No, we will go kicking and screaming, covered in blood and guns blazing, whether we win or lose! A lot of people who try to stop us are gonna end up cold and dead."

CHAPTER 28

STEWING IN SCHEMES

Hastul lifted his hand to his face, forming an "O" shape with his forefinger and thumb. He blew into the center of the circle causing a few bubbles to fly out and float in the air before popping. It was always a fun distraction. When he did it, he'd sometimes wonder what his life would be like if he chose elemental magic over color magic, but that was just frivolous daydreaming. He'd never have been able to choose differently than he did.

His bathroom was garishly luxurious and yellow. The tub itself was cozy but large, plated in gold and filled with warm water and bubbles that were formed from therapeutic skin-smoothing formulas. A golden plate holding both his favorite mirror and an array of nutriorbs sat easily within his reach on a small table. Hastul himself was wearing a green paste mask on his face, and a large television screen hung above him, displaying the purple-embroidered end credits of a *Vivvedell's Blossoms* episode.

It had been an exceptionally good day for the Yelo leader. His magic training was going well; he had humiliated the Marauders, furthered his plans to remove their stink from his city, several deserters were turned into powerful examples of what not to do by his loyal Huntsman, and to top it all off, Vivvedell ended up with his preferred choice of Bachelor. It really was a great day.

Hastul reached over and grabbed an orb from the platter. Any minute now, the elites of Yelo would begin to gather here in order receive their updated postings for the next phase of Operation Cassilda, and they would then scurry off to where they should be like the good little ants that they were. He threw the orb into his mouth, biting down with a crunch. It was a subject of serious consideration for him as to whether or not he should leave the tub for this meeting, but, in the end, he realized that he really earned this today and wasn't going to get out just because he had to have a quick little meeting—besides, there were a lot of bubbles in the tub.

The yellow door burst open with the sound of an alarm blaring for a second before being swiftly muted.

Vice-Commander Lawndel walked in, quickly saluting his soaking master. "Vice-Commander Lawndel, reporting as requested!"

Hastul glanced at the clock in the corner of his television. It was the exact time he had requested for the gathering to begin. Lawndel had been waiting out there for it to arrive.

"Thank you for coming."

"It is my pleasure, sir. Am I correct to assume that this meeting is in regard to Cassilda? If so, you will be pleased to know that I have already made all the necessary pre-preparations, and that overseer Thirty-Two is currently seeing to it that the consolidation of Yelo forces in Yellow Light goes as planned."

"Ah, good. Thirty-Two has always been a reliable overseer. Really got the Yelo spirit. You know what I mean?"

"I do, sir."

The door opened once again followed by the clacking of boots. Ten identical masked figures marched into the room. They organized themselves into a perfectly straight line before giving an in unison salute of their own. Each of them carried an energy rifle tipped with a Raiga blade bayonet that they could flip on with a switch.

Hastul reached for another of his orbs as he examined the Lem's entrance, trying to figure out if there were any imperfections in their stances. He ate the orb when he was confident that there were none.

Only one more to go, he thought to himself, just as the door opened again, and the smell of burning filled the room.

The Huntsman entered with a courteous bow. "Greetings, my most marvelous master. I have come as you requested."

Hastul smiled deviously. The time had finally come for the next stage of his glorious plan to cleanse Board City of its filth. "I have called you all here, the highest ranking members of Yelo within the great walls of Sinistus, aside from myself, to enlighten you as to the details of the next step of my ingenious machinations." He raised his arms out of the water. "As you know, we have long been losing precious territory to the Marauders and are left with only one major territory left under our complete control, Yellow Light. However, as of today, I am happy to announce that the tables have started to turn."

Hastul began to flail his arms rhythmically in the air, getting droplets of water and bubbles everywhere as he spoke. "We have given the Marauders two things today. On one hand, we gave them the punishment they deserve, and, on the other, we have handed them a test." Hastul brought his hands in closer to himself, curling them into fists and closing his eyes. "A test that they failed miserably. It took them hours to respond to an attack which was in their own front lawn. This is a sign of weakness, and an opportunity that we cannot dare let pass us by. From Yellow Light, we have long held a pristine strategic position for us to stage an invasion of the valuable manufacturing district Grandmin, and also to cut off their supply to all of its wonderful resources while taking them for ourselves. With Grandmin under our control, the rest of the city will follow suit in what will seem like the blink of an eye."

His eyes whipped open, and he threw his hands into the air triumphantly. "Now that we know that they have finally weakened, the time has come for us to finish this! Operation Cassilda is now a full go! We are going to call our forces from all across Board City and funnel them into Yellow Light! Then in one fell swoop, we will take Grandmin by surprise with the whole of our might, restore our power, and send the Marauders spiraling! We invade in four days."

The group of collected underlings began to clap for Hastul. When the clapping subsided, first to speak was Lawndel. "Excellent explanation, sir."

"Thank you. I know."

Hastul carefully grabbed his mirror off the side table and pointed it at the Lems. He traced a line across all of them. "I will be splitting the Lems into two groups. A group of five that will stay here and continue their normal duties, and a group of five that will be heading to Yellow Light to assist in the assault of Grandmin. As for you, Huntsman, I will need you here to help make up for the lack of Lems."

"As you wish, my master," the Huntsman croaked in his dry voice, his sharp yellow teeth forming into a hideous smile.

"Lawndel, you will continue your duties as normal, but with the addition of updating Thirty-Two daily on new developments and spreading the word to our cells that they are to head to Yellow Light as soon as possible."

"I will work it into my schedule, sir."

"Good; I want this invasion to be ready for launch three days from now. Now, Huntsman, Lems, you are dismissed. Return to your posts." Soon the room was empty, save Hastul and Lawndel. Hastul leaned forward in his foam-filled bath before asking his ever-staunch Vice-Commander a question.

"How long until the next batch of Lems will be ready? I know we will lose some in the assault, and they don't last more than a few years as it is."

"I have already begun selecting viable candidates. The survivors of the assault and those stationed here should last another six months to a year before the drug cocktail begins to cause serious mental and physical degradation, sir."

"Will you have them ready for use by then?"

"Yes sir."

"Good, now leave me."

Lawndel saluted before exiting the room. Hastul let out a deep breath before reaching for another candy. He pulled one bubble covered hand out of the water, a small magic projectile hovering above it. He fired it at the TV, harmlessly hitting a button near the bottom and causing the channel to change to one that only had soft instrumental music playing. He stretched out in the tub, feeling the oils in the water soak into his skin; he really did deserve this.

Chapter 29

Interesting Infirmary

The room was a crisp and sterile white, and was covered in an array of rectangular tiles from floor to ceiling. There were two hospital beds propped up against the wall of the room, with only a pulled back navy curtain and small table with a vase holding a white flower between them. Sitting up in the bed closest to the open door was a woman with bandages wrapped around her mouth. She sat up perfectly straight in her bed, completely unmoving and with a glaze over her eyes, and in the other bed lay Queenie.

She looked down at the bandages that wrapped around her hand, and at the gray smudge of disinfectant that was slowly soaking through them. It didn't hurt anymore, but the back of her head still had a dull pain from where she hit the floor. It was quite embarrassing, but the fact that it happened didn't surprise her at all. Still, the whole ordeal of getting it removed wasn't that bad of an experience. Artex was definitely the nicest Marauder she'd met so far. Their conversation was actually a pretty fun one before she fainted.

Queenie learned a lot of things during their talk. She remembered the exact moment that the conversation started to be about more than the thing in her hand. It was when the giant ran at Bishop.

"Oh, god! That's Butler," she remembered Artex saying, cringing as he did. "And he's yelling about Lode, isn't he?"

"That guy actually asked me if I had seen whoever Lode is earlier. He seemed pretty broken up about the whole thing."

"I'm pretty good friends with Lode. It would really blow if he died in this mess, but honestly, he might just be taking advantage of it and hiding."

"Hiding?" she asked, as Bishop dispatched Butler outside.

"Yeah." Artex looked her in the eye and pointed to the weeping giant. "You see that guy, Butler? Him and Lode have been a thing for years, but from what Lode told me last night, he's been getting real clingy these past few months. Like, sometimes stalking him type of clingy. Which of course, he's bad at—I mean, look at him, he's massive! Where's he gonna hide? Behind four light posts? But that's beside the point. Lode wanted out bad, like real *real* bad. Me and my other buddy, Zoog, had tried to talk him into ripping off the Band-Aid and just ending it last night, but he still felt sore about how Butler would respond to do it. I wouldn't be surprised if he's just dipped to get away from Butler at this point."

Artex shook his head while he tried to pull the machine out of her again. Queenie forced her hand to stay still; she could see her flesh lift up with the machine. She pulled her hand back out of instinct when she felt something tear. Blood squirted from her hand and onto the lumi-tattoo on Artex's cheek. The tattoo flashed red for a split second before returning to its normal placid blue color.

"Oh, Providence! I'm so sorry!" Queenie squeaked, cupping her good hand over her mouth. From what she had read on Artex in the mission files, he was the least physically dangerous member of the Marauder leadership, except for maybe Patho—but he was good with a gun and reportedly had quite the temper.

"No, it's fine," he said, wiping her blood from his face. "It's not like you can help it. We've gotta get this out though, especially now since there's a tear."

Queenie internally breathed a sigh of relief. The report, for all it was worth, seemed to be mostly wrong about him, but she wasn't sure how wrong it would stay if he ever found out where she actually came from and why she joined. The pain in her hand was like she was holding a hot coal and gripping it as hard as she could. The torn skin and flesh from his latest pull and the swelling was turning her palm an ever-darkening shade of blue. She really did appreciate his help. She really did, but she didn't see anything about medicine in his file, and he was proving that part right.

"Is there an infirmary you could take me to?" she blurted out. "Like, a place where they could maybe numb it?"

"Yeah," he answered, not taking his eyes off of her palm. "Patho probably wouldn't like anybody else seeing this thing though. If it were anything but this particular machine, I'd have you down there right now."

"Oh," she said sadly, her momentary hopes crushed in an instant.

The crowd outside was now silent, entranced by whatever speech Bishop was spinning for them. Queenie wondered about the chain-haired woman; her tattoo was similar to the one Artex had. She'd seen people with them before when she was young, but she forgot about them completely during her time in Yelo. They were kind of pretty.

"Is the "M" for 'Marauder?'" she asked him while he was planning out his next assault on her palm.

"Yeah, I got it after we captured Lentald from Yelo. First time I really felt like we could really back up what we were saying. Felt like I had to celebrate somehow, I always wanted one before that, and it seemed like the best time."

"Oh," Queenie responded. "That's where most of the nutriorbs are made, right?"

"Yeah, after that it was Grandmin, then Monochro—we just kicked a smaller gang out of Unric a few days ago, but that's probably what got you to join up with us, so you probably know that."

"I, uh—"

"Yeah, we always get a surge of recruits whenever we have a victory like that," Artex interrupted, unaware that she was trying to answer. But that was probably for the best. Queenie knew her being in Yelo wouldn't be kept secret for long, seeing as a whole mob of people already know about it, but she didn't want to sour his opinion of her while he was in the middle of helping her. She would always be an outsider here. She knew that, and that's why she wanted to try and get out of gang life before she got completely sucked in again.

"Aside from that, I'm definitely gonna have to rip this out. I don't think there's another way to remove this. It wasn't made with our flesh in mind." Artex grabbed her arm and pulled it closer to him. "I'm gonna count to three, and then I'm gonna pull it out, okay?"

"Okay." She nodded.

"One."

"Two."

"Three."

There was a gross ripping and squelching sound, and it felt like a knife was driven through her hand. Then Queenie remembered nothing. She woke up, but then she fell asleep again not long after when the initial panic of being somewhere new was soothed by a nearby doctor.

She looked over to the dull-eyed woman in the bed next to her. She tried talking to her when she woke up for the second time, but after a few minutes and no response to be found, she gave up. The way the woman sat there really unnerved Queenie. Her eyes were dull like those of a corpse. It made her skin crawl, and the perfect posture that the woman had been holding for hours sent a chill down her spine. But the worst part was the amount of drool that was soaking through the bandages around her mouth and covering the bed cloth beneath her. It made Queenie want to vomit.

There were a lot of weird things and people in the Marauders. She learned that pretty quickly. That guy being held by Patho, and this woman in bed were two of the worst, but the crying stalker giant was up there too. Out of all of them though, what freaked her out the most was an implication she picked up on the night before. Artex told her that the crab machine wasn't made with "their" flesh in mind, and that same machine made her look exactly like the guy who made it when she accidentally activated it. Queenie knew what the glove guy in the basement said was ridiculous, but Patho was definitely more than just a Human that happened to join up with a Varse gang. No, he was hiding something, and Queenie was perfectly happy not to find out what it was.

A doctor rushed into the room, then stopped abruptly in the middle of the floor. She was wearing a white lab coat with a blue shirt barely visible underneath, a black skirt, bags under her eyes, and a look of mania. She had a clipboard in one hand and an IV sack with a needle in the other. A long, clear tube was wrapped around her body and connected to a canister at her side; the tip of the tube was positioned near her mouth, and her eyes bugged so far out of her head that Queenie thought they might pop out. Her thousand-mile stare flicked from the wall in front of her to Queenie.

"Oh good, I was hoping you'd be awake. My name's Nilka. I'm a doctor here, in case you couldn't tell by the outfit. Haahhahaahahahaha-hahahahahahaha." She laughed like a machine and spoke like rapid fire sprayed bullets. She looked like she belonged in a hospital herself.

"Hello," Queenie said with her best smile, trying very hard not to escalate the encounter.

"Hello indeed! I bet you're wondering about your roommate? Don't worry about her, she does this from time to time. At least, that's what I've heard. I never actually worked on her before, but hey, everyone has a different way of dealing with bad hangovers, right? You look like the type of gal who likes to vomit when you wake up with a case of the head stabs. Am I right?" Nilka took a large drink out of the tube, and a clear liquid flowed from the canister into her mouth.

"I've never actually been drunk." Queenie managed to work in an answer before Nilka could keep yelling.

"Never been drunk? Religious one, are ya? Didn't take you for the science type, but guess I can't judge a book by its cover, now can I? Stupid Ol'Nilka, am I right? Hahahahaha." She drank again from the tube. Nilka walked over and hooked the IV up to the bandaged woman's arm. "This should get her up and kicking again. Girl, have you ever had liquid caffeine? It really keeps you going, but oh boy does it taste bad. I've put sugar in mine, but that makes it taste too good and now I can't stop drinking it. I feel like garbage anyway. I might as well have fun doing it, right? I've been up for forty-eight hours, and honestly, I feel like my insides aren't solid anymore."

There were no words Queenie could think of on how to respond to the barrage of words that she was being bombarded with. She didn't want to be rude to a doctor, though she was pretty sure this wasn't the one that calmed her down in the middle of the night. Eventually, she settled on the first question that came to mind.

"Why so long? The attack only happened yesterday."

"Ohohoho!" the doctor laughed as she threw herself wildly into a pose on one of the walls, causing Queenie to jump in her bed. Nilka lifted a finger toward her and pointed while continuing to laugh. "You have no idea how much a response like that reveals about you. You obviously don't know what yesterday was. Allow me to enlighten you.

Yesterday was the season finale of the modern work of art that is *Vivvedell's Blossoms*. As a true Blossomer myself, I devoted my last two days to watching the previous ten seasons start to finish. Then, Yelo had to go and attack us and flood this place with the dying and injured. Do you have any idea how hard it was to get a break yesterday?! But I did it, and I saw the finale! Let me tell you this! True love prevails baby!"

Nilka struck a triumphant pose, stood still for a few seconds, then flipped her head back to Queenie.

"Oh, that's right," she said in a much softer tone than usual.

"What?"

"There is somebody here to see you."

"Really?" Queenie asked, her mind racing. Who could be visiting her? Could it be Rook trying to threaten her for yesterday, Butler coming to apologize, or is it Artex coming to check on her? Out of all of them, she really hoped it was Artex. "Who?" But Nilka had already left to go retrieve them when she finished asking. So Queenie sat and waited.

Nilka returned. "Here he is," she said in her usual tone, before stepping aside for the mystery guest.

A man walked in. He wore an outfit as black as the desert night. In one hand he held the chained vest, and in the other a strange machine covered with wires and suction cups. His gray-white skin was wrinkled and aged, and his eyes were serene in an unnerving way, more reminiscent of a stagnant lake surrounded by dead trees than a relaxing babbling brook full of life and wonder. Queenie recognized his face immediately.

In Yelo, there was a thing called Ration Bounties. Ration Bounties acted like normal bounties, but only for Yelo members, and instead of money you'd get an increase to your rations for a number of days or weeks for turning it in. Yelo had both types of bounties out on this man, as did most of the smaller gangs. His name was Silt, otherwise known as "Silt the Silent." He was a famous assassin in Board City.

She felt like her heart had stopped in her chest. Was this really how they were going to get rid of her? And in one of their own hospitals, no less. Should she feel honored that they felt that she was worth the Zel to hire Silt? She didn't know, but she did feel like crying and begging for her life. Still, despite all of this, she couldn't help but glance at the vest.

"Ahh, you must be Queenie," Silt greeted in a warm tone. "I'm here on the request of Sir Patho."

"Y—you are," Queenie managed to squeak out.

"Yes, he had quite a few requests regarding you, actually."

"Did he, now?" she forced the words hoarsely out of her mouth.

"Yes," Silt answered, laying the vest at her side. "The first was to return this to you. The second and third requests I'm afraid are a bit less easy, but only a bit. If you comply, this next task shouldn't take that long."

Queenie managed to nod, and Silt set down the machine on the table next to her.

"Can you please attach those to your head, wrists, and forehead?" Silt produced a pen and paper from his pocket. "He has asked me to ask you a few questions regarding the Yelo compound, Sinustus. That machine will tell us if you're lying, so please think before you answer." Queenie nodded.

"Lastly, I've been asked to be your chaperone of sorts. Can't just trust someone with a background like yours after recent events, I'm afraid."

"Di—did they hire you just to watch me?"

"Oh my, no, I've been a Marauder for five years now—ever since they rescued my grandsons from a Yelo slave market. Although, I mostly just act as an advisor to the new infiltrators now. I'm also available to gather potentially valuable intelligence like what I'm doing right now, plus a few rare executions."

"Oh, I see. That's a relief." She let out all the breath that she had been holding in. "I thought you were here to kill me."

"Only if you try anything funny," he answered with a kindly smile.

The woman in the bed sprang to life. She reached behind her head, and with one mighty rip, she tore the soggy bandages from her face. She sat holding them and panting slightly.

"Much better," she panted. "Feel like a million Zel."

She twisted her head toward them. Her eyes were alive now, like those of a predator, and filled with a blazing fire.

Vara looked at them giving them a huge sharp-toothed grin. Her formerly shattered teeth were now repaired with ones of solid gold.

"Be honest," she asked, as it dawned on Queenie who she had been rooming with. "How do they look?"

CHAPTER 30

THE RIDE

The model of the car was incredibly sleek, with a deep red hue painted over it. The vehicle made a soft hum as it drove and looked as if it glided on the road. The seats were a leather dyed blood red, and the windows were tinted black. A hood ornament in the shape of a "T" sat proudly on the hood; three small spouts of wispy blue Raiga erupted out of the top of the ornament, causing it to resemble a trident.

When he was younger and lived in a world brimming with his own kind, Patho had always preferred to move by foot, but now, in this new world of sand and cities, learning to drive was sadly a necessity. But he admittedly did like the customizability.

Today's ride wasn't for fun, though. In fact, it was part of an errand that had found its way into his lap during last night's rousing bout of arguments. Well, not actually into his lap. Patho had no actual obligation to be going where he was going. His passenger, on the other hand, had wholeheartedly agreed to this task without knowing all the details. Patho loved when people did that—it made his nonexistent heart sore.

The streets leading to Lentald were like most streets in Board City: packed with a variety of different and annoying vehicles. Navigating this mess, although easy for him, had always been too time-consuming for Patho to humor driving more than once in a blue moon. But he wouldn't miss seeing this for the world.

The sun was sending rays of heat and light down to the city from its diamond-shaped body. A blue flash of light and a bang came from one of dozens of alleyways that he drove past, but it was probably the fifth time he'd seen that today. People were screaming and fighting with each other on the streets over bags containing who knew what. Many of the people had brown trails leaking out of their eyes. There were people who were painted silver and gold dancing on sidewalks and hoping for a generous passerby to throw them a spare Zel or two. A disheveled man was walking through the streets, shrieking about utter nonsense and holding a sign of painted cardboard that read: "The Provider is returning soon! Will we be ready for his gifts!!!" All around, it was quite a beautiful day to be driving though the city's pulmonary streets.

"Ah, the Provider," said Patho's passenger, referring to the man with the sign. "I still can't believe what you told us about that whole thing."

"Yes, I almost felt bad bursting your bubble." He flicked his false eyes toward Bishop briefly before returning them to the road. "It is overwhelmingly likely it was just another survivor of my kind that told your people about how to produce and use Raiga, not some divine messenger sent to aid you in your quest for survival."

"You sure they're dead?"

"This half of the planet isn't living under a technocratic god king. So, yes, I'm quite sure."

"That's a funny way of putting it," Bishop laughed. "Is that what you're going to do when we're gone, become the machine king of the Varse?"

"Oh, I hardly have the mind or patience for that. I might be a genius compared to any species alive today, but I am of quite average intelligence for an Eatherial."

"Yet here you are, alive in the present."

Patho smiled, savoring his position as the last of his wretched kind.

"Yes, here I am, benefiting from the length of my own sentence, safe in stasis, inside my cell while they have all died out free in the open world. Serves them right."

"What were they like?" Bishop asked. "The first Marauders?" Patho looked sad for a moment before answering, while Bishop fought back the urge to apologize to him for bringing it up.

"We weren't like the ones we have now. We fought for the cause of freedom, refusing to live by the rules others set out for us. Our leader was a great and powerful embodiment who wielded gray color magic with the utmost skill. I don't know if our species died out before or after the Marauders were stopped, but I do know that we were losing our battles more and more. I was captured during a siege of a city, and swiftly tried for my crimes in a fixed court before being shoved into what was supposed to be an eternal sentence." Patho's voice was low and somber as he spoke before picking up again. "Then a bunch of Varse scientists found the prison I was trapped in, freed me by coincidence, which caused a kill switch to kill all the other prisoners. Naturally, I then killed them, and now here we are."

"Embodiment?"

"It's a magic term," Patho answered.

"For what?"

"It's a color magic equivalent for a Magician, just as powerful a state when reached, but there is a catch. An embodiment is, well, an embodiment of their own negative emotions. When they become their true selves, the 'gunk' in their souls causes them to take on a monstrous appearance. It's not something you choose to be, but end up as. A good sign that somebody is or is becoming an embodiment is an unnatural obsession with a specific physical object. During their magical growth, the aforementioned soul 'gunk' begins to flow into the object and it basically becomes a part of them. Without it, they can never unleash their full potential if they do actually reach true embodiment status, and if they bind enough with it, the magic user will always be able to feel where it is—no matter how far away."

"You see, that right there is why I don't want to use magic. Too many unspoken rules nobody tells you about."

"The templates that existence functions under are quite odd."

The district of Lentald opened up before them. Back during the "Golden Age," before Varcia fell apart, this district was meant to feed the entire city state of Board with an endless supply of nutriorbs. Now, it was still used to provide food to the city, but it was also home to a large number of unsavory manufacturing practices. The buildings were a mix of the normal alabaster and gray of Board City and a blend of intricately carved wooden buildings and carved brick. Thanks to a long defunct gang of Human fetishists, the whole district had been sprinkled with buildings and culture that looked like it had been ripped straight from the other continent. Greenhouses and factories were dotted frequently around the district and were never far from one another. A stream of people in identical white uniforms and safety masks walked in and out of both, and into each other constantly, always pushing or pulling something or some collapsed colleague behind them. A fast-growing disparity in this district had made it into an elitist's dream with rare recreated Human Culture, expensive restaurants that served both the finest grade of nutriorbs and actual foods cooked to the finest standards; to top it all off, they could watch the peasantry walk around below them as they ate.

Bishop never liked places like those, but one of those restaurants was where they were meeting the arms dealer that day. So, he'd have to stomach it at least for a little while.

"I haven't been here since we took it from Yelo," Patho commented, tapping his fingers on the smooth leather of the wheel. "I forgot how mismatched everything is. It's disgusting."

"Yeah, it seems like just yesterday that we razed that music hall to the ground."

"Good times."

The car came to a slow stop in front of a gray brick building that was built to look like a castle with a single tower rising up from its center. At the tower's top was a glass dome made up of several different segmented windows. A sign out in front read "Bubble Delight" in a bright pink, glowing calligraphy.

Patho moved the car into the adjoining building, which was a large gray rectangle lacking any of the details that its neighbor showed off so proudly, handing the man out front a few luminescent blue coins as he did. The parking garage resembled any other that one could find in Board City. It was mostly empty, save a few other expensive-looking cars, though there were some Marauder guards walking around keeping the expensive cars out of inexpensive hands.

"It's easy to forget that it's us who are in control here," Bishop commented as he nodded to the guards. "There's so damn many of us."

"Yes, it must be surprising for you to see how the gang actually functions outside of Monochro," Patho replied.

The two Marauders exited the car and began making their way toward the doors of Bubble Delight. The air in Lentald was infused with the overwhelming scent of the nutriorb plants, which was a constant assault on Bishop's nose. It was a sickly sweet smell doused with a good chunk of chemical cleaner that made his eyes begin to water. He brought his metal hand to his face, clutching his fingers tightly together to try and block the scent out as much as he could.

"I suddenly remember why we left here for Monochro," Bishop mumbled through his hand. "This is going to give me a monster of a migraine if I'm out here any longer."

"Lentald assaults your nose and eyes. I can't say I've missed this town of swollen vanity."

"Which dealer are we meeting up with again anyway? Onda? Ran?"

A massive smile ripped its way across Patho's face. This was what he was waiting for: the information Bishop had neglected to search out when he accepted Patho's conditions of cooperation the night before.

"Oh, didn't Artex tell you when you took over this job for him?" Patho answered, his satisfaction dripping from every word.

"No, he didn't."

"It's Winal."

Bishop's expression told it all. Anger and frustration had birthed themselves from nothing inside of him as soon as he heard the name. It was the exact reaction Patho was looking for.

"You're kidding."

"Not at all."

"Why?"

"I told you last night. You can't just emerge from your cave in a new outfit and pretend like that undoes several years of degradation and non-existent leadership. The other two might be willing to believe it is the case just so they can finally welcome you back to the world of the active, but I'm going to need more proof than just a good speech and a punished subordinate."

"You're a complete monster, you know that?" Bishop hissed through his fingers, glaring swords into Patho.

"People keep telling me that."

"You're going to love every agonizing minute of me talking to this scumbag, aren't you?"

"Oh, no! Of course not!" Patho corrected, pretending to be offended by the question. "I'll enjoy watching every agonizing *second.*"

Bishop marched to the door, leaving Patho behind to laugh at his own joke. He pushed it open with enough force to cause it to slam into the wall with a loud thwack. The waiter standing at the podium flinched at the sound.

The waiter's eyes widened in surprise when he saw who threw the door open, and the widened further when they saw the still giggling Human who walked in behind him.

"B—b—b—Bishop!" he muttered through a high pitched yell. "How can we help you today, sir?"

"I need a table for three."

"Yes, of course! Right this way, please!"

The waiter led them up the staircase, which was made to look as if it were lit with torches and had heat blasting down on them from the ceiling.

"If I may ask?" the waiter cheeped. "What is the name of your third, sirs?"

"Winal," Bishop groaned while Patho stifled another laugh.

"Ah, yes of course, I should have known! Please forgive my question and me for being so stupid."

"There's no need to act like that," Bishop dryly stated, walking ahead of the waiter and toward the dining area. "We will seat ourselves. Go back down to your perch."

"Yes, sir!" the waiter said with a bow before scurrying down the stairs.

"You can't tell me you're not excited to see Winal again, can you? It's been years since you two last met face-to-face," Patho prodded.

"I could live eight lifetimes and it still wouldn't be enough time for me to feel okay about interacting with it again."

"It? Why Bishop, how rude of you. You're the leader of the Marauders, our face to the world. You must be a bit nicer than that. Especially to a valued weapons dealer," Patho continued to prod.

"Why do we even need dealers? We have factories pumping out guns and bombs, and you whipping up who knows what in your lab," Bishop grumbled as they reached the top of the stairs.

The dining area was beautiful. It was furnished with a deep blue carpet, and there was a large bar in the middle. Some of the tables even had live cooking, and the light seemed to always stream in at the right angle.

"Grandmin is quite useful indeed for mass producing basic things, and I as much as I love inventing and creating new ways to kill people, I am only one person. Dealers are a necessity if we want to get a taste of what Inner Varcia and the Church of Conort are whipping up. Besides, I love vastly improving on their little 'breakthroughs.'"

Bishop mumbled something under his breath and sat at a table very close to the glass windows of the dome. He sat facing the stairs, waiting for his loathed guest to arrive.

"Patho, you better not expect me to pay for him," he said, "and I hate you."

Patho cracked an unflinchingly sly smile. "If your hate is the price that I must pay to watch this, then so be it."

Chapter 31

A Loving Rage

The Yelo captain listened intently to the printer as it painted the ink into the paper. It had barely been a day since they took over this hideout, and almost immediately after securing it, they were informed that they were to begin moving out to Yellow Light as soon as possible. It seemed like a waste to the captain, but he was not of the rank where questioning an order was a possibility. He wasn't even sure such a rank existed.

The paper slid out of the printer and into the tray waiting to catch it. "Operation Cassilda," it read. The captain skimmed the document to get the gist of the plan before he abandoned the post that his men—and possibly women—died for. It was hard to tell with the uniforms. No matter what, there were only six of them left, eleven when they first arrived, and he was not very keen on moving his troops through the city again before they had a chance to properly rest. He had asked for reinforcements before they fully cleared out the enemy, but he had heard nothing back on the matter. It was always hit or miss with command when it came to requests like that.

The operation, as much trouble as it would be to carry out, seemed pretty sound to him. If this worked and Grandmin fell to Yelo, then their grasp on the city would be basically guaranteed. As much as he didn't want to push his troops, the risk was looking more and more like it was worth taking.

He placed the document down on the table next to the broken radio. The room he was in was an awful eggshell color, but was a welcome sight compared to the deluge of yellow that made up most things in Sinustus and Yellow Light. There were two Bans in the room with him, and each of them were armed with either a high-powered single-shot shotgun or a rapid fire. He turned to address them and tell them to prepare the others to move out, but he was interrupted by a knock on the door.

"Sir," one of his men called from the other side of the door. "There are people outside who claim to be the reinforcements."

The captain felt a small rush of elation in his stomach. Some fresh bodies would make leaving this Provider-forsaken maze all the easier. He opened the door and walked down the stairs, past the Ban who had informed him. The downstairs consisted of three rooms: a small kitchen that connected to the main room via an open wall, and a main room that was littered with trash and sleeping bags. Lastly, there was a hallway next to the stairs that branched out of the main room and led to a deep closet where their enemy had made their last stand with a couple of rapid fires, each was littered with blood spatters and bullet holes. They had dragged the corpses—both of the enemy and of their own—outside, for whatever person or thing might want them. He acknowledged the Bans that were taking aim at the closed door, waiting for their captain's orders on what to do next with a nod. The captain peered out of the peephole. Sure enough, there were two Bans standing side by side, waiting to be let in.

He motioned for his men to stand down and opened the door. "Welcome," he said to the waiting minions. "We appreciate you coming on such short notice. Are there only two of you?"

"Yes," the Ban on the right answered. "Any number higher was too much to be spared."

"Ah, I see," the Captain said, his voice muffled by his mask as he led them inside.

"I'd say make yourselves comfortable, but we won't be here much longer. You can stay down here or head upstairs. The choice is yours, just be ready to move out at a moment's notice."

"Yes, sir," the other Ban responded. "We would like a refresher on the mission. I'm afraid we were sent out to reinforce this position without receiving all the necessary details for the mission."

"Are you unaware of Cassilda, then?"

"Yes, sir. We were only told to head here and nothing more."

"Best if you come up with me, then. I'll inform you on the basics so you don't have to catch up from nothing."

"Thank you, sir."

The captain waved a hand at the Bans who had been guarding the door. “Stay here while I catch these two up. Be ready for an in-depth briefing in the next few hours, then be ready to relocate to Yellow Light.” The Bans did the Yelo salute for their captain.

Chapter 32

All is Fair in Confusion and War

The rage inside him boiled and churned, ready to explode at any moment. Last night had not been his brightest moment, but Butler appreciated Bishop forgiving his outburst. He appreciated the mission he was assigned to soon after even more. Butler had spent hours searching for and calling Lode, trying to ignore the obvious. Lode was dead. He didn't find a body, but there were a lot of people crushed into a fleshy blue paste when the buildings collapsed. From reading Lode's phone, he knew that he was meeting a friend of his—Pawna, he thought her name was—to discuss the Vivvedell finale, in a building Butler knew had been reduced to rubble. Yelo did this. They took his love from him and they had to pay for the lake of tears he cried, in double the amount of blood.

Butler hated The Brooks. Its smell was always moldy and he could feel hundreds of eyes staring at him all the time. The only thing keeping him from being swarmed by the hungry and destitute was probably the two massive rapid fires hanging at his side. He loved his guns. They made problems go away and put food on the table. He was very excited to use them to put dozens of holes in the pathetic slime that made up the ranks of Yelo, though he doubted that this would be enough retribution for Lode's death. He'd need the entire gang to go up in agonizing flames for him to feel like they were even. Still, this should put at least a bit of pep back into his step.

Grumbling, he reached into his pocket and pulled out a crumpled piece of paper with a list of addresses written on it. A single address in The Brooks was like a needle in a haystack. Luckily, with a list of them like this, finding the address would only be hard instead of impossible. Butler had left his car on the bridge and walked in. He knew what would happen if he drove in and got out. Even if it was for a few moments, that car would be gone. He had heard a story of someone that came back to find their car stripped clean by a man so off his rocker that he was eating the rubber from the tires. The man, of course, shot the tire eater at the end of the story, and it probably didn't really happen. But a lot of things like it did. Butler came to a stop outside of a large dark building that was crammed between two other identical buildings. This was it.

He walked up to the door as quietly as his massive frame would allow. He grabbed ahold of the two guns on his sides, ready to fire them at any moment. He was going to relish this next part; he always did. Butler kicked the door, and it splintered under the force of his strike. As soon as he could see even an inkling of what was past the threshold, he put his fingers in the triggers and fired twin sprays of energy bullets into the room.

The sound of gunfire echoed through the streets as Butler filled one of the three Bans left to guard the door with hundreds of bleeding holes. The Ban fell like a rag doll. Butler turned his sprays to the left and right, catching another Ban who was trying to ready his own gun in the hail of bullets. Butler stopped firing, and the silence fell hard. He examined his work just as the last Ban rose from behind the counter, shotgun in hand. He fired a blast. Butler had noticed just in time to move his giant body out of the way. He was much more agile than his frame would suggest. The baby blue scatter of Raiga put dozens of holes into the wall.

Butler moved to fire at his assailant, but the Ban had already loaded another blue crystal into the chamber, dropped the empty gray one to the ground, and clicked the trigger. The shot came fast, but Butler was faster. He threw himself to the ground as soon as he saw the finger move, and the holes in the wall were given a matching friend. He pulled both triggers and released a torrent of solidified Raiga energy into the Ban, who then slumped, dead and unrecognizable, behind the counter.

He stood up. He could feel his heart in his chest beating hard, but nowhere near as hard as it had beat for Lode. Butler dusted himself off, reloaded his own crystals, and turned his eyes to the stairs.

***

The Yelo captain had barely returned to the room with his new recruits before he heard the crash of the door being kicked in. He swung violently toward the door as gunfire erupted from below him.

"Men!" he yelled in a panic, but still managed a commanding tone. "Ready your weapons!"

But the Ban to his right only fell to the ground with a coin-sized hole in his head. The captain instinctively stepped back just as the Ban to his left fell. He looked down at the new corpse, and then to the reinforcements who stood in front of him, holding sighted handguns with thin, cone-shaped barrels.

Before the captain could say a word, they silently filled him with holes, hitting all his vital areas with ease due to the close range. He was dead, and Jeff and Joff removed their masks. A screaming giant burst into the room, gun aimed and ready to fire.

"Don't shoot, it's us!" the twins screamed in unison, terrified.

Butler put his guns down, the blue leaving his face slowly. "Oh, it's you," he panted. "I forgot you were on this too."

"Forgot?!" they gasped in their nasal voices. "How could you forget?! You almost killed us!"

"I've got a lot on my mind."

The twins mumbled to themselves. Then they shook their heads and Joff turned to retrieve the document from behind them.

"What's that?" Butler asked, slightly embarrassed.

"We don't know yet," answered Jeff. "From what the captain was saying, it sounded pretty big."

Joff looked back at his brother and Butler. He was as pale as a ghost and his legs were shaking.

"Joff?!" Jeff gasped and ran to catch his brother before he fell. "What's wrong? Did you get hit?"

"How would he have gotten hit? You were the only ones to fire shots up here."

"I don't know, Butler?" Jeff hissed. "Maybe somebody was shooting two guns like a mad man downstairs and a stray bullet—"

"The document," Joff interrupted, shaking the paper in the air. "It's their plan. It's Cassilda."

"What about it?" Butler questioned, furrowing his brow.

"It is a plan to take Grandmin, and it could work. Hell, it sounds like it would work."

The other two stopped speaking. Then Jeff produced a small sphere from his pocket; it looked like a metal eyeball. Jeff pressed a button on the back as a beam of red light scanned the words up and down before stopping with a little ding.

"We need to get back now," Butler said, already trudging down the steps. "We need to warn the others."

"You're right," Jeff replied, helping his brother to his feet. "But I just sent the warning."

Chapter 33

Lunch Hate

Bishop clicked his metal fingers against the hard wooden table. He didn't legitimately hate many people. Sure, there was Yelo, but they were a group, not a single person. Winal, however, was somebody that Bishop absolutely hated with every fiber of his being. Arms dealers in general were a hard-to-handle bunch, but most of them at the very least could put their Zel where their mouth was. Winal, though—he was just a loud-mouthed coward. He had met him only once before. Bishop had made it a point since then to never work with Winal again, if at all possible.

The restaurant, for what it was worth, had been very accommodating to them. They'd refilled Bishop's water several times and offered Patho a list of different options every time he turned down a drink. That was the one silver lining to the situation—the face of the waitstaff at any given restaurant reacting to Patho's lack of hunger, and the half-hearted excuses he'd given to get them to leave, had always been fun to watch. That day, he had told them that he couldn't eat or drink on certain days of the week as part of a new diet. After that, they sadly left him alone.

The other diners would give them nervous looks every once in awhile, always afraid that something bombastic might occur and put some actual life into their dry, upper crust lifestyles. He knew it made them uncomfortable that he wasn't trying to rub elbows with them like some of the other gang bosses had done in the past, but he didn't need to put on an act to keep them cozy and their Zel with the Marauders. No, as awful a way to keep power as it was, he could see and smell, that just by looking at them, and the sickly, sweet-smelling, dry brown smudges around their eyes that many of them had badly tried to hide, that a lot of them were already trapped in Patho's narcotic web. And nobody in the city could hold up to what Patho brewed up.

Bishop leaned over to Patho. "It looks to me like your work is quite popular around here."

"It would seem so."

"It's a shame isn't it?" Bishop asked, kicking his feet onto the table and reclining in his chair, earning himself even more looks in the process, "that the best way to keep control over our territory outside of brute force is to give everybody enough happy poison to shut them up."

"The degradation does result in a waste of resources," Patho mused. "I'm planning to move into all non-addictives in the near future, but that still won't do anything to stop their bodies from falling apart."

Patho's dark lips curled into a smile. "That's what I thought until recently, anyway."

"What do you mean?"

"It's just a theory at the moment, but I think I might have found a formula that can cure addiction altogether, and on top of that, it can spur on a fast recovery to the damaged bodily systems. The only thing is I need a research specimen that is in the middle of a severe withdrawal in order to accurately test my theory. That's a process I attempted to start yesterday, but like most things, it ended in more of a mess than I'd have hoped for. Luckily, I reclaimed my test subject."

Bishop's expression of boredom shifted into a grin. "That would be amazing, Patho," he exclaimed, keeping his voice down. "I literally can't think of a reason someone would buy from anyone else if we took away the consequences."

"I doubt the formula could be replicated by anyone else," Patho continued. "It's going to need things that only Eatherial could ever dream of producing while still using Raiga power, but if this works, it will be like a trident piercing through the veil and allowing us to see new horizons for the first time."

A male Human with pale skin walked up the stairs; he was followed by a large Varse man who was carrying a rapid fire. The Human was wearing a finely tailored dark black suit and a red-and-white trimmed cape around his neck, like that of a king. His hair was a light brown in color, and his eyes were a sickly green. He talked incredibly loudly on his phone with a voice that sounded like glass shattering, and as he walked toward the two Marauders, Bishop's grin faded to a barely hidden frown.

"Yes, I'm here now. Yeah, I know, I'm surprised too, he actually came out of his cave," Winal commented to his caller. "I guess those bombs must have shook more loose than just the rubble."

Winal laughed like a crow at whatever the caller had said to him before saying his goodbyes and hanging up. "Bishop! It's so good to see you! It's been . . . well, it's been at least five years since I was last graced with the presence of the original Marauder himself. I'm honestly surprised to see you. I had heard you'd become a shut-in and never left Monochro anymore."

"You know how fast rumors like that spread."

Winal gave a dreadful laugh. "That I do, but I don't think it was a rumor. Honestly, I don't care about your personal life or your shattered reputation, but I think we can all agree this is a time to celebrate." Winal reached into his jacket and produced a purple-banded cigar. He tried to hand it to Bishop, whose nostrils flared at the scent before he turned away. At that exact moment, Bishop decided he was going to kill him.

Winal pulled his seat out and hopped into it. "Ah, Patho, it is so good to see another Human face around here. I get so many bouts of that type of loneliness that can only be felt when one is away from their own kind for too long. I'm sure you can understand."

"Yes, it can be quite different at times from what I was used to in the past, but I've grown quite fond of Varse culture during my time within it," Patho answered without batting an eye.

"Inner Varcia can be endearing at times, I'll admit, but it out here it's just so blah. It's hard to believe that had the Black Stone Event not happened, then this half of the planet would still be covered in us, and Varse might not have even crawled out of the ground or wherever they were, before half the planet died."

Winal looked up at his still standing guard. "No offense." The guard simply grunted back to him as a response.

Bishop silently unholstered one of his pistols and began to quietly drag its barrel across the bottom of the table. That guard hadn't done anything to him. Sometimes people were in the wrong place at the wrong time, or they were hired by the wrong people at the wrong time. That was life. He'd have to die first, though. Risking that rapid fire going off while he went for Winal wasn't going to happen.

“So,” Bishop started, shoving his irritation to the pit of his stomach. “What did you have in mind for this meeting you arranged with us for today, Winal?”

“Well, I’ve got to correct you there. I didn’t set this meeting up with either of you. I set it up with *Artex*, and to be quite frank, I wish it still was with him. No offense, but if there is one thing that Inner Varcia has mastered completely, it’s the art of the TV drama, and I was hoping to work out a nice little deal between your group and myself while discussing that heart-wrenching season ending to *Vivvedell’s Blossoms* with Artex.”

“Ahhh, I see. Neither me nor Patho are dedicated fans of the show. So—”

“I can tell,” Winal interrupted with a self-righteous scoff. “The two of you don’t look like you’d understand the deep emotional philosophy of the show. It’s nothing to be ashamed of, though, not everyone has the sheer intellect to understand the meaning of its symbolism. Why, in the beach episode alone I could write a whole list of things that almost brought me to tears.”

Bishop slammed his free hand onto the table, causing the silverware to shake, and he forced a smile. “That’s very interesting, Winal, but do you think we could get down to business before we are old, wrinkled, and dead?”

Winal rolled his eyes with a sigh. “That attitude right there is why I would have preferred Artex over the agoraphobe and the scientist. But yes, Bishop, we can get down to business.”

“Great, Winal! I was hoping you’d say that. What do you have for us?”

“As always, I am on the cutting edge of weaponry,” Winal answered with flair and excessive hand motions. “The finest advancements from Inner Varcia brought here to your little backwater city. ‘Use them, abuse them, I don’t care as long as I get my pay’—that’s my motto.”

“Yes, but what do you have?” Bishop said, hoping to stop another monologue before it could start.

“You really don’t have any patience for good branding, do you? Fine, I’ll just tell you since you want to be that way. I’ve come into the possession of a few Raiga shells, a new model of shotgun, a nice little selection of land mines, and thanks to a beautiful new supplier, I'm getting a big influx of high-quality Raiga crystals within the next few months."

"Good to hear," Bishop said, pulling the trigger of his pistol, and sending a Raiga bullet straight through the head of the man with the rapid fire. Winal's guard collapsed into a heap. Bishop stood up, throwing the table to the side. In an instant, he had his metal hand wrapped around Winal's neck and was lifting him up into the air.

Bishop took a moment to look around the diner. The other diners were screaming and some were running out, and the waitstaff was not far behind. They were cowards one and all, but he couldn't blame them for running. This was not their life; they lived sheltered from the true brutality of this city, and from the very thing that made it run. Patho was still sitting in his seat, eyes wide, watching the scene unfold. Bishop could tell from the look on his hologram that he hadn't even thought of the meeting going to anywhere near this level of violence. Good. He loved when he was able to outsmart the Eatherial genius. Although, to be fair, he hadn't seen it coming either, but then Winal had made the move that changed everything.

"That cigar," Bishop growled into the face of his terrified, struggling captive. "Did you really think that I wouldn't be able to smell the poison laced in that cigar?"

Winal squeaked. "I'm sorry. I'm sorry, you can't blame a guy for trying though, right? Yelo posted a big bounty for your head—I just wanted the money, man, it wasn't anything personal. I just wanted the money, please let me go! You know how cutthroat this place is. Please!"

"I understand. Money is quite alluring for spineless creatures like you, but you won't have to worry about money anymore. Since you're gonna die here."

Winal croaked something that sounded like a laugh. "If you kill me, you won't get any of my stock, and your reputation among my ilk will plummet. Will you really take that risk, losing every dealer you have? They will swarm to Yelo and leave you helpless with outdated weapons."

"Oh, but Winal, the thing is I don't care about what the other dealers think of me. They will still line up for business just like always when I tell everyone that you tried to kill me. It makes this whole thing justified, you see."

"The stock! You still won't get the stock!" Winal hissed, trying to pry himself from Bishop's grip. "Especially the Raiga! I don't even have that in yet! Imagine what you could do with it—the number of bullets you could fire before swapping crystals!"

"Patho," Bishop ordered. "Break the window." Patho put his hand on the glass; his holographic face had returned to its usual placid expression, and a red pulse shattered the window. The air was immediately filled with the smell of Lentald, but Bishop was able to stifle the tears in his eyes as he reached for Winal's pocket.

"You know, Patho, I've been thinking about what you said to me a bit ago."

"And what's that?"

Bishop took Winal's phone from out of his pocket. "These things are a bit of a security risk."

Winal's eyes widened into sickly green saucers. "No," he whimpered. "That's not fair. You can't just take that! It's not fair!"

"Oh, shut up!" Bishop responded with a roll of his eyes. He threw Winal with all the force he could muster into the pavement below, and he shrieked before his head burst like a balloon. Red blood covered the pavement outside.

Bishop turned to Patho and asked, "So, did I meet your expectations?"

***

Patho's car drove through the central street of Monochro. Life had resumed in the area as normal despite the piles of rubble surrounded by crews of Varse working to pick it all up, and a few more blood stains that were not present a few days ago. Of course, this meant more traffic.

The trip back wasn't eventful in the slightest. The same old sights over and over again made up another reason that Patho disliked driving. It was so boring. Bishop had proved himself to be serious about the change, though. That was good. He had even called Vara about clearing out Winal's warehouse. The address, to nobody's surprise, was located right in his phone's tracking map. Despite his dangerous job and the value of what he sold, Winal didn't even have a lock on his phone, much less any serious security.

Patho pulled into the rows of secured garages that sat near the tower. He made sure that they were all as secure as possible with defense systems and alarms of his own design. This was especially true of his other garage, which was in the same complex, but contained a few pet projects that he had been working on in his free time. They werew nothing he wanted anyone to see yet, much less steal.

"Now," Bishop said, stretching as he got out of the car. "I'd say that the whole trip went a lot better than I thought it would when you told me that I was meeting Winal. I just can't seem to think of how that could have gone any better than it did, actually."

Bishop kneeled down and smiled at Patho, who was still seated in the red car. "Now all we gotta do is figure out how to deal with Yelo."

A beeping sound came from Patho's pocket. He reached in and pulled out a metal sphere that looked like an eye. A red light was blinking in its pupil.

Chapter 34

Due for a Wake Up Call

Claw walked down the hallway with an almighty smirk on her face. She was dressed in her usual get-up and was counting her blessings that her night of sudden responsibility had finally come to an end. If there was one thing in the entire world that Claw hated more than anything else, it was being responsible for anyone other than herself. Everyone else was just too damn fragile for her liking, and the only reason she was even in this gang was because all of the mercenary work dried up when they started to take over.

The bottom layers of Monochro Tower were bustling with activity. Everyone wanted blood for what happened the day before. Claw, of course, didn't care all that much, but more jobs were always good for starving off the ever-creeping sense of boredom that plagued her most days. However, getting work was not why she was down here today. No, today she actually had something to look forward to. You see, if Claw had one weakness, one personal flaw she couldn't expunge, it was a love of romance—not in her own life of course, attachments like that we're unhealthy in this line of work. Just look at Butler. But in the lives of *others,* it was fair game.

Claw had gotten quite good over the years at predicting romances before they even happened. She could tell that Bishop and Vara were an item before she had even seen them together. She knew Lode and Butler wouldn't last in the long run. Granted, Lode dying in a bombing wasn't what she saw coming, but it still counted as an end in her book. And even though it was just a TV show, she knew that Vivvedell would end up with Garn. That last one was why she was here today: to rub her victory in the face of the romantically challenged.

A press of a red button was all it took for the door to open. The room was metallic and uninviting, perfect for a war room. A large table sat in the middle of the room with some chairs around it and a map of the city draped over it, and a single occupant, Artex, who paced back and forth from one wall to another mumbling to himself about something she was sure she wouldn't care about. He looked up at her after a few minutes of pacing, and her smirk widened.

"What is wrong with your face?!" he gasped.

"What?"

"It's all contorted and looks like it's about to fall off," he answered in a tone brimming with snark. "Oh, wait. Are you smiling? I don't think I've ever seen you do that before."

"Can't a girl just be happy?"

"I've known you for four years, and I've never seen you happy."

"Fair point, but today is a special day. How could I not be happy?"

"Why, what's today?" Artex asked, puzzled. "The day after we didn't explode?"

Claw's smirk grew into a grin of sharp Varse teeth. He didn't know. This was going to be better than she'd imagined "Why, Artex?" she maliciously cooed. "You're not telling me that you don't know, are you?"

"Don't know what?"

Claw tried her absolute hardest to stop herself from laughing at his growing frustration, but she knew that if she just kept it up a bit longer the payoff would be worth it.

"The thing," she replied, before biting her inner cheek as hard as she could to contain herself. She could feel her coppery blood beginning to pool in her mouth and flow down her throat. she was at her limit.

Artex leaned over the table, spreading his arms wide before addressing her. "Claw, I have no idea what you're trying to accomplish by acting as vague as Priests of the Provider do when asked if they know when he is going to return, but fine, I'll bite. What is this *grand* thing that I should know and that has you, the epitome of the word stone-faced, so happy?"

A flood of immense satisfaction flooded over her as the words left her mouth. "Just how the Vivvedell season finale ended."

Artex froze where he was standing; he looked like he was about to be sick and she could see the beads of sweat already forming on his face. Artex had the same awful weakness she did, but he held none of the talent when it came to love predictions. She could tell that he already knew what she was going to say, but he was hoping beyond hope that he was wrong.

"You didn't see it, did you?"

"No," he wheezed.

"She chose Garn."

Artex didn't respond immediately. "Claw," he whispered, his tattoo glowing bright red.

"Yes?" She replied, the wave of satisfaction already beginning to crest over her head.

"You'd better move to your left."

She did as he said, sliding a few steps to her left. Artex screamed and flipped the table. The map flew off and floated to the ground, some of the chairs screeched across the floor when they were hit, and the table itself smacked into the wall before bouncing back to something resembling its original position.

"You know?" he started, "this is just typical. I get trapped in my own home with no way of watching my favorite show, so that I could at least be there when Vivvedell ruins her life, and of all the people on this husk of a continent . . . no, this whole damned planet, you are the one who delivers the news to me. That's exactly what I need after the worst day in the history of our gang, to be told more bad news by the enemy of love itself. I hope you're happy, because this is by far the lowest point in the series. It was the last good thing to come out of Inner, and now it's gone. Now all that's there is pompous idiots who can't even write good television while they get fat on exploitation, and while the Church of Conort keeps their little bubble of paradise safe from us mongrels outside. I hope you realize that we've just witnessed the death of an entire culture. The only thing that justified the existence of Inner Varcia has literally evaporated into nothing. And if you are wondering about your money, you'll get it when you get it.

"Poor Vivvedell, she doesn't even know the full extent of Garn's past as a Courier in Travat City. How can you expect her to stay with him if she doesn't know about the experiences that shaped him? Stelvo has been her friend since childhood! They were perfect for each other and held a special bond like no other, but that selfish bitch goes for the bad boy, and now what is Stelvo gonna do? He already left Alrla to be with Vivvedell! Alrla will never take him back, and she already skipped town!"

He just kept going and going. It was amazing how much he could talk before stopping for breath. Needless to say, this was better than what she was expecting. Romance might be her first love, but ruining people's days had to be a close second. It was a feeling like no other to watch someone crumble into a heap of screaming madness.

She'd seen him like this more than a few times, and it never wasn't hilarious. The best part of it all was the epithet he accidentally developed. As one of the leaders of the gang, he had to stand next to the likes of "Twin Razor Vara," "Red Demon Patho," and "Blue0Eyed Bishop," but Artex was just "Artex the Angry," a fact she loved and he hated.

The tantrum was stopped by the sound of Bishop fixing the table. He moved frantically and his eyes were wide with panic. Claw never had much of an opinion about Bishop, he was always just kind of there. Even before she heard people talk about him becoming lazy and repetitive, she never really cared about his existence. Vara, too, was somebody that Claw just couldn't get herself to care about, aside from proving herself right when she found out they were together.

Bishop began to move the chairs back into place as he talked to his friend. "Artex, I heard you yelling from outside. I'm sure you have a good reason to be waking up everyone in the infirmary below us, but I'm afraid it's going to have to wait. We have big bad news."

Patho strutted into the room, and he moved as if he were just slightly perturbed by something. Claw had never seen him not calm. It was very unnerving—almost scary.

"Yelo has a plan to take Grandmin," Bishop said. He placed the map back on the table, and he gestured to Yellow Light. "They are starting from here, and from what I've seen it looks like it will work."

Artex stopped rambling. "What are we going to do?!" he asked, his voice still a yell.

"I don't know, Artex, that's kind of why I'm in the freaking war room right now."

"Where's Vara?"

"Currently killing a warehouse full of second-rate thugs," Patho chimed in, his voice uncharacteristically raised. "It's not like she would be much of a help drawing up a game plan."

Bishop slammed his hands down on the map, his eyes drifting toward the compound on its edge. "Gotta agree with that. Love her to death, but she ain't the planning type. Now, executing plans—that she can do in spades."

Reading romance might be her specialty, but reading rooms wasn't that hard either. Claw, knew it was time to leave. She made for the door but was blocked by Patho.

"Claw?" he asked.

"Yes?" she responded.

"Where ya going?"

"Out of here."

Patho smiled that sinister smile she'd known him for. "Now, why would somebody with your years of urban warfare and combat expertise want to leave the war room in the middle of something like this? Why, I'd have thought you'd be overjoyed to help plan an assault you'll undoubtedly take part in?"

Her face was its normal expressionless frown, but inside she was screaming with rage. All Claw wanted to do in her life was get through it, not sit around a table and come up with battle plans. But with three out of her four bosses in here and the most intimidating of them directly asking her, she didn't see herself returning home anytime soon.

"Fine," was all she said before turning toward the map and taking a seat.

CHAPTER 35

WORKOUT

Vara stood atop the stoney gray building and looked down eagerly at the warehouse below her. She gave a quick lick to the dark green nutriorb that she had impaled on a toothpick. It was high in protein like all her snacks, and the taste reminded her of her Wasting. Bruteil was a brutal art, and the cost on its user's body is incredibly steep.

To Vara, the Wasting had seemed like one long continuous moment, but from what the monks had told her, she'd been strapped to that bed for several weeks before her muscles reconstructed themselves into a more fitting form for the martial art. The monks would dump buckets of a high protein pink sludge into her throat, and the throats of the other initiates that made it that far. She was the only one that survived the process that time. It was a defining experience, to say the least.

When she had left the infirmary with her new smile, she also took the chance to change into something other than the dress that she had been wearing for two days. Vara was now wearing a fashionable black vest with some type of fur sewn into the edges. She didn't know what it was from, but it was gray. She also wore baggy black pants, combat boots, and her silver hilts were hanging off of a silver belt with an "M" in the middle.

She could feel her heart pumping already. From what she was told, there were only eight guards in the building, and she'd already seen two of them walk in and out during their rounds. Winal was probably trying to keep a low profile, which was always a good idea for somebody in his trade. But she didn't really think that mattered for him anymore. Eight would be enough for this to count as a decent workout, though it would undoubtedly be more fun with actual combatants instead of the pieces of metal that flew at her in her gym.

The rusted doors to the warehouse opened up and two men in dirty green jumpers walked out. One was holding a rapid fire, but the other was undoubtedly armed with something. Good.

Vara threw the nutriorb into her mouth and spit out the stick before swallowing. This was where the fun began. She smiled a gilded smile as she let herself fall from the building.

This was always a fun way to make an entrance. It was fun because she'd die if she messed up, and if she succeeded, she'd be able to launch herself like a rocket. It would feel like flying. The wind whipped her face and across her hairless head as she judged exactly when she should kick off. Life, she had learned growing up, was not about surviving. No, life was about proving you were alive, and there were only two ways to really do that. The first was to push your body to its limits and feel it scream, and the second was to use the strength gained from the first to prove yourself in combat over other living things. Only then could you be considered truly alive.

That's why Vara only respected those with strength, and the exact reason why she only listened to what Bishop had to say after he managed to break her arm in a bar fight. He wasn't stronger than her, of course, but actually injuring her like that was a signal of him being a quality person. She never expected to fall in love with him a few months after they met, but hey, that's how life worked.

The guards still hadn't noticed her yet, or if they did, they probably just thought she was just another gambler who had lost it all. Vara figured she'd gathered enough momentum, and now it was time to see if she screwed up and if she would die. Again, always fun.

Vara maneuvered her feet to the wall and kicked; she left a small crater as she flew through the sky like a rocket. She ignited her hilts, and the daggers left a trail of blue light behind her. When the guard with the rapid fire saw her, he sent a hail of bullets in her direction while his friend reached for a pistol that Vara could now see holstered at his side. She moved in midair, avoiding the spray while she prepared herself for the landing. The guard was just beginning to adjust his aim when she hit the ground in front of him in a crouched position; she buried her dagger in his head.

The man went limp just as his friend pulled this pistol out and fired. Vara shielded herself with the body of the guard, and the bullet sent a spray of gore and blue blood into the air. That was something Vara wished her blades would do, but that was the tradeoff for having three-sixty degree cutting.

She threw the corpse aside and moved for the pistol-holder. She moved with force and speed as she removed the arm that was holding the gun in one stroke, and his head with another. After that, she sprung into the building. Every once in awhile, she'd hit the ground again to keep her speed up. The world moved slower for her when she was like this, and she felt truly alive.

The inside of the warehouse was old and decrepit. Boxes were stacked everywhere and each one seemed to vary heavily in condition. There were raised pathways made out of chain-link, and a few staircases that looked to be made of the same.

It wasn't long before she saw a woman on one of the stairways. She was clutching a shotgun and looking out the window, trying to see what all the commotion outside was about. By the time she saw Vara, it was too late. In one slash, Vara had liberated the top half of her skull from the rest of her. Again she lamented the cauterizing nature of her daggers—this would have been really messy.

Now there were only five guards left, and she hoped they would put up more of a fight. She knew they wouldn't, though. A flash of blue lit up her vision. She dodged the blast of Raiga, which easily ripped through the metal wall of the warehouse and flew a bit outside before dispersing. Without a doubt, that was from an energy rifle. Vara had a love-hate relationship with energy rifles; she *loved* seeing what they could do, but she'd *hate* to be hit by one. She steadied herself and found the gunman.

He was a floor above, holding his rifle toward her. He had a cigarette hanging in his mouth and large streaks of brown leaking from the sides of his eyes. He fired another shot at her when she jumped to the platform in between them. Again, she avoided it, and yet again it blasted through the wall. Despite his condition, Vara could see that this guy had good reflexes, or perhaps it was because of it.

She dodged another slug as she ran toward him on the platform. Then she felt the platform shift. He had hit one of the chains holding it up. The rifleman took note of her moment of weakness and fired again, his eyes worn and tired. She shot him a golden smile as she dropped to all fours and blasted herself into the air. The Raiga shot ripped through the chain-link of the platform.

Vara twisted in the air so that her feet hit the ceiling, and then she launched. The old man didn't get another chance to fire before she plunged the knives into his chest. His mouth gaped open as he gasped for air before dying. That one was more trouble than she had anticipated, solidifying this as a good day.

Only four remained, and she was excited to see who would find who first. She began to hop-run again, blitzing through the building and searching for her next victim. Then she found one. He was a heavier man with an uncertain look in his black eyes. She could see his white pupils whipping around. He was trying to figure out where the assailant was so that he could throw the grenade he cradled like a baby in his hands. Holy shit! It was the guy from Pawna's floor. She made quick work of him anyway. Some people were just hired for anything nowadays, she guessed.

The next one managed to fire her pistol at Vara. Too bad for her, though, that she turned out to be bad with moving targets, like her head and arms would be considered as they fell to the ground.

The old man was definitely the best guard here, from what she could tell. Everyone else was just okay or disappointing. Her rematch with Patho had been fun, but she knew they could never have a good old fight to the death, despite how much fun it would be. She often thought that the others would see it as one-sided, with Patho being able to regenerate and all, but she had actually figured out how to kill him a while ago. Well, at least, she thought she knew one way.

Vara ran toward an open door that she had noticed on the upper levels, easily predicting the spray of Raiga that would burst forth from it. A man with a rapid fire was standing guard over the foreman's office. It was a great strategy, she had to admit. A rapid fire in a straight, confined area was hard to get around, but unfortunately for him, it was also a very common strategy .

She jumped into the air and whipped a dagger into his head before he could react. He slumped against the door behind him. Vara retrieved her dagger before taking a good long look at the door. If she had been in that office, and if she used firearms, she knew that she'd be waiting to fire off something nasty as soon as that door opened. So she left, and she took the grenade that the guy from Pawna's place had been holding, with her.

Mart had been waiting for Windel to return for a few hours now. He knew that traffic in this wreck of a city could be bad, but this wait was ridiculous. He didn't mind being here that much at first, and then somebody got into the building and began killing the rest of his squad. Now he was waiting here, rifle pointed at the door, so that he could put an end to whoever the hell had been doing this.

There was a shattering sound from behind Mart. He turned around to see a clear plastic, oval-shaped object that was filled with a bubbling and hissing blue liquid. He recognized it immediately. It was a grenade, it went off, and then Mart was dead.

***

Vara watched the blue explosion rip through the windows of the room, leaving a massive scorch mark in its wake. Explosives weren't as satisfying as the personal approach she liked taking, but they were fun.

"Done and done," she said, whistling to herself and dusting off her hands. The emptying of the warehouse would be somebody else's job. It had been a great day so far, and she couldn't help but wonder what was happening in Monochro.

CHAPTER 36

THE BEST DEFENSE

The air in the room was rife with frustration. Ideas were being thrown into the ring and thrown out just as fast. Things like these didn't go smoothly under the best conditions, much less ones like these. Bishop had come up with his own plan back when he first fully processed what he had read on the eyeball thing. He still wasn't sure what it exactly was. The idea was not one that would be widely considered "wise." In fact, it was downright stupid, in his own opinion. Still, it was the only one that ended with an actual victory for the Marauders instead of just another day to fight on. But holy nonexistent Provider, he did not want to take the flack for suggesting it.

"The best option," Patho announced, peeling his eyes away from the map, "is to move everyone we can spare to Grandmin, reinforcing it. This will weaken the other districts temporarily, but Grandmin is by far the most important single district in terms of pure strategic value. The others will have to make do."

"You obviously spend too much time in your lab," Claw grumbled, her tattoo glowing as red as real flames since she had sat down. "Nobody in their right mind would waste a force of that size once they had it put together. As soon as they realize Grandmin is going to be harder than they bargained for, they will switch targets and head straight here to get the morale boost of taking Monochro."

"Better here than Grandmin."

Claw slammed her good hand onto the table. "Tell that to everyone yesterday!" she yelled. "I'd rather be shot than go through that again, and I know what it feels like to be shot!"

Bishop looked over to her, trying to work up the courage to throw his idea in the ring. "I didn't expect you to have such a visceral reaction to the attacks. Did you lose anyone close?"

Everybody looked at Claw and saw her freeze. He could swear he saw the gears turning underneath her chains.

Claw opened her mouth and no words came out. "No," she finally managed to say before the silence returned.

"That aside," Patho yelled, trying to put things back on track. "Does anybody else have a better idea?"

"I think that if we move some heavy firepower to Grandmin, and reinforce all the districts equally, we will have the best chance of coming out of this thing in one piece," Artex added in.

"The heavy fire is a good idea, Artex, but not every district is of equal value to Grandmin. Even most of our clothes are made there, and that's not mentioning the crystal supply."

If Yelo was really amassing a force capable of retaking a whole district all at once, then their home base would be the least guarded it had ever been by necessity. It would be the perfect time to invade. The only problem with that was that the cannons of Sinustus could blast any force they sent there into oblivion. When the tide first turned against Yelo, they tried to raid Sinusitis, and the casualties from the turrets alone became too high to even consider it again. Bishop could still remember the way his heart palpated every time he saw and heard the shells explode. Until now, the best course of action seemed to be to starve them out.

Bishop stood up from his seat. He couldn't wait any longer. He said to himself that he would not be a coward anymore, and that meant suggesting this plan even if everybody hated it. It needed to be said, even if only for the sake of his own sanity.

Bishop clasped his hand together and prepared to use his leadership voice. "Lady and gentlemen," he began. "I think you are missing the big picture, here. Getting this information on their Cassilda plan is not something to be looked at as a warning. No, this is nothing more than an opportunity.

"They are planning to attack us in three days—two and a half, if you wanna get technical. They also don't know that we know about what they are planning. So I have two propositions for you. One is that we attack them with a force of our own while they have their pants down. I highly doubt Yelo is actually ready to actually defend Yellow Light right now because they are planning to use it as a jumping off point. So it's the perfect time for us to not only take it, but to also inflict devastating casualties onto Yelo. My second proposition is that we finish this all at once. In my speech last night, I had promised that we would finish Yelo once and for all. This is our chance to do just that. Sinustus is weakened, and if I'm not correct, please do correct me, but don't we have a recent defect within our ranks? You know, somebody that might *know* what to do about the massive cannon problem?"

Patho snapped his fingers. "Yes," he gasped, his ruby eyes wide. "I haven't thought about it like that. This is a great opportunity to finish them, and I have already obtained key information about those cannons from that defect."

"You mean the girl who kidnapped Rook, right?" Claw interjected. "I honestly thought she'd have been killed anyway after her little stunt yesterday. I guess it's a good thing that I settled the crowd down."

"Yes, it is," Patho responded. "It's a great thing because I know the make and model of those cannons now; I have always had my suspicions, but now I have no doubt."

"So, what does that mean?" Artex asked.

"It means that they are Varcian Three Hundred and Sixty Degree Raiga Shell Defense Cannons, probably mark two or three. I knew the shell part, obviously, but the circular movement is what I'm really excited about."

"Why?"

"Because technology like that needs to run off of a core mainframe if it is going to function at all, and if we upload a virus onto that mainframe, then we can have them turn around and fire right into the compound. I can probably make the virus rather quickly, although it will have to be manually uploaded for this to work. This was meant to be a long-term plan, after all, but I guess it's now or never."

"No, it's not," Claw spat with a confused look on her face. "Patho, we don't know how to get past the cannons, much less inside of Sinusitis."

Patho opened his false mouth but did not speak. Bishop felt the hopeful tone that had slowly been growing in the room die with those words. At least, it was looking like the Yellow Light plan would be a go, but sadly, Yelo itself would have to wait a bit longer.

"Patho?" Artex asked, scratching his head. "Did you ask her if there was a way into Sinustus besides the main gate?"

Patho's eyes narrowed. Bishop could see the unmistakable look of embarrassment on the false face of the Eatherial.

"No . . . no, I did not."

"Well then!" Bishop piped in. "Can somebody find her and do that, please?"

The sun was shining beautifully upon the outdoor Monochro cafe where Queenie was sitting. She was wearing a white sundress, something she had never worn before and was quite happy to be wearing, and the vest was resting on the table. Queenie had a new bandage on her hand, and she held a glass cup filled with a green caffeinated tea in her hands. It tasted okay, but it wasn't really her cup of tea. No pun intended.

The cafe had been Silt's idea. He said that if he had to watch her until told otherwise, then he was going to at least try to make it fun for the two of them, instead of demeaning. Silt, Queenie had found out, was a very interesting individual to talk to. His life story sounded like a movie. The man had slews of romances that ended in tragedy, and his family had been reduced to his two grandchildren and himself. He had been an assassin for over fifty years, and according to himself, was only a little bit rusty since mostly retiring. He reminded her a lot of her own grandfather—if he had a lot more blood on his hands and didn't die in an accidental car bombing.

"Oh, yes," he laughed. "In a place like this you'd never guess what this city was really like. At least, if you don't look behind you at the rubble and blood stains from yesterday. That would really ruin the illusion this cafe provides."

"You know," Queenie replied. "I really wish I was born in Inner Varcia. Even if I was dirt poor there too, I bet my family would still be alive."

"I'm sure everybody in this city has thought the same thing once or twice," he replied somberly, but with a hint of grim cheer, nonetheless. "You know what always annoyed me? Nobody ever talks about Mid Varcia. It's always Outer or Inner. I've been to Mid Varcia and it's still much better than here, at least in terms of gang violence. Where it's much worse, though, is with the Conortionists."

Queenie blinked at him, confused. "The what?" she asked.

"Conortionists," he continued. "It's some strange religion that, according to the rumors I've heard, basically runs Inner Varcia behind the Monarch's back. They also go on 'conversion' runs into Mid Varcia. Which, I must tell you, are not a very nice event, especially if they are rejected. The size of the gangs in Outer Varcia actually scare them off. One reason to be happy to live here, I suppose."

"Did you see any when you were there?"

"Only a few missionaries; none of the soldiers, thankfully."

Queenie barely knew of the world outside Board City. The years in Yelo did not help with that. From what she did know, most of the other large cities were just like this one. The gangs had different names, obviously, though all still shared the same goal of dominance. She would love to see it all one day—the world, that is, not the other Husk Cities. Sadly, it was looking like this chapter of her life belonged to the Marauders . . . at least for the time being.

A beep came from Silt's pocket, and his face turned blank as soon as he heard it. He pulled out something that looked like an eye. He pressed the pupil and a note of red light projected out. She watched his eyes move as he read it. They moved disturbingly fast, and then he put it away.

"Queenie," he started, his voice eerily tranquil. "Please finish your tea. Your presence is requested in Monochro Towers."

Nervously, she finished the drink. Silt threw down a few pieces of Zel on the table and helped her up. She followed him toward the looming shape in the distance that was Monochro Tower. She began debating in her mind how far she would get if she ran. She had herself partially convinced that this was going to be some kind of torture interrogation, but if she ran, Silt might just kill her.

The door to the war room opened and Queenie stepped in, holding the chained vest around her right arm. She saw the chain-haired woman's eyes widen before she looked at Patho, who put his finger over his mouth and winked at her. This was off to a good start. Silt was waiting outside for her.

Going solely on appearances, the only normal-looking person in this room besides herself would be Artex, who actually looked pretty good in that shade of blue. She would say that Patho looked normal for a Human, but she knew that was not really what he looked like. Again, she did not want to know. She tried to smile at the chain-haired woman, but she was only given a glare back as a response.

"Queenie," Bishop yelled, slamming his hands down authoritatively on the left.

"I—it's fine," she answered.

"We need to know if you remember there being another way into Sinustus—aside from the main entrance, of course."

Queenie wracked her brain before answering. "I, uh, I think there was a pipe near the back that was used to drain the sewage. Why?"

She saw Bishop swear under his breath when she said the word "sewage." He looked at her again before answering her question. She hadn't gotten a good look at his arm before, but now that she saw it up close, she could tell that information she had been given about him was wrong. It was definitely not a standard prosthetic.

"Why do you think?" he chuckled before continuing. "Another question for you. Have you ever seen a room with a big computer in it while you were there?"

"I mostly worked in the greenhouse, but I think I mopped outside of something close to what you're describing once."

Bishop smiled at her, and then he looked at the others. "Here's the plans, ladies and gents. We have two groups. One will consist of the vast majority of the gang, which will be led by Artex." The chain-haired woman breathed an audible sigh of relief at this. "And they will be going to Yellow Light. The second group will be smaller, more elite, and they will handle the killing of the Yelo leadership and the destruction of Sinustus. That group I want to work on a bit more, but myself, Patho, Vara, and Queenie will be in it definitely."

"Me?!" Queenie yelped. "Why would I be in that group? There's nothing elite about me."

"I'll take that into consideration, don't you worry. But you, my dear 'Yelo defector,' are the only one who knows where we're going."

"I barely know!"

"Hey, barely is more than nothing, and that's how much we know. Meeting adjourned."

She wanted to say something back, to do anything she could to avoid going back—to make sure that all the crap she went through the past day and a half didn't amount to nothing—but the room was already emptying out.

She felt somebody place a hand on her shoulder. She turned, expecting Silt, but hoping for Artex. Instead, it was Patho, his red eye piercing into her.

"Hang onto that," he said, nodding to the vest. "It could save your life one day." Then he walked off.

Chapter 37

Thirty-Two

Overseer Thirty-Two pressed her hand against the massive glass window of her office. Yellow Light, formerly Red Light, shined with well . . . yellow light. After they took over, she personally saw that each of the lights were changed to a more appropriate color, as per Hastul's orders. Machines sprayed mist into the air, and light-casting machines played an endless stream of adverts for the clubs and brothels that littered the district. A large chandelier-like building hung in the center of everything, held in place by powerful and thick wires, and right outside of her window was the beautiful sight of Bans running around frantically while their superiors hollered orders at them. The invasion would be soon, and she would do everything in her power to make sure it was a success. Even if it killed her.

Thirty-Two had grown up in this district. She was one of the many poor souls who had to work in the brothels just to barely scrape by. She remembered every bit of the abuse like it happened only yesterday. Her sister died doing that work, and that's when Thirty-Two decided to escape. When she left, she had known nothing else but Red Light, and the constant fear of a pimp's wrath. Yelo promised a life free of worry in exchange for simple labor. Joining was not a hard decision for her to make, considering the alternative. She got more than she could have ever dreamed of bargaining for.

She was fed and given a place to live just like any other Ban would have gotten, but the loss of her previous identity wasn't a loss for her. It was a massive boon. In Yelo, she could act as if her former life didn't exist, and could let her worries dissolve into the placid lake of sameness that was being a Ban. Day after day, the reality that she had actually escaped her past life dawned on her more and more, until eventually that realization became a flame of ambition. She could succeed here; she could do what nobody would have ever thought possible of her. So she did.

Climbing the ranks wasn't too hard. All you had to do was know your place underneath Hastul, respect those above you, and work hard enough to distinguish yourself from the others. She became somebody that could be relied on, and now she was the one that they relied on to run the same district that was her living hell growing up.

Now all those pimps feared her—all but her old one, though. He was very much dead at this point and well beyond the capability to feel fear. Back when this place was Red Light, people would say that the flow of warm bodies and alcohol never stopped, but Yellow Light did. It stopped three times, in fact. The first time she did it because she could, and she wanted to watch them all squirm. Second time was when one of the brothel owners disobeyed her, and the third was right now. The district had come to complete halt as Cassilda prepared to launch.

Cassilda was a beautiful name for a beautiful plan. It was a plan as beautiful as the woman it was named after, as beautiful as her sister. Even when the plan was being drawn up, the use of Yellow Light was always a certainty. So, as its overseer, Thirty-Two was given a seat at the planning table. She knew that it was only a formality and all the actual planning would be done without her, but she was given the honor of putting in a suggestion for the operation's name. Hastul happened to love it, and the rest was history.

She liked to think of it as her sister's revenge, as if her spirit rose from the pits of this den of sin and led the charge to Grandmin—as if her sister was here with her and benefiting from the same system that she did.

Overseer Thirty-Two stepped back from the window and wrapped her arms around herself. She began to dance wildly around the room as she hugged herself, almost tripping over her desk. It was going to be so satisfying to retake Grandmin. The Marauders were a threat to the success she built, to the life she ripped from the gutter, and for that, they had to die. *All* of them had to die. Nobody would be allowed to threaten her anymore. Now she was the one that did all the threatening.

She stopped her mad dance and readjusted her cloth mask, making sure the goggles were aligned correctly with her eyes. She blinked a few times then sat at her desk. She had reports that needed to be read, and others that needed to be sent out. Thirty-Two was a very busy woman. She'd have time to celebrate later.

CHAPTER 38

READYING AND LAUNCHING

The night was cold, and the day and half before it had come and gone like sand running through fingers. The preparations had been made and the troops deployed. Queenie stood with those few as one of the "elite" who were meant to take down Sinustus. The entire group consisted of her, Bishop, her old roommate from the infirmary who she now knew was Vara, Patho, the giant lovesick man with two rapid fires, Butler, and her chaperone: the deadly assassin, Silt. Everyone was waiting patiently outside of the garages.

All but Butler and Patho were wearing a special type of body armor that Patho had made. It consisted of a skintight black suit with flexible hexagonal plates concentrated around the torso. Patho was wearing the fiendish armor from his lab, with his false appearance, suit and all, still worn underneath. Butler was simply too big for the body armor. Queenie herself had a black bag around her waist that held the vest, and Bishop was wearing a very ugly helmet that blended in with his skin. She could faintly see the blue glow from his eyes underneath it.

Bishop walked in front of the group, the strong scent of roses wafting in the air as he passed. "Now," he began. "Everybody is aware of the plan, yes?" They all nodded before he continued on. "Good. Patho, will you please hand out the virus."

Patho handed each of them a silver flash drive with a black necklace cord attached to it. "These will be your prime directive," Bishop continued. "We figured the more we have, the higher the chances of success. *Someone* has to get this into the mainframe. I really don't care who does it as long as that whole damn place goes up in flames. Once it's in, you will have fifteen minutes before the cannons start."

Patho walked over to the garage behind them once he had handed out the last of the flash drives. He entered a code into the keypad and the door began to rise. Three pitch-black motorcycles sat inside of it. The motorcycles were sleek, incredibly sleek, sleeker than anything Queenie had ever seen, and there were no wheels, just large black spheres where they should be.

"I'd like to introduce you all to a pet project of mine. I call them the Dark Horses," he exclaimed with immense pride. "Silent all-terrain vehicles."

"There are only three of them," Butler pointed out. "How are we going to get all six of us there?"

"Simple," Patho answered, a pep in his voice that Queenie hadn't heard before. "Partners."

"They don't have wheels; how are they going to move?" Silt asked.

"Yeah, how do they move?" Vara chimed in, her eyes shimmering like those of a child who just got a new toy.

"Watch and find out," Patho replied, motioning to Butler.

Patho got onto the bike followed by a wary Butler. Seconds later, the Dark Horse lifted a few inches off the ground, kicked up some dust, and then sped off into the streets of Monochro.

Vara let out a rapid slew of excited swears. "Yes! Yes!" She ran up to one and grabbed the handlebars. "Bish, get on now! There is no way in hell we are letting Red beat us there."

"Vara, I think I should drive since your stop is before mine."

Vara's smile weakened before immediately picking up again. "Fine, but I get to drive back, and we are racing them back here. And we are going to win."

"Sounds good to me," he said, returning with a large smile of his own.

The two of them rode after Patho and Butler. Queenie stood there, watching them fly through the streets and dreading going on one of those things herself. Silt floated up to her, already on the Dark Horse.

He gave her a small smile. "Be sure to hold on." He laughed. She returned the smile with an apprehensive one of her own before taking his hand. Then they were off, and she was screaming.

Queenie never felt anything close to the feeling of being on the Dark Horse— it felt like she was flying through the air. Monochro turned into a blur of light around her as she held tightly onto Silt. Before she knew it, her screams turned into laughter. They dodged smoothly out of the way of cars and civilians. They moved past them as nothing but a blur of black. Provider, these things were fast.

It wasn't long before they caught up to the other two Horses. Both Vara and Bishop looked like they were laughing, but Patho and Butler looked as silent as Silt was. They drove all the way through Monochro and turned down a pulmonary street. The three Dark Horses zipped through it smoothly, moving out of the way of every obstacle in their path, until the neon sky of Board City was gone, and the only thing left in front of them was a bridge with flickering street lights that led to a large dark patch with a dim neon sky of its own. The Brooks.

She watched Patho turn and drive down the stairs to the reservoir. Butler's swear was just audible over the wind. Bishop and Silt followed soon after. Going down the stairs felt exactly the same as driving on the road, but with a tiny hint of falling mixed in. Patho turned again, and this time it was from the path next to the water onto the water itself. The Horse sped gracefully over the water, kicking up a spray behind it.

Soon, they were all on the water riding to the other end of the reservoir. The moonless sky was a beautiful void filled with the few stars that shined bright enough to get past the light pollution, and every once in a while, a few drops of water would fly over or onto Queenie's face while she looked up.

Then the water was replaced with sand. She shielded her eyes and noticed that Silt had put on the pair of goggles. Lucky him.

A black blotch began to appear on the horizon. The closer that they got to it, the more detail appeared on the blob. Blinking lights outlined the shape of massive cannons, and a slightly illuminated massive stone wall that otherwise looked like a wave of shadows, and a large gate in the front appeared. Rising out of the middle of the shape was the top of Hastul's abode, the largest building in the compound.

Sinustus loomed on the horizon, but Queenie oddly didn't feel afraid. To her, it felt like all those years spent there just blended together into one agonizingly long day, but the past few days—despite all the chaotic nonsense that filled them—were some of most memorable out of her entire life. Looking in that restaurant window restored her sense of self, and it sent her on a circular journey back here. The only difference was that this time when she got back she wouldn't run back to the greenhouse with arms full of gardening supplies, but instead she would be part of the group that was going to destroy it all.

She'd never had any friends in Yelo; unnecessary communication was frowned upon, But she still felt a bit bad for the other people in there who were just like her. It wasn't about them now, it was about her. She needed to make sure that she walked out of this so that she could keep enjoying her life, as weird as it may be.

They drove past the dark walls, and she saw some Bans patrolling on top. Not one had an idea about the silent riders below them. Bishop slowed down his Horse and pulled something that looked like a crossbow out of his coat. He fired a metal spike out of it and into the wall, and then he dropped the crossbow into the desert sands. Vara stood up on the bike and leapt for the rod, causing the bike to temporarily unsteady. She jumped onto the spike. Then she leapt up the wall. There was a quick flash of blue before the pieces of the Bans fell down the wall. Bishop steadied and sped up again.

The group rode around to the back of Sinustus, where the sewer waited. The Dark Horses came to a graceful stop, and the riders dismounted. Surprisingly, it was only a slightly disorienting experience. In front of them was a circle-shaped hole with yards of dark grimy sand around it. Luckily, it was just big enough for Butler to fit in if he really tried. It smelled awful.

Bishop walked up behind her, and again she smelled roses. "You sure this will get us in?" he asked quietly.

"Yes," she replied.

"Guards?"

"Not usually."

"Good." He motioned the rest of the group over to him. "Here's the planL Silt and Butler will protect Queenie as she leads them to the place where she remembers that the mainframe is stored. Patho and I will be gunning for Hastul. If we are going to take Yelo out, then we have to make sure the leadership is absolutely dead."

"What was all that with Vara?" Butler asked.

"We have good reason to believe that there is at least one Bruteil user in Yelo. If they are anything like Vara, they will seek her out first.

We don't want to have to deal with them while we search. She is the bait and a trap at the same time."

"Okay then, but what if we get the cannons going before you guys kill Hastul?"

"Don't worry about us. Just worry about getting your part done; everything else is just an afterthought until that job is complete. Do you understand?"

Butler nodded. "Yeah. I just want you to know that I'm setting those things off as soon as I get the chance., Lode needs to be properly avenged."

"I understand, Butler. Make sure that he is."

"I have a question," Queenie piped up. "Why do you smell like that?"

"I must confess," Silt added in, "I've been wondering that as well."

Everyone looked at Bishop, but he didn't flinch. "I'm sorry," he said angrily. "I was told we were going into a sewer, and I happen to have a sensitive nose."

"So you covered yourself in perfume?" Patho asked.

Bishop gesticulated wildly. "Yes, and I won't hear any more about this. I wouldn't be questioning all of you if you suffered from a similar condition."

"That's not going to work," Butler contributed with a shake of his head. "The smells are just going to mix."

"I can barely smell the sewage right now, so I think I'll take my chances."

Patho climbed into the tunnel first, and the rest followed suit. The waters of the tunnel were thick, slushy, and up to their knees. Thankfully, whatever material these clothes were made out of didn't let the water or sludge soak into them. Bishop was trying his hardest to stifle his gags, but everyone heard them. After a few minutes of maneuvering through muck, the water level dropped. It wasn't long before the group came across a sealed door that was used for maintenance. On the other side of it was the subterranean portion of Sinustus, an array of linoleum tunnels that connected to most buildings, conducted repairs, and housed important equipment like heaters and air conditioners.

A bright red pulse from Patho's hand blasted open the door, and they were in.

CHAPTER 39

INFILTRATION

The hallways of Sinustus's underground were absolutely covered in propaganda posters. Some sang the praises of Yelo, while others derided the outside world for being backward and full of agonizing choices. The Marauders quietly stepped out of the tunnel. Their special clothing was entirely clean of muck, leaving no trail of waste behind them. Queenie watched Bishop look down each of the three hallways that branched out from where the door was. He looked kind of pale and was still covering his nose. This whole complex was just a maze that the only truly dedicated and experienced could easily traverse. Queenie was neither of those.

"Okay," he said. "Which of these leads to wherever Hastul will be?"

Queenie took a moment to get her bearings, but eventually she thought she recognized where they were. "We are pretty close to a basement area that he spends a lot of time in. If you take the path to your left you should find the entrance to it fairly soon. I've had to wheel rocks into that room a few times."

"Excellent," Bishop replied in a hushed tone. "You three head straight for where you think the computer is. Silt, try to take care of any threats before they become a problem. Butler, if they do become a problem, solve it, and Queenie, guide them the best you can."

"Got it," she and Butler replied, while Silt only nodded.

The group split up. Despite her time in Yelo, Queenie had done most of her work on the surface level. She had only been given tasks down here when she had to fill in for somebody else. Luckily, one of the few details she did remember was that the room with the mainframe in it always had two large posters out front.

"So, have you decided what you are going to do after this?" Silt whispered to Butler. "I know that Lode was the second love that you lost to violence like that."

Butler slid his eyes over to the old man beside him. "No, I haven't."

"Nobody would blame you if you wanted to retire after this. I know from experience that the loss of a loved one hits one like a rifle blast to the heart."

"Retire?" Queenie asked, piping in.

"Yes. Retire," Butler replied gruffly.

"Can you just retire from the gang whenever you want?"

"Unless it's in the middle of a firefight, then pretty much yes. Although you should probably do something of worth first or nobody will give you any respect in retirement."

"Oh," she responded.

The group got to another intersection, where there were three other paths. Queenie motioned to keep going straight, and the other two followed without a word. It felt weird being the leader; she was so used to just sitting there and letting the wind throw her where it wanted to that actually being taken seriously without the assistance of a gun was quite a shock. She couldn't lie to herself, though. She liked it.

They heard footsteps coming from their left. Silt smiled at them reassuringly, and then prodded them to go against the nearest wall. He hid on the wall closer to the footsteps, a pistol with a conical barrel in his hand. Two Bans walked out of the hallway, and before they could see either Queenie or the giant next to her, Silt had already ended the life of one of them. He flicked his wrist slightly to adjust the shot and silently killed the other.

"We better move before they find the bodies," he whispered, and Queenie couldn't have agreed more. They hurried into the next hallway, a bit of time passing before Butler picked up the old conversation where it left off.

"I'd love to leave this all behind me and live a more peaceful life. After I give these bastards the bullets they deserve. The only problem with that is, once I'm on my own, what will stop me from falling into a deeper and darker hole within myself? I might stay in the gang just to have something to channel my energy into."

"Understandable." Silt nodded. "Still though, if you do find love again, being a part of the Marauders won't make them any safer."

"I don't even want to think about love right now. It would be too disrespectful to Lode to even consider moving on so soon." Butler's tone became somber, and his face began to slacken. "He had a close call a few months ago with one of his clients. They weren't willing to pay and got violent about it. Lode was never a fighter, but luckily he had a guard at the time who put the client down. After that I swore to myself I'd protect him, but some job of that I did."

"You can't blame yourself for what Yelo did, Butler. There was no way you could have been everywhere at once."

"But I could try."

They came to yet another identical intersection. Queenie began to point right, when a figure blurred at the group and swung down with the object in its hand, creating a large blue arc of light as it went. They narrowly dodged it. The attacker was a Lem. Their Raiga bayonet was activated, and ready to cut them to pieces. Silt drew a small hilt from his side and ignited a blade no bigger than a letter opener.

The Lem went to cut at Butler. Silt blocked the blade with his own and blue sparks flew as the two blades met one another. Queenie fearfully backed away from the fighting, watching the two try to slice into each other. Butler had his guns drawn, but the Lem was being very careful to keep Silt in front of him during the duel. Silt was grabbing one hand with the other to match the strength of the Lem, and his struggle was visible on his face.

"Just go," Silt grunted as they clashed blades again. "I'll catch up with you later. Just go!" Butler and Queenie did as they were told and ran.

She heard Butler curse under his breath as they ran through the halls. Queenie had no idea how he had found them. Lems rarely patrolled the underground; it was mostly Bans down here, and unless the Lems were instructed otherwise, they mostly just stood guard around Hastul's building. Even if the bodies had already been found, it would still take a while for a Lem to get this far down.

They kept running and running. Every time that she thought that they needed to change the direction, she'd yell to Butler. Both of them were completely forgoing stealth at this point. Every once in a while, they would run into a Ban or two, weapons drawn, but the grunts just couldn't keep up with the blitzing giant next to her, who would almost immediately fill them with holes. Thank the Provider that Butler was a quick shot. Queenie felt her lungs burning from all the running. She hadn't run like this since she was small. She took a deep breath and coughed. The air tasted like smoke.

Bishop and Patho moved quickly through hallway after hallway. They were no closer to finding the door. In hindsight, he probably should have asked for a more detailed description of where they were heading than a general direction.

"We took over half a city, and we can't even find one door," Patho commented, half in jest and half in anger.

"I honestly wish that this surprised me. We were always more front-line fighters than infiltrators."

"And here I thought Vara's perfume would help your sense of direction."

"Now you're just being mean," Bishop retorted. "It's not like I have a bad sense of direction either. It's just that I've never been here before, and it all looks the damn same."

"I guess that's fair, but I won't let you live down the roses."

"I didn't expect you to, honestly."

They crouched against a wall as a horde of Bans ran through a hallway in front of them. At least one of the other Marauders had to have been discovered for a crowd like that to be running around. He was hoping it was Vara and not the search team. He knew Vara wouldn't go down easy, if she went down at all. The other three being as capable as the two of them were, he was not as confident in.

"That doesn't bode well," Patho remarked. "We should kill them."

"Normally I'd say yes, but we can't risk ourselves getting discovered. If they find out either of us are here, they will do everything in their power to kill us or alert higher-ups. It will make finding Hastul impossible."

Patho grumbled underneath his helmet. "Fine."

A few more guessed turns laterm and the duo finally came across a golden door. It was carved intricately with patterns of snakes writing on it. Bishop turned the handle, and they walked in. The room was large, and unsurprisingly, yellow. Piles of rubble covered the floor, there were stairs at the other end of the room, several fans were turning slowly on the ceiling, and there were some vents up there as well.

They walked up to the stairs, carefully stepping over the loose rubble. The floor above them was another hallway, and Bishop came to the conclusion that he had seen enough yellow to be satisfied with the color for at least several lifetimes. This hallway was much more decorated than the other, and he considered this a good sign. There were several grates on the right side of the ceiling, where they could see somewhere else in the compound that was also disgustingly garish.

"I think we are close," Bishop said, his iris expanding and contracting as he peered out of the grate. The room looked like a fairy tale throne room, but there was no throne atop the staircase that waited at the end, only a wall. With his enhanced vision he could see that the wall was fake, and that something lay behind it. He had a good idea of what. The problem was that the throne room had three of what Bishop recognized as Lems in it. Each of them wore a strange clear, plastic-looking garment over their normal attire. Bishop had no idea what that was about, but nothing these freaks did anymore could surprise him after the mile of propaganda he had just walked through.

Bishop tapped Patho. "They have three of those elite soldiers that they tout around so proudly, guarding that room. If they have that many there, then they must be guarding something important."

Patho opened his palms at the grate, red energy swirling around them. "Excellent." He blasted the wall, and with a loud bang there was a large hole where the grate once was. "We can have some real fun then."

They climbed through the cloud of dust and over the rubble. Guns had been drawn, magic wrapped around an Eatherium, and claws were clenched. The battle was about to begin—or it would be, if there was anyone else in the room.

Chapter 40

Order Versus Chaos, and Then More Chaos

Quick and almost immediate flashes of blue preceding a lack of Bans returning from their posts presented a problem that even an idiot could figure out. There was an intruder. When this was first reported to him, Lawndel had sent two teams of three to investigate and put an end to whatever was going on. Neither returned. Now, sufficiently angry at the reordering of personnel he would have to oversee, Lawndel was preparing to accompany a third team to solve this little problem.

He had been able to piece together from where the light appeared and disappeared, and some of the movements that the intruder on the wall had used to dispatch the second team. He recognized them because he had done them so many times himself. It was Bruteil, but the effectiveness of the user was still very much up for debate. Bans were nowhere near a match for anyone even half-trained in the art. So Lawndel had thought to design a proper test for their guest.

Two Bans and Lem would be the next to engage the mysterious martial artist. The death of the Bans would provide the Lem, who themselves were trained in the rudiments of Bruteil, enough time to strike. The results of that strike would decide if Lawndel would intervene himself.

Sinustus was lit up in a sheen of yellow by hazy lights that didn't reach up the wall. The ladder leading up the wall was tall, sturdy, and a sickly yellow. Lawndel wouldn't allow something as vital as this to be subpar. The group of four ascended into the night sky. He watched the searchlights move across the silver sand outside and saw no obvious vehicles inside their beams; whoever was up there was crafty enough at the least to hide their tracks. Then, the first Ban fell with a flash of blue.

Their head separated from their shoulders, and the second one soon followed. The Lem fired a shot from their energy rifle. The powerful blue sphere of solidified Raiga whizzed through the air and at the black figure standing over the dead Bans. The figure, who Lawndel could now tell was female, most likely Vara of the Marauders, leapt over the shot in a true demonstration of beautiful Bruteil, and kicked the Lem in the side of the head, causing his mask to fly off. He fell off the wall. Lawndel could just barely make out the brown stains on the man's face as he fell into the foggy lights of Sinustus. The woman looked to him next, preparing to strike.

Lawndel was already ready for her though, and launched himself at her, delivering a powerful kick to her stomach. Instead of the hardened muscle he expected to give way under his boot, it was some type of armor that broke under his strike instead. He was intending to not kill her immediately with the kick, but instead, he wished to wound her lethally with enough time left to answer a single question. No matter—even if she wasn't on death's door, she would still be able to answer him, and would still be dead before she knew it.

She slid backward across the walkway, kicking up a cloud of dust in front of her as she went. He could swear she was smiling.

"How long was it for you?" he asked. "Your Wasting."

The woman looked up at him, grinning from ear to ear. "A few weeks. You?"

"A month and a half."

She reignited her daggers and lunged at him. He could see now that her teeth were made of metal. He caught her blades with his own, and the sickles and daggers sparked off one another. She jumped over him, keeping her blades on his. Lawndel followed her movement by turning in place and thrusting his arms apart to get her off of him. She landed on the other end of the walkway and flew at him again. She slashed at him with her left dagger, and he deflected the blow with their curve of his sickle. The right one came next, and again he swayed out of the way.

She was quite skilled, and her speed could match his own—a worthy opponent, but one that could be overcome. Lawndel swiped at her, managing to get a thin slice into her abdomen where he had broken the armor. The woman, like any true Bruteil practitioner, didn't let a minor injury distract her. Instead, she went for a thrust of her own while he was busy attacking. Lawndel used his other sickle to move her blade out of the way before he himself stepped backward.

They ran at one another again. Blades clashed repeatedly, sending blue sparks into the air, the two fighters appearing as dancing black silhouettes, aside from their weapons, to anyone who was watching. Vara attacked Lawndel violently, and he defended himself by attacking when he was able. Occasionally, the two would nick each other, but a battle between their ilk was always really about whose stamina would run out first.

He caught her blade in the bottom of his curve and slid it through the hole of the sickle. This broke Vara's form. He went for her neck with his next slice. She ducked underneath as the sickle made an arc of blue light above her. She put her hand on the ground and pushed herself up, trying to drive her daggers underneath his rib cage, but he slid backward to avoid it.

Vara kicked at him, and Lawndel kicked in return. Both feet slammed into one another. Their owners used the opportunity to propel off their opponent's foot. Each landed with a metallic bang on the walkway before assuming a sprinter position and springing at the other again.

***

Yellow Light was in flames, and holograms of exotic dances, adverts for shitty alcohol, and subpar restaurants played on the smoke. The once-decadent district was quickly being reduced to blood-splattered rubble. Claw had never seen this many destroyed buildings and flipped vehicles, and other cars and motorcycles were screeching through the streets accompanied by a never-ending cacophony of gunshots. This was her life. It always had been. She had been born into this, and she knew that she had to keep going until the day that this life eventually killed her. Some part of her wanted to leave all the violence behind her and move onto something that didn't involve blowing skulls apart every other week, but this was all she knew. This was all she was good at, and Claw had already accepted this truth about her life. All she could do now was get through the gunfights and enjoy the little things in the time in between.

She had lost track of Artex early on in all the chaos. If he died while he owed her money, she would never forgive him. A Marauder had just swung by, screaming, on a cut wire while firing a rapid fire at a building full of Yelo members. He was quickly gunned down by them. His corpse was just a fleshy stain in the street now, waiting to be run over and lose its last traces of recognizability. Claw herself was huddled behind a collapsed wall and holding a rapid fire of her own. It was down to its last crystal, and Provider be damned she wasn't wasting another one on this piece of junk. Things had to calm down a little before she'd consider moving again. She would have to calm them down.

Her good hand gripped tightly on the gun. Claw moved from behind the wall, firing her gun at the Yelo0controlled building. She saw at least two unprepared Bans go down. The rapid fire clicked empty, and Yelo members inside regrouped. She threw the gun aside; she just needed a few good shots at them. Then she'd move on and leave the cleanup to somebody else.

Raiga bullets began to punch through the wall behind her. One grazed her arm. She swore, and then she reached into her coat and pulled out a string of three grenades. She threw one blindly behind her, knowing that she wouldn't hit the building. It went off with a bang and left a blue smoke cloud in its wake. The gunshots slowed down while the Yelo reloaded and tried to see past the smoke. Claw used this time to throw the other two grenades into the building. She didn't know if she would actually hit anyone with the bombs, but all she really needed was the chaos from the blasts.

The building was in disarray from the grenades, and Claw looked for somewhere new to perch. Eventually, she settled on a shattered balcony over her. She pulled the middle finger of her prosthetic back and aimed it at the balcony. When she let go, her hand shot on a wire up to the ledge and grabbed onto it. Her chains rattled, and blue blood trailed from her wound as she zipped through the air.

She ducked beneath her brick banister. Claw allowed herself a quick glance at the destroyed apartment behind her. She could see a ruptured waterbed, a dual colored green and red shag carpet, a ripped up bead door, and poster for "Sneaky Snoodles," obviously a Yellow Light strip joint. Everything about Yellow Light was repulsive to her, but this guy's sense of interior design was really something abhorrent.

Claw reached into her coat and clicked something. She pulled out the handle of Cherry Picker. The other pieces of the gun flew out to meet it, each one glowing blue at their axis. She positioned herself like a sniper, and then Claw fired the first shot. The shell went through one of the broken windows with a bang. It exploded into a blast of hot Raigic plasma. She could hear the gurgled screams of those not immediately killed by the blast. She fired at a different part of the building. Light blue plasma burst out of the windows.

She doubted there were much, if any alive in there after that, but they were not her problem anymore. There were hotter zones of conflict than this, and she needed to find them.

Chapter 41

The Invisible Hand

Bishop and Patho stood still in the empty room, and neither was sure what was going on. Cautiously, they began to walk forward toward the fake wall. Their footsteps echoed throughout the massive gold-plated room. Then Bishop's nostrils flared, and his face scrunched up.

"Are you sure you saw people?" Patho asked.

"There are still people here," Bishop replied. "I can smell their eye trails."

A rifle blast hit Patho right in his chest plate. He flew backward through the air, spinning wildly. He wrapped his upper arms in magic and rocketed them into the ground to catch himself in place. There wasn't even a scratch on his armor.

"What?!" he growled, picking himself up.

Bishop tried to scan the room again with his eye, but another blast was already headed for him. He activated his eye as he moved out of the way. He wasn't fast enough to completely avoid the shot, and his left forearm was taken off. Blood began to burst from his mangled, pulpy stump, but it was soon slowed by an eruption of steam. His body began to try and repair itself. The disembodied hand landed with a soft whump and the gun slid smoothly across the ground.

Bishop grunted and swore. Limbs always took a while to grow back, and the wounds would still bleed while they healed. He kept himself moving to avoid being an easy shot. His eye was active now, and he was starting to see them. It was still hard to make them out, and what he was seeing wasn't exactly the Lems themselves, but the imperfections around the walls they were mimicking. He could see all three of them hugging the walls—even their silenced rifles were coated in whatever it was that let them mimic their surroundings.

"Patho!" Bishop called out, as he ran around the room.

"Yes?" Patho replied, blocking the brunt of a third blast with his arms and being pushed back several feet.

"They're invisible."

"Bishop," Patho said. "The sky is blue."

"Funny." Bishop narrowly dodged another blast, which left a messy, debris-surrounded hole in the floor behind him. "Don't worry about them. Go straight for the back! I'll keep them out of your hair while you go and take care of Hastul."

Patho glanced at Bishop with his red holographic eye. Then he wrapped himself tightly in a large amount of red and launched himself at the fake wall like a missile. The Lems turned in unison to shoot him out of the sky.

Bishop fired his remaining pistol, and the solid Raiga bullet dug right through the skull of a Lem. What was left of his brain spilled out onto the floor along with a waterfall of blood. His body was still undetectable, aside from what looked like a sudden head wound in the fabric of reality. The other Lems turned back to Bishop, invisible rifles raised. Patho broke through the wall and Bishop smiled at them.

"You're gonna have to kill me if you want the chance to help your boss." He grinned.

The Lems immediately began trying to kill him. Bishop dodged the first blast, leaving a trail of steam and blood droplets in his wake, but without Patho to help divide their attention, both Lems were reacting to one another's shots. The second blast was fired at the same time as the first, right where they thought he would dodge, and they were right. Bishop raised his Eatherium arm to block it. The impact sent him hurtling back and knocked the gun from his hand.

He recovered quickly, and the Lems continued to try and rip him apart. He had noticed that their primary targets had switched from his vitals to his legs, but Bishop didn't have a doubt in his mind that if they got them, then the targets would switch back. On the bright side of things, his arm wound had stopped bleeding, and even if he died it would cost Yelo a lot of money to repair this floor.

Bishop blocked another blast with his metallic arm and regained his footing. He needed to strike back at them. He knew that, but the opportunity just wasn't presenting itself. A shot grazed through the side of his left calf, and steam began to flow out.

The bombardment stopped momentarily as the Lems reloaded. Bishop didn't waste any time—he'd be a much easier target while his legs healed, and he would be able to reach one of his guns before they reloaded. He grabbed a shard of scrap from the ground. With all the might in his body and all the accuracy in his eye, he threw the shard at one of the Lems, getting them in the neck. Blood spurted from the wound as the Lem clutched at it, and not long after, they fell limply to the ground.

***

Hastul sat on his throne, looking at the scar on the side of his face. The Marauders had somehow found a way inside of his citadel, and, even more outrageously, they had the gall to actually invade. This scar was the first insult that they had given him. Taking Board City from him was the second, and now a third was in the form of this invasion! The first alone was absolutely unforgivable, much less the other two.

Of course, he had heard the blast in the courtroom. He had faith in his guards to handle the situation, but he wanted to be here just in case he would have the delicious opportunity to kill some of those beastly creatures. None of them could even dream of matching his magical prowess, much less even understand what he was using to kill them. He smiled at the thought of their confusion before his magic ripped them apart.

The wall in front of him blew apart, throwing leaves of stone all around his well-maintained bedroom. Hastul jumped in his chair. A Human wearing a quite malicious set of armor rose out of the dust. Hastul recognized the man despite the armor covering him.

"Ah, Patho," Hastul said snidely. "The Marauders' resident Human. To what do I owe the—"

Patho blasted a beam of red at Hastul, who in turn immediately shrieked and met the beam with his own. The red and yellow energy collided with a shrill humming sound, and after a while, both exploded into a shock wave that caused Hastul's robe to flutter.

"Magic?!" he screamed and summoned up his flaring yellow aura.

Patho lunged at Hastul; his hands were covered in red magic. Hastul shot a projectile at him. The projectile hit Patho in the chest and sent him flying upward.

Hastul sneered. "Your only chance was that surprise attack," he hissed at Patho, almost laughing with every word. "There's nothing you can do now that can result in you winning, Human!" Hastul fired another projectile, sending Patho into the wall. He created a small crater where he landed.

Hastul cackled madly. "You are nothing compared to me! I will become the greatest Magician who's ever lived, and you will not even be a thought in my mind when that day comes! A stepping-stone so small that it's not even worth remembering." Hastul created and then launched four more magic ovals from his aura. He launched each of them like a cannonball into Patho, driving him deeper into the wall and creating a large cloud of dust.

Hastul's laughing stopped sharply when he heard, "Oh, shove a trident in it," come from the hole. Patho peeled himself from the wall, his distinguished appearance fluctuating back and forth between itself and a blinding white light. He landed on the ground and ripped something from the back of his neck, and his form shattered in front of Hastul.

Patho stood up, now with his true appearance. He spoke, his voice emanating from his entire body. "You broke my face, and I quite enjoy my face. I got to *pick* my face. Do you know how many people get to pick what they look like? It's not a high number, Hastul. Sure, there is a spare back home, but I *liked* that generator. I got quite attached to it over the years. And *you* broke it."

Hastul took a step back. He could feel his heart racing in his chest. This wasn't a Human. This wasn't anything he'd ever even *heard* about. Hastul could almost see *through* parts of him, the eyeholes of the helmet just had a solid red behind them. He looked like an unblinking demon. Maybe that's what he was.

"What are you?" Hastul managed to ask.

"What I am isn't important. All that's important is that I'm going to take you apart piece by piece." Patho jumped at Hastul, using his magic to boost his momentum. He held out a clawed hand and pierced a finger through his cheek. The pain was searing. Patho ripped through his entire cheek and left only a crudely cut, bleeding gash, before landing behind Hastul.

It was impossible. They did it again. They scarred his beautiful face again. A hot, burning rage began to flow over Hastul, and his aura began to whip around madly. This could not be allowed. Not in his own home. Not anywhere. Hastul stopped caring about whatever type of monster Patho actually was. He was still going to be the world's greatest Magician, and nothing would stop him from reaching the heights he *deserved* to reach.

Hastul began to float off the ground. His aura formed tendrils at his back and flew to connect to his mirror that was still lying in his serpentine-throne. The mirror glowed yellow and flew onto his back. Yellow electricity became visible underneath his light gray skin. Hastul grinned a wicked grin.

"I'm afraid, you're confused, my dear insect," he chortled, reinvigorated by this new intoxicating power. "*You're* the only one who'll be dying here today."

Chapter 42

Sword and Sorcery

Vara blocked a slash from Lawndel. It had been years since she felt a rush like this—she hadn't actually fought with another Bruteil user since she was still in the monks camp. It was an exhilarating experience, and she was savoring every moment of it. She went for a slash of her own, bringing her blade down in an arc of blue. Lawndel deflected it with his sickle, and immediately went for a counterattack. Vara parried and threw him back.

He came at her fast, swinging both sickles upward in a fluid movement. She threw her blades against his and rode the momentum of his strike so that she could jump over him. She knew what he was trying to do; he was trying to cut off her arms and cripple her. Vara really didn't want to be reduced to just kicks. She liked kicking people, no doubt about it, but she imagined that they were a lot more fun when you are in one piece.

Speaking of which, she went to kick his legs out from under him. She hit them, and Lawndel flipped himself in the air until his feet were facing her. He then went to kangaroo kick her in the face. Vara blocked with her forearms. She could hear her bones fracture underneath the force, but she didn't have time to let that slow her down.

Vara ignored the pain and lunged at Lawndel. She went for two stabs at his chest. He pulled his sickles together and pinched her daggers in between. This could go either way now, she knew this. A hold like this could make or break a battle. She grabbed her daggers as tightly as she could, and pain radiated through her arms. She gritted her teeth and pulled to her left with all her might.

He flipped and smashed hard into the ground. He let go of her blades. Vara went for him again. Lawndel shot his leg up like a cannon. She just managed to jolt her head out of the way before he broke her jaw. It missed her by less than an inch. He used this as an opportunity to spin himself to a safe distance. He jumped back onto his feet and held his sickles out in a fighting stance.

She was at the disadvantage now, and she knew he knew it. Her arms were injured now, and she had missed her chance to finish him. Vara smiled, this was the end of the fight; they both knew it, but she still had one trick up her sleeve.

She hopped away from him, and he followed after her. They were both blurs of blue moving on top of Sinustus's wall. She needed to move and get his mind focused on something else before she struck. Lawndel flung himself against a cannon, then used it to launch at her. Vara burst into a full sprint to avoid him.

She slammed her foot full force into the ground, causing it to crack. Vara changed directions, running right at him. The air stung her eyes as she rocketed at him with all the force she could muster. She picked up her feet and flew through the night like an arrow of blue light. Lawndel moved to the side to avoid her.

Vara cracked a smile. It was just like she predicted. She held her daggers out to her side and clicked both blue gems. Her daggers became swords just as she passed by him. The sudden extension caught Lawndel off guard. The blue of the sword ran through his arms and abdomen. Lawndel came apart, and his torso fell off the walls and into the compound below. Vara began to kick her feet lightly into the ground, and she kept hoping the inevitable until she came to a controlled walk. She couldn't keep the smile from her face. That was everything she wanted in a fight, and for her to come out alive at the end of it was a nice plus.

***

Queenie heard Butler swear. They were standing in the middle of a four-way intersection between the hallways, and small wisps of smoke were slowly filling the air around them. There were two Bans at every pathway, each armed with either a shotgun or a pistol.

"Queenie," Butler whispered. "Get down."

She did as she was told, and Butler held his guns out to his sides. He screamed as he spun, unleashing twin streams of Raigic destruction upon the Bans. When the shooting stopped, Queenie looked up into the smoky air. She saw that Butler had been hit several times by the Bans. There were wounds in his left thigh and right shoulder. Butler opened his mouth to speak to her.

The ceiling tile behind Queenie fell to the ground with a smack, followed by a thick plume of black smoke. Butler raised his guns again, preparing to unload into the plume. The tile behind him fell, and the Huntsman dropped after it, his scaly face twisted in an expression of glee. He was holding himself upside down with his tail wrapped around a pipe. He fired a shot from his rifle, and it blew a massive hole through the giant's chest. The blood flew all over a mortified Queenie.

Butler fell on top of Queenie, barely managing to catch himself before he crushed her. "Run," he croaked.

Queenie almost slipped on the blood when she began to crawl out from under him. The Huntsman placed his foot on the back of the dying man's head and smashed it into the ground. Butler didn't get back up. Queenie ran over the corpses of the Bans, not stopping for a look behind her.

She ran through the long narrow hallway, a cloud of black smoke quickly gaining on her. Queenie was panting and holding back the instinctive urge to begin bawling. The Huntsman was the bogeyman that every member of Yelo feared, a beast that would emerge from smoke and take the heads of those that deserted back to Hastul. He was the almighty deterrent against abandoning ship, and it looked like he knew about her jumping overboard.

She ran by a connecting hallway, and a shape stepped out in between her and the approaching cloud. It was Silt. Everything came to an abrupt pause, and an eerie silence came over the hall. Silt was pretty banged up, but the blood covering him was not his own. He had killed the Lem.

He stared into the cloud and raised his gun to it. "Queenie," he said, in a voice void of emotion. "Keep going." But she couldn't make herself move anymore. She didn't want to leave Silt on his own again, and if he killed that monster, she wanted to be here to see it.

Black silhouettes appeared in the fog, and Silt immediately began to gun them down. Each one dissipated into smoke when hit. Somewhere in that cloud, the Huntsman was lying in wait for his prey. Silt continued to fire into the cloud until a knife flew out of it. It glinted briefly in the light before planting itself in Silt's hand; he dropped the gun. Another dagger flew into his head, and Queenie was running again.

The cloud formed into a grotesque face behind her, its smoke jaws were chomping at her heels. Queenie pulled the vest out of her pack. It worked on the gauntlet guy, but she doubted throwing it at the Huntsman would do anything. Still, if Patho had made sure it found its way back to her then it must be good for something right? Blackness enveloped her and she was tackled to the ground.

The smoke around her became thin again, allowing light to pierce through, and the Huntsman flipped her on her back and slammed her to the ground. The vest flew from her grasp and slid across the floor.

He vomited more of the foul smelling smoke onto her face. "Your scent," he rasped. "It was your greenhouse scent that led me to you all. It was you who let me know where to find you filthy intruders. We know about all of you and are killing each and every one of your Marauder scum heaps as we speak, but you are a traitor. So you are mine."

He wrenched open her mouth and placed his hand over it. "Leading the enemy back here deserves a special punishment, don't you think?" The smoke seeped from the scales of his hand and into her mouth; it moved on his whim and began to flood into her lungs. She was reaching for the vest with her waning strength. He chortled at her struggle.

Everything was black, and Queenie was falling. Suddenly a great orange light pierced through the darkness. Queenie covered her eyes as the light swept her up into it. The orange light moved around her like gentle water, it soothed her and filled her with strength. She knew what the light was. It was her soul. It was magic.

***

The black around Queenie's white pupils filled with the orange light. A wisp of the light exited her fingertips and entered the vest, lighting up small carved grooves on the material with orange. It all felt as natural as breathing. There was a flash of an orange aura around her torso, and the chained vest was now on her. The Huntsman frowned in confusion at the new outfit his victim was suddenly wearing. Queenie widened her orange eyes; she knew what the vest did.

One of the blade tipped chains popped off of the vest, surrounded by an orange glow, and shot in between the ribs of the Huntsman. He let out a screech as it dug its way inside of him. The smoke inside her stopped moving, and she sat up coughing and wheezing. The Huntsman was trying in vain to rip the chain out of him, but his red blood made it too slippery, and it went inside. He writhed and contorted on the ground, shrieking. Queenie could move the blade like it was her very own limb, and she was using that limb to tear his organs apart.

He clawed at himself, ripping his clothes and cutting his flesh, trying with all his might to somehow get her out of him. It was too late, though; his movements became sluggish and blood began bubbling up from his throat. The Huntsman died screaming, and a wheezing Queenie passed out.

CHAPTER 43

BLOOD WITH BLUNDERS

There was only one Lem left, and Bishop was running toward him. The wound on his leg, although healing, was throwing his steps off. Bishop slid out of the way of a blast. He had no weapons left, but he didn't need them. He could handle one Lem on his own, and Bishop had already decided how he was going to kill him.

Another shot of blue appeared from the shimmering air where the almost invisible Lem stood. Bishop raised his arm to clock it. The Raiga shot shattered on his arm and pushed him several feet backward. Pain throbbed though his leg. Bishop continued his sprint. The Lem fired again, and Bishop ducked under it. A blue streak entered his injured leg, causing his flesh to twist painfully before his leg was completely torn from his body.

Then, Bishop's face hit the ground hard. Blood was pooling from the injury and steam was slowly stifling the flow. Bishop could feel that he was getting dizzy, and the regeneration was slowing. The Lem fired again, this time for the head. Bishop shoved the ground with his hand and still-steaming stump. He flipped backward, just managing to avoid the shot. Bishop landed using his three remaining limbs to keep himself balanced. He kicked the ground with his good leg and used his arms to balance. He ran like an animal at the Lem, ignoring the pain from his injuries the best he could.

He tackled the Lem to the ground. Up close, the pungent smell from his eye trails was almost worse than the sewer. Bishop slammed the healing stump on his left forearm into the Lem's face, breaking the bones that were growing out of the wound. He ripped the rifle from the Lem's grasp and threw it across the room; Bishop then straddled the Lem's chest. Over and over he drove his Eatherium fist into the Lem's face.

The goggles broke, and the black eyes underneath them burst. Blue blood mixed with the fecal brown streams of rot on the Lem's now indistinguishable head. Bishop thought it was a man, or maybe it was a woman. He didn't really care. Whatever they were, they stood in the way of the Marauders, and threatened their way of life. This Lem and all the others that still held the creed of Yelo close to their hearts wanted him and everybody that was associated with him dead, and to subjugate everyone that they didn't kill into being the same type of soulless drone that they were. He would die before he allowed that to happen.

Bishop threw his fist into the soup that was once a face until the back of the skull cracked open. Pieces of the Lem's teal brain floated across the floor on a small wave of blood.

Bishop weakly turned his head to the hole Patho made. Yellow light was pouring out of it. He began to try and crawl toward it, leaving a trail of both his own blood and his victims behind him. The room was spinning so badly at this point that his eyes were starting to lose focus. Bishop collapsed, exhausted, onto the floor and listened to his body steam.

***

The staircase was narrow and the flames from outside caused an orange glow to dance across the peeling yellow wallpaper. Artex had spent more time during the invasion than he'd like to admit trying to find where the Yelo overseer was stationed. The main problem was getting a Ban that was still alive to be interrogated, but the actual questioning process went surprisingly well. He was expecting to have to torture the guy a little bit, but when he asked the first question, the Ban just told him the location and mouthed off about his boss in between sobs. That's what you get when you don't let your members vent their frustrations or communicate with one another, he figured; they will hate you without you ever knowing.

Artex looked outside from one of the many small portholes that dotted the wall. The massive figure of a holographic woman dressed in cabaret-style dress danced seductively in the smoke in front of a burning brothel. Bodies from both factions lay bloody on the streets, and a Marauder crawling out of the carnage was mowed down by sniper fire. They were terrible things, fights like these—he had no idea how his sister could enjoy stuff like this. To him, it was another tragic necessity of living in Outer Varcia, but then again, the monks never really tried to indoctrinate him. Instead, they just taught him how to shoot and tolerated his presence. He couldn't say it didn't bother him, not being as gifted as his sister, but he did like the greater sense of right and wrong that he developed on his own.

A gray car full of Bans pulled up in front of the brothel. Artex broke the window with the pummel of his Blunderbuss and fired a shot at the car. The blue explosion consumed the car, and the shock wave sent some of the corpses rolling.

Artex began running up the stairs. He had no information on this overseer, but then again, very few in Yelo actually stood out. Still, getting up that high in rank meant you were very good at something, and he was just hoping it wasn't combat. The top of the stairs took him to a suspended hallway, which in turn led to a circular dining room that was suspended above the district like a giant chandelier. The room was filled with the bodies of dead Marauders and a Lem with two Ban underlings behind them standing in the other hallway.

Artex swore when he saw the Lem, but it was too late. The energy rifle was already being pointed in his direction. He could fire the Blunderbuss again and still have one shot left, but if he blew up the halls then the building would fall, and he'd have to find another way to the Overseer. The Bans sent silent twin blasts of energy into the Lem's head. They fell, and Jeff and Joff took off their masks.

"You two?!" Artex gasped.

"The correct response is 'thank you,'" The twins replied, slightly out of sync. "We did just save your life."

"But why didn't you kill him sooner? You were standing behind him."

The twins rolled their eyes. "We needed a good opening. Those things are fast."

Artex let out a deep sigh and walked into the room. "Look," he said. "I don't have time to argue with you two, and you don't have time to argue with me. I'm going to find and kill the overseer of Yellow Light, and you can come with me or leave. I'm blowing this place up as soon as I leave so no other Yelo members can get across."

The twins rolled their eyes again and followed Artex to the other side. "I don't see any bombs on you," Jeff pointed out.

"Don't need 'em." Artex replied smugly. He fired the Blunderbuss and blew out one of the halls. The building metal creaked and groaned before the entire structure collapsed into a big yellow heap of scrap in the street.

"Great way to warn them," Joff chided.

Artex's smugness faded. "Shut up."

The trio entered a beautiful sitting room decorated with intricate golden tapestries that depicted a Varse woman lying with her eyes closed on a bed of flowers. The chairs were made out of fine velvet. They opened the engraved door and turned a corner; it was much less nice in here, with only pipes and dim lights.

They came across a black door with the number thirty-two emblazoned on it. The twins moved to cover its sides and Artex went for the handle. A spattering of small holes appeared in the door. The shotgun blast hit Artex in the chest, ripping through his clothes and being met by the body armor Patho gave him. The metal hexagons bent under the blast, some of them puncturing into Artex, but they succeeded in stopping the blast from being immediately fatal. The force threw Artex like a piece of paper in the wind. He crashed into the wall, which was only steps behind him, breaking several pipes with his head and slumping to the ground.

It felt like somebody had driven a knife into his brain; the world was a spinning blur. Artex saw the shapes of the twins move for the now-open door. He moved his hand awkwardly for the Blunderbuss, watching the twins get off two shots before the overseer fired the shotgun again. The spray of bullets hit the twins and sent their blurred forms reeling to the ground. He couldn't tell if they were dead. Artex was trying his best to aim while the shape in front of him loaded a new shimmering blue crystal into the gun.

"You will not take this from me," the figure angrily stated. "I will not let you or anyone take this from me. I will fill you all with a dozen bleeding holes before I let even one bullet hit me! Do you hear that trash? Yelo will . . . no, *I* will end those who stand ag—"

Artex fired the Blunderbuss. He hit the floor in front of her, and the explosion began to expand around the room. The shockwave hit the screaming overseer and sent her hurtling through the window. Everything in the office was covered in a blue fire that was quickly turning a shade of orange as it found more and more fuel for itself. Artex watched the flames dance in front of him like a circus of fairies that were threatening to make aging him a part of the show. He couldn't move.

Two silhouettes pulled themselves in front of him, blocking the fire from his view. Artex felt hands on his shoulders, and everything went black.

CHAPTER 44

RED RUNNING

The aura flared around Patho's whole body like a ruby inferno. If he was going to get out of this alive, he'd have to do everything in his power to outlast Hastul. He kicked off the ground and shot up like a streaking red bullet. He hit his arm off the ceiling and began ricocheting himself around the room.

Hastul flicked his wrist and sent a dozen projectiles flying around the room, each failing to hit their mark, and punching clean holes in the decorated walls. Patho remembered his own First Binding, when the piece of his soul that put itself in his trident reunited with his body for the first time. In the original Marauders, when an aspiring Embodiment underwent the process it was a cause for celebration, but now in the present and seeing Hastul undergo it, Patho didn't feel much like congratulating him.

"It's hilarious, really," Hastul spat from his torn mouth. "I am standing here at the pinnacle of my own existence, only a few measly steps away from becoming a Magician, and you still think you can avoid your own death." Hastul held both his arms out as if to hug the air. An egg-shaped yellow object formed within his aura like bubbles in water. He waited for Patho to bounce within sight and then released.

A storm of magic headed toward Patho, and he curled himself into a ball to power through it. Red and yellow met one another in the air. The force of the impacts knocked his hands away from his head, but his chest plate held strong under the volley. The force was immense. If this wasn't Eatherium, he would have been reduced to a fine red mist and a pile of scrap metal by now. One of the smaller ones hit his leg in the opening of his armor. Hastul's magic easily and painfully took the limb off and sent the boot clattering to the ground.

The volley stopped. Patho fell to the ground with a clang, his leg regrowing, and Hastul hung in the air in front of him panting, still pulsing with energy.

"Let me tell you a secret," Patho said standing up. "Better yet, let me tell you a fact that you've neglected to acquaint yourself with. If you kill me, all the Marauders, and anyone anywhere, will stand against you. You will never become a Magician. It's already too late for you, it has been since you picked up magic. I can see it from the mirror on your back. You are like me, an Embodiment. And you are still oceans away from being anywhere near a full one."

Patho stood up on his new leg and sent a sphere of red at him. Hastul growled and met the sphere with a beam of his own. They met one another and for a second they were even in force, but then the sphere came apart like wet paper and the beam hit Patho in his chest. He hit the back wall; his chest plate was left unscratched.

"You think *you* can lecture *me* on the ways of magic?!" Hastul screeched like an animal, warm blood still dripping down his face. "I've trained with it since I was a teenager and you think that you, some Marauder demon, can lecture me about the ways of the arcane? It's like you don't even *want to survive*!"

Hastul's aura shifted around him wildly. It began to twist and writhe around his right arm, and Patho began to ricochet himself again. Hastul could hit like a truck. After that, he seemed vulnerable, and he would wager that the more magic he expended now, the less he could use to counterattack. It was at times like these when Patho was incredibly thankful that he used physical over the more expensive ranged magic.

Hastul started shooting magic from his arm like a rapid fire would shoot bullets. Each one put a large dent in the walls. Patho loudly bounced off the walls, leaving a trail of red behind him, while Hastul chased him with a constant stream of magical bullets. The room was lit up with the glow of magic, and the light was constantly churning between yellow and red.

Hastul threw his other arm into the mix and launched a twin stream of magic. Patho didn't see the new attack and was caught in its path. The magic was weaker than the last, but he didn't have time to try and defend himself. His helmet flew off of him and took his head with it. The other stream caught up with its sibling. Patho's bare leg was shredded, and his left arm and gauntlet were torn away. The pain was incredible, he could feel it in the gas of his reforming limbs. It radiated through him like electricity.

The hail fire stopped when Hastul's aura began to dim. Patho made absolutely sure to land in front of Hastul on his feet, and as gracefully as possible. The sensation of standing on his new leg felt like he was shoved into a blazing bonfire.

"Yo-you don't have a face," Hastul gasped, before his own face returned to a crazed sneer. "You really are some kind of freak of nature, aren't you?"

"Says the one made of meat," Patho retorted.

Hastul's eyes narrowed. "Enough of this," he panted, each breath a struggle. "I have had enough of this." The aura flared back to life, completely condensing itself into a single spinning projectile in Hastul's hand. It flew at Patho.

Patho tried to move again, but his new leg wouldn't budge—the pain was too great. He wrapped his right arm and both legs in red, then with his palm splayed, he rammed his fingers into the magic. His gauntlet was shaking on his hand as he tried his hardest to stop the arm from twisting off entirely. He could feel the force of the projectile and knew that if it hit his chest, it would twist the breastplate around him and cut all of his limbs off at once, killing him. Hastul floated to the ground gently in front of him, one arm held out to control his magic.

Patho poured all of his remaining magic into his arm. It began to glow brighter but did not change its shade. He ignored the pain from his bad leg as he began to slide backward. He couldn't let this beat him. He wouldn't die without his trident. The place where his fingers met the projectile began to give; he felt the magic start to come apart. Patho whipped his faceless head into the air and looked straight at the straining Hastul. All that magic in his hand released in a blast that tore apart the projectile. The beam slammed into Hastul, sending him sliding across the floor, and shattering his mirror.

Hastul's eyes widened in horror as he slowly picked himself off of the ground. Patho watched him reach for the glass shards on the ground behind him and try uselessly to put them back into the mirror. it was a terrible feeling, to lose the item in which you had poured a piece of your soul, and it was one Hastul absolutely deserved to feel.

"You know," Patho mused as he approached the now-weeping Hastul. "It's actually quite funny."

Hastul turned away from his broken mirror and stared daggers into Patho's blank face. "You think this is funny? An insect like you thinks that my tears are funny! You should consider yourself lucky you even got to see me like this before I put an end to your miserable life."

Hastul struggled to his feet, only to be met with a blaring laugh from Patho that filled the entire room with ominous tones. "I thought that last blast was it"—Patho happily exclaimed as he curled his hand into a fist, a ruby glow slowly climbing from his wrist to his fingers—"but it turns out, I still have some left."

Hastul pulled his arms back and shot them forward, trying to blast Patho with his magic, but only producing a small little puff of light from his palms. Patho dove his magic covered fingers into Hastul's neck, and blue blood sprayed out like a fountain. Then swiftly, but brutally, Patho liberated Hastul's head from his shoulders.

"Left." Vara heard Queenie say while she dragged her behind her.

"Is this the last left? You've given me a lot of 'lefts' today."

Queenie coughed. "I think so. I think I can walk now, can you let me go?"

Vara dropped her and turned left. The wall was much more fun than this dumb maze thing Yelo had underground, and no one down here had been a challenge for her. The new girl, to her credit, killed some Lean guy, but she couldn't walk when Vara found her. In fact, she was out cold. Nothing a few good slaps couldn't fix . . . the bruises, on the other hand, might take a while to heal.

A sliding door sat between two large posters depicting Bans with their arms locked around one another and the sun rising behind them. Queenie came crouching behind Vara.

"That's it," she said. "Be careful it might be guarded."

Vara walked in. The computer was massive and covered the cold gray of the room in a light blue haze; security monitors covered the screen. A lone Ban turned around in their chair, saw Vara, looked back to the monitor of the wall, looked back to Vara, and then shot his hands up in surrender.

"Get out of here," she sighed, disinterested.

The Ban ran past Queenie, and Vara shoved her flash drive into the disc drive. "This isn't working."

"That's not the right place."

"Ahh."

Vara poked the flash drive into the console until it finally found its place. The computer screen turned black. Pixel by pixel, a red trident began to form, and once it was fully on the screen a clock counted down from fifteen.

Queenie coughed. "How are we going to get out in time? The sewers are all the way back there and we can't fight our way out the front."

Vara laughed. "Are you calling me slow?"

Vara scoped up Queenie and began to hop-jump through the maze. Bodies were strewn about, and the occasional Ban looked at the blur that moved by them in confusion while they cleaned. Vara passed the places where Butler and Silt died. Their faces were frozen in death. Silt was straight-faced, and Butler was strained in sadness and frustration. She debated dropping Queenie off and going back for them, but she couldn't risk it. She was okay with dying in combat, but not in stupidity. They'd have to be remembered without their bodies. Being buried at the site of one's last battle was an honorable resting place, anyway. At least, it was in her book, as of right now.

Queenie whipped her head around in terror from the ride. Vara could see that her eyes were watering from the air, and the chains in her weird vest were clinking annoyingly. This was why Vara hated giving people rides, but she couldn't let this poor girl just wander around down here blindly until she died. Finally, they came across the busted sewer door, and splish-splashed through it.

At the other end, waiting for them, were Bishop and Patho. Bishop looked like he had been thrown into a woodchipper and then had put himself back together again. His suit was missing the fabric around his left arm and both his legs; his cheeks were sunken in. Patho was without his hologram, and he was holding a round object wrapped in cloth under his arm.

Vara looked at Patho. "You're nude." She laughed, dropping a wide-eyed Queenie to the ground.

"Combat has a way of taking one's face off . . . whether they want it to or not."

She turned to Bishop. "You look like you had fun."

"It was something, but I wouldn't call it fun. Where are Silt and Butler?"

"They didn't make it," Queenie cut in, staring at Patho.

"Shame, that's gonna be a hard one to break to the twins."

Vara moved toward the Dark Horses, and with a smile she looked back at the group. "Queenie," she said, getting on a bike. "You're going with Patho."

"Okay," Queenie whimpered, slowly shuffling toward him, the Eatherial.

"Will you hold this for me while I drive? I don't want to lose my souvenir."

Queenie cautiously took hold of the dripping cloth from Patho, her face scrunched up in disgust. "What is it?"

"It's Hastul's head," Patho answered merrily.

"Ready, set, go!" Vara yelled, taking off before Bishop could get on his bike.

"Very fair, Vara," Patho commented before starting after her. "It's good to see tonight's events haven't made a change in your excellent sportsmanship!"

Bishop swore and limped to his bike. "A win like this doesn't count, dammit."

Behind the gliding Night Horses and in front of the rising diamond sun, the cannons of Sinustus began to turn inward. The barrels retracted as they repeatedly fired massive Raiga shells into the commune with loud booms. Blue splashed over the walls, scorching them, and as the last of Yelo was laid to waste, Vara won the race.

CHAPTER 45

EPILOGUE

Everything was dark as his eyes began to regain their focus. It was cold down here, and the Crimslo was finally beginning to wear off. The world above buzzed with the sounds of heavy machinery. Golden Rose Lode didn't know how long he had been trapped underneath these rocks. He figured suffocating while on a Crimslo trip would be preferable to being conscious for his death, but the drug must have slowed his breathing . . . a lot. Lode had always wondered what it was like to use what he sold. Luckily, Crimslo was non-addictive. Not that it mattered for him anymore.

His phone was crushed under one of the rocks, a fact he both lamented and celebrated. It sealed his fate down here, but he wouldn't have to see the bombardment of texts and calls he surely had from Butler. At least there was a silver lining to all this. He would never have to have that awkward break-up.

The rocks above him began to stir and shake. Lode pulled himself into the fetal position, hoping not to be crushed when they fell. Although, now that he thought about it, it would be faster than suffocation.

A crack of light appeared above him and swiftly grew into a hole. Lode shielded his eyes from the daylight, and he heard the surprised voices of a construction worker. A smile crept up his face. He was going to make it.

As one person escaped darkness, another was still trapped within it. Zoog had lost track of how long he had been imprisoned in this lab, with only the red light from the lava lamp thing in the back, and the constant brain-numbing sound of dripping to keep him company. After his short-lived breakout, Patho had welded him inside of a large metal box that was made of the storage bins that the girl had been looking through earlier. Only his face was exposed to air.

It was like hell; he could never even dream of worming his way out of this. Even back during his performing days. Zoog's body had started to rebel against him. He had felt it try before, but always had a syringe nearby to lull it back to a sweet sleep; now he was feeling it worse than he had ever felt before. His body was shivering like he was standing naked inside of a freezer. Every part of him rang with a dull ache that at random moments would become a shrieking pain. His tongue was dry and swollen in his mouth, his breaths shallow. Sweat drenched his body and pooled at the bottom of the box; the dripping was driving him mad with how consistent and endless it was. The trails around his eyes were at first gushing with the brown degradation, but now they had dried into trails. Each and every second was its own eternity for him while he sat in the dark. All Zoog wanted in the whole of Mekebe was to get something into his system that would make it all go away.

The door opened and the lights were switched on, causing Zoog to hiss in pain and shut his stinging eyes from the light. He heard the familiar sound of Patho's footsteps clicking against the metal floor.

"I think enough time has passed," he heard the Human man remark. "You should be in a suitable state of withdrawal by now."

When he slowly peeled open his eyes, Zoog could see clearly his captor walking nonchalantly over to the array of beakers and tubes that had been producing the dripping that had been tormenting him for so long.

"It sure looks like you're in a sorry state," Patho commented, briefly glancing at Zoog with his ruby eyes. "Let's see if my new drug can put an end to it."

Zoog felt his heart flutter as a wave of excitement rushed throughout his body. Drug? Was he really doing all of this to him just to test out some new kind of drug? If that's what this was all about, how potent of a dose was Zoog about to get? He said it would put an end to the symptoms, so it must be one hell of a drug. Zoog could hardly wait.

Patho seized a beaker of red fluid from the chemistry stand. "I'd prefer to put this into pill form before I give it to you, but I think that would just be a waste of time if it doesn't work."

Zoog watched him walk forward and licked his dry lips in anticipation. His black eyes were fixed on the beautiful beaker in Patho's hands.

Patho smiled as he moved the beaker toward Zoog's mouth. "I bet you're wondering about a name?" he mused. "Well, I was too, but I think I found the perfect one." Zoog strained his face forward, trying to get his lips as close he could to the red fluid.

"Panacea."

***

"Ow." Artex, who was lying down on a new leather couch in the Monochro Tower penthouse, winced as Queenie dabbed at his gut wound with an alcohol-soaked cotton ball.

"Sorry," she responded, reapplying the bandages. "At least it's not that deep."

"And at least I have a good nurse," he chuckled, causing Queenie to blush.

"You two make me wish that Yelo killed me," Vara yelled down from the second floor, a massive grin on her face.

Artex's face shifted in anger as he tried to stand and yell at his sister, only to yelp in pain and fall back onto the couch.

"Please don't try to move!" Queenie called out, moving to block Artex from moving again. "Leaving the infirmary in this state was bad enough! If you tear something again, you could bleed out before we get you back down there."

"Queenie," Artex managed to say through the pain. "I think you're overreacting."

"Yeah, he'll be fine," Bishop yawned, walking up next to Vara and putting his arm around her. "A lot worse has happened on that couch than getting a little blood on it."

Queenie looked up at the pair with a confused look on her face. "Th-the couch has only been here for three days," she stuttered.

"We know," Vara replied smugly.

***

The courtyard of Sinustus was unrecognizable. The heat from the liquid Raiga shells had caused what was left of the buildings to twist and warp into spires of metal that stood out awkwardly in the sunlight. Large blue stains coated the ground and walls, leftovers from the evaporated Raiga, and above all of it were the cannons, which still clicked to fire ammo that wasn't there.

Overseer Thirty-Two fell to her knees amongst the rubble, her broken right arm hanging limply by her side. Tears began to well up in her eyes as the thought of a life without Yelo began to become a reality to her, a life without the power she once held so dear. Thirty-Two grabbed her mask from her face with her good hand and held it tightly. This had to be a dream—there was no way that the Marauders could have defeated them this soundly. It just couldn't be real. She looked up to the once-grand walls of the compound and remembered how safe they made her feel when she first joined Yelo. Now, Thirty-Two realized that they could help her be safe from the world once again, this time permanently.

She searched the wreckage slowly, taking in the serene and sorrowful atmosphere as she went. Several bodies had survived complete annihilation and lay charred throughout the compound, identifiable features seared off, but all with mouths open in screams. One surviving ladder was all she needed for her one-way trip, but she couldn't find one. Hours went by, and the sun began to set. Thirty-Two just kept retracing her steps throughout the courtyard. She refused to believe that this plan was also going to fail.

"Oh sweet child," the voice was androgynous and seemed to sing out from all around her. "So lost and alone."

Thirty-Two whipped around frantically to try and find the source of the voice. "Who's there? Are you a Marauder?"

A long shadow fell over Thirty-Two, only exaggerated by the now setting sun. She turned to see the source of the sound. The figure wore a cloak of pulsating white flesh. Its arms were covered by heavy gauntlets of green sinew and brown bone, and its face was covered by a white, seed-like mask that depicted ten luminescent green circles in the vague shape of a tree.

The creature spoke calmly as a long crack appeared down the middle of its mask, gradually opening to reveal the featureless green, slightly translucent face underneath. "Fear not, for ***I*** shall provide for you."

www.ingramcontent.com/pod-product-compliance
Lightning Source LLC
LaVergne TN
LVHW091133080826
845145LV00008B/2136

* 9 7 8 1 7 3 5 6 3 5 7 1 2 *